# GIFT WRAPPED

# GIFT WRAPPED

## Peter Turnbull

This first world edition published 2013
in Great Britain and in the USA by
SEVERN HOUSE PUBLISHERS LTD of
19 Cedar Road, Sutton, Surrey, England, SM2 5DA.
Trade paperback edition first published
in Great Britain and the USA 2013 by
SEVERN HOUSE PUBLISHERS LTD

British Library Cataloguing in Publication Data

Turnbull, Peter, 1950-
  Gift wrapped.
  1. Hennessey, George (Fictitious character)–Fiction.
  2. Yellich, Somerled (Fictitious character)–Fiction.
  3. Police–England–Yorkshire–Fiction. 4. Murder–
  Investigation–England–Yorkshire–Fiction. 5. Detective
  and mystery stories.
  I. Title
  823.9'2-dc23

ISBN-13:  978-0-7278-8262-2 (cased)
ISBN-13:  978-1-84751-477-6 (trade paper)

*All Severn House titles are printed on acid-free paper.*

Severn House Publishers support The Forest Stewardship Council [FSC],
the leading international forest certification organisation. All our titles that
are printed on Greenpeace-approved FSC-certified paper carry the FSC logo.

MIX
Paper from
responsible sources
FSC
www.fsc.org  FSC® C018575

Typeset by Palimpsest Book Production Ltd.,
Falkirk, Stirlingshire, Scotland.
Printed and bound in Great Britain by
MPG Books Ltd., Bodmin, Cornwall.

# ONE

Tuesday, 30 May, 11.37 hours – Wednesday, 31 May, 22.10 hours

*In which postcards in many languages lead the police to a murdered man and Detective Constable Reginald Webster is at home to the dear reader.*

The woman, so Reginald Webster rapidly thought, had clear possession of a certain warmth about her; she had, he further thought, a very naturally giving personality. She seemed to Webster to also have a genuine sense of care for others about her, which he felt went a long way to explain why she had gravitated to the unpaid voluntary work she informed him that she did at the 'drop-in' centre, where advice and companionship was offered to the lonely and needy, and to the troubled of the city of York. The woman, Webster saw, had a ready smile, a pleasingly balanced face and eyes with dilated pupils. She was also, Webster felt, the sort of person who, had she been a schoolteacher, would have been loved by her pupils, or if a curate or priest then equally cherished by her parishioners. Her auburn hair was worn in a wild and straggly manner but was, Webster saw, wild and straggly in a controlled, designer sense. Her clothing was of the type which Webster believed to be termed 'office smart' – a brown jacket, worn open, beneath which was a cream-coloured blouse, both of which gave way to a brown three-quarter-length lightweight summer skirt. Light-coloured nylons encased shapely slender legs and her feet were, in turn, encased in dark brown 'sensible' shoes. She carried a large brown handbag which she had laid gently on the carpeted floor beside her chair upon accepting Webster's invitation to sit down. She was married, by her title and her rings, and wore an expensive-looking watch among the bracelets on her wrists. Delicate and expensive perfume wafted gently from her and in

terms of age she was, Webster had hazarded, probably in her
mid-forties. The woman had, upon her arrival, given her name
to the constable at the enquiry desk as Mrs Bartlem, Mrs Julia
Bartlem. She gave her home address as being in Selby and had
said, matter-of-factly, that she wished to report a murder.

Upon being invited into the interview suite she had, once
seated, reached beside her into her handbag and extracted four
postcards, then handed them to Webster.

Webster once again carefully pondered the postcards which
had been presented by Mrs Bartlem, who sat silently and quite
still as he did so. All the postcards, Webster noted, were of
the nearby coastal resort of Scarborough and all were identical,
showing what Webster thought to be an intelligently composed
photograph of the harbour looking out to sea, over which a
deep red sunset had formed. All the postcards had been
postmarked 'York', although he knew there was nothing
significant in that because, from his own experience, Webster
had found that all postcards and letters which were posted in
Scarborough would be postmarked 'York'. The postcards
would in all probability have been purchased in Scarborough,
but they could have been posted anywhere in North Yorkshire.

Mrs Bartlem continued to remain silent and quite still,
patiently waiting for Webster to pass comment about the postcards, cutting as she did a slender figure – about six feet tall,
Webster had estimated – sitting upright in the chair with her
long legs pressed together at both knee and ankle and angled
gracefully to her right side.

'Murder.' Webster raised an eyebrow in a non-threatening
and slightly humorous manner. 'You say murder?'

'Yes, sir.' Mrs Bartlem spoke little, but when she did she
spoke with a soft speaking voice with just a trace of local
accent that Webster could detect, as if she was, Webster
guessed, working class in respect of her background but had
risen and had entered, or had married into, the professional
middle class, and who by now, with sufficient time on her
hands, was giving herself to those people who, out of one
need or another, walked through the ever-welcoming doorway
of the 'drop-in centre' which, she advised, was situated in a
church hall near the city centre.

'"*Der Mord*".' Webster read aloud the words which were written on the rear of the first postcard, then on the reverse of the second postcard he read the word '"*assassinio*"', on the back of the third card he saw and read the word '"*meurtre*"' and on the reverse of the fourth card he read the word '"*homicidium*"'. He looked up questioningly at Mrs Bartlem, who remained expressionless. 'I'm sorry, I can't claim to be a linguist but of the four words I can only guess that the last, "*homicidium*", is Latin for "murder"?'

'And you'd be guessing quite correctly.' Mrs Bartlem smiled warmly. 'Apparently.' She paused. 'Note I say "apparently". I can also speak only English but I am advised that the words in the order which you have just now read them out are German, Italian, French and, as you say, Latin, for "murder". So I . . . so we . . . were advised.'

'Very well,' Webster murmured softly. 'We will certainly verify the meanings, but what about these numbers I also see on the cards under the word for "murder"? The words are different but seem to mean the same thing . . . "murder" . . . but the numbers are . . . yes . . . yes, they all are the same in each case – the same numbers have been written on the back of each card. Do you perhaps know what the numbers signify?'

'They are in fact map reference numbers.' Mrs Bartlem beamed confidently. 'It's a map reference. Apparently so.'

'I would not have guessed.' Webster felt a trifle embarrassed by his ignorance. 'Though I dare say that we would very soon have identified them as such. Of that I am in little or no doubt.'

'Again, as with the languages,' Mrs Bartlem added, 'I also would not have recognized them as being map references, but my lovely dear husband teaches geography in a secondary school and he saw them for what they are in an instant. 1-1-1-3-5-4-0-0. Apparently it's a location just north-east of York, quite open country – my husband consulted the Ordnance Survey map, you see – so "murder" in four different languages, but each postcard giving the same very precise location . . . of something.' Again, she paused and drew a deep breath. 'It could, of course, we thought, be someone playing silly, stupid games – some person or persons with a questionable, a very questionable, sense of humour and a weak grasp of ethical correctness . . .

or . . . or . . . it could equally be someone or some persons pointing to such a precise location because it has some connection, some relevance, to a murder. Whatever it is, we decided that it is not a job for the volunteers of the drop-in centre at Saint Chads on Gilleygate, and so chose to surrender them to the police with myself being the messenger, for my sins.'

'For your sins?' Reginald Webster echoed as he smiled his response. 'Yes, I understand. Thank you. You did the correct thing in the circumstances. When did they arrive? I notice they have different postmarked dates.'

'We received them at the regular rate of one a day. Today is Tuesday, as you know . . . one arrived yesterday and one arrived on Saturday last and the first arrived on Friday last. As you see, they arrived in the order of German, French, Latin and Italian, though whether or not that is significant is of course not for me to speculate.'

'No . . .' Webster murmured, 'but it may be of some significance. Time will tell.'

'One of our volunteers is a linguist and it was she who identified the languages, but none of us had any clue at all about the numbers and so I took the postcards home to show my husband and, as I have just told you, he immediately recognized them as map grid references used by the British Ordnance Survey. He looked up the reference and found it gave the location as being north of York, between the villages of Gate Helmsley and Warthill.'

'Delightful-sounding name,' Webster growled. 'Warthill, indeed.'

'Indeed, isn't it?' Mrs Bartlem grinned, showing a set of perfect white teeth as she did so.

'Have you . . . did you,' Webster enquired, 'visit the area?'

'Oh my heavens, no,' Mrs Bartlem replied defensively. 'No, I . . . no we didn't, we thought it wasn't our place to do so. I returned to the drop-in centre this morning and waited until the post arrived to see whether or not it contained a fourth card, which it did . . . so . . . after four cards had been received we thought it high time to bring them to the attention of the police and I was despatched, as I said, for my sins.' Mrs

Bartlem then allowed herself a glance around the room to take in her surroundings – the hard-wearing, dark orange hessian carpet, the walls in two shades of orange, the coffee table which stood on the carpet between her and DC Webster, the comfortable but armless chairs on which they both sat.

'Typed,' Webster commented. 'The words and the numbers are typed.'

'Yes.' Mrs Bartlem smiled. 'We also commented upon that. None of us at the centre thought that typewriters existed any more but evidently someone has still got possession of one. Quite useful too, I would imagine.'

'Oh?' Webster raised an eyebrow. 'What do you mean?'

'Well, I am of course not a police officer so it isn't for me to say – clearly it isn't – but I would have thought that a typewriter is a very useful tool to have if you want to disguise your handwriting. You can't put a postcard into the printer of a word processor – you can't put one into my word processor anyway – but that is of course your area of expertise. I do so apologize.' Mrs Bartlem lowered her head slightly. 'I am sorry.'

Webster held up his hand. 'Please don't worry, you are being very public spirited. There really is no need to apologize, no need at all.' He paused. 'I doubt whether we'll get any useful prints.'

'Prints?' Mrs Bartlem queried. 'You'll copy the cards?'

'No.' Webster smiled. 'I meant latents . . . fingerprints. I doubt if we'll get any useful fingerprints off the postcards but we'll check anyway.'

'Ah . . . I see.' Julia Bartlem returned the smile.

'The cards will have by now been handled by so many people – yourself and the staff at the drop-in centre, myself . . . the postman who collected the card, possibly, the postman who sorted the cards ready for delivery, certainly . . .'

'My husband as well,' Mrs Bartlem added. 'He has handled them.'

'Yes, he also, and I can pretty well guarantee that if these cards were posted by a felon he would have wiped them clean before dropping them into the postbox. We can also be certain that the stamps will have been wiped clean of any thumbprints,' Webster commented dryly, 'but of course we'll check them anyway, as I said. We'd look very foolish if the cards did transpire to have the fingerprints of a murderous felon upon them, but really no one who is even slightly forensically aware is going to press down on a stamp and leave his or her beautifully preserved thumbprint all over the image of Her Most Gracious Majesty . . . But, as I said, we'll check them anyway, just in case we really are dealing with a prize idiot, but I do doubt very much that we'll get a result.'

A short silence ensued.

'I don't think that I have any further information.' Mrs Bartlem once again permitted herself a quick glance round the interview suite. 'I have told you everything.'

'And I don't think that I have any further questions either,' Webster replied quietly. Then he added: 'But should you, that is, should the drop-in centre receive any more cards, cards like this . . .'

'We'll let you have them immediately,' Mrs Bartlem anticipated him as she and Webster stood at the same time.

'Thank you for bringing these cards to us. It's very public spirited of you, as I said. I'll take them up to my boss, but we'll definitely be following this up.'

'Good. Well, I've done my bit.' Mrs Bartlem bent at her knees to pick up her handbag. 'I dare say it's over to you now.'

Detective Chief Inspector George Hennessey studied the four postcards slowly and carefully as though, Webster thought, he was searching for something beyond the typewritten words and numbers. He then slowly reclined in his chair and placed the cards one by one on top of his desk. 'I confess that I cannot say that languages are a speciality of mine either, so don't reproach yourself, Reg. No need to do that. We would have had them translated anyway; in fact, as you know, we will still have to have it confirmed that they do mean what the lady, Mrs . . . ?'

'Bartlem, sir,' Reginald Webster replied promptly. 'Mrs Julia Bartlem.'

'Yes . . . we'll still have to have it confirmed that the words all do mean "murder". Mind you, having said that, I think that even I could have made a fair and a reasonable guess that "*homicidium*" is indeed Latin for "murder".' Hennessey took a deep breath and exhaled slowly. 'So . . . where on earth is 1-1-1-3-5-4-0-0?' he asked.

'5-4-0-0 is bang on the fifty-fourth parallel, sir, and 1-1-1-3 is just west of the second meridian,' Reginald Webster replied enthusiastically.

'In English, Reg,' Hennessey pleaded. 'English will do very nicely, if you please.'

'Well, sir,' Webster leaned forward, 'my map reading . . . my reading of the map puts the location exactly where Mrs Bartlem said her husband had placed it, halfway between Warthill . . .'

'Delightful name,' Hennessey growled, 'utterly delightful.'

'Isn't it, sir? In fact that's just what Mrs Bartlem and I both said . . . a delightful name.' Webster grinned. 'But I feel that at least it must have some ancient meaning. In contrast, you know, sir, there is in the fair town of Rotherham in South Yorkshire, a road on a fifties green field housing estate with the astounding name of "Gallow Tree Road". The name has no provenance at all, as if it was dreamed up by someone having a bad day one wet afternoon. But to continue . . . the location indicated seems to lie pretty well midway between the village of Warthill and the nearest neighbouring village of Gate Helmsley.'

George Hennessey ran his fleshy, liver-spotted hands through his silver hair and glanced to his left-hand side out of the window of his office as he did so. He espied a group of T-shirted youths excitedly walking the walls, each of whom was draped with expensive-looking photographic equipment. He pigeonholed the group as being overseas students. 'So,' he turned to Reginald Webster, 'tell me, what is the lie of the land like round Warthill and Gate whatever . . . do you know?'

'Helmsley, sir, Gate Helmsley,' Webster responded. 'I just know that it's agricultural land, sir, going by the map. There is no indication of it being a built-up area.'

'Fair enough.' Hennessey once again read the rear of the postcards then pondered the photograph on the front of the cards. 'Scarborough,' he said softly. 'Anything to be inferred from the choice of postcard, do you think? The very popular resort town of Scarborough . . . the North Sea, the sunset, summertime . . . is there some message in the photograph that we are supposed to pick up? Do you have any thoughts there, Reg?'

'A little early to say yet, sir, I'd say.' Webster sat back in his chair. 'I think all we can do is to keep an open mind on that possibility . . . on that issue.'

'Yes, yes, of course it is . . . of course it is.' George Hennessey patted the cards as his eye was caught by another tourist walking the ancient walls which stood on the opposite side of Nunnery Lane from Micklegate Bar Police Station. The tourist was a loner on this occasion, a middle-aged male, wearing a white, wide brimmed hat, a loud yellow T-shirt and also with an expensive-looking camera hanging from his shoulder. American, George Hennessey thought, for no clear or identifiable reason. The man just looked to him to be a 'cousin'. 'So we don't know the area?' Hennessey turned back to look at Webster.

'Seems not, sir,' Webster replied. 'No police activity there at all.'

'Warthill and Gate Helmsley . . . it does sound like the rural north of England, which will now be in all its summer bounty and splendour.' Hennessey paused. 'Who is in the CID rooms at present – any idea?'

'Just Thompson Ventnor, sir,' Webster informed.

'All right . . . all right . . . myself and Ventnor have to deal with any and every emergency that might come in for the CID this afternoon while you, Reg, have a trip out to the country to arrange and look forward to.' Hennessey smiled at Webster. 'You lucky man.'

'Yes, sir.' Webster grinned his reply. 'And just when I was about to address all that lovely, lovely paperwork.'

'Oh that lovely, lovely paperwork won't go away.' Hennessey smiled broadly. 'You don't need to worry on that score. Her Majesty's Home Office wants its statistical returns, and by hook or by crook Her Majesty's Home Office will have its statistical returns.'

'As you say, sir.' Webster returned the smile, equally broadly. 'So . . . you don't need a large number of bodies, I would have thought. Just two sniffer dogs, their handlers, six constables, a sergeant and yourself. That will be quite sufficient.'

'Yes, sir,' Webster replied promptly.

'Take an Ordnance Survey map of the area, as large scale as you can find . . . you can draw that from stores, and get the crew as close as you can to the grid reference. Then release the dogs and see what, if anything, they find. You know the drill.'

'Yes, sir.' Webster stood smartly and left Hennessey's office.

What the dogs found within fifteen minutes of arriving at the grid reference was an area of soil at the edge of a field, in which both animals demonstrated great and excited interest. The two brown and white Springer spaniels pawed at a small section of the ground, barked enthusiastically, turned in tight circles and wagged their short tails. One of the dog handlers turned to Webster and gave the thumbs-up signal, calling out, 'They've got something, sir. They've caught an interesting scent all right.'

'Thank you,' Webster replied as the dog handler, a tall and lean constable in a white short-sleeved shirt and serge trousers, clipped the lead back on to the dog's leather harness and led him to one side, gently patting the dog's flank as he did so. The second dog handler then retrieved his dog and stood by his colleague.

Reginald Webster then took one more last survey of the wider area and again he saw a patchwork of lovingly cared-for fields, lush with crops, being wheat in the main, but he noticed a bright yellow field of rapeseed on the skyline in the far western distance. The area, he noted, was interrupted here and there by small stands of isolated trees, all under a vast blue sky and with only the occasional thin wisp of white cloud to be seen. Webster turned his attention to the small area of ground which had so interested the dogs and walked slowly towards it. 'So,' he said amid the birdsong, 'you think something is under the surface just here?'

'It's definitely going to be rotting flesh, sir, that is certain,' the first dog handler replied. 'That's the only scent that they are trained to respond to . . . but whether it is human or not, well, I'm afraid that only honest to God hard sweat and hard graft will tell.'

'I see.' Webster noted the location of the grave as a bead of sweat ran off his forehead, if it was in fact a grave. It lay amid a small group of young oak trees, all, he thought, to be about ten years old and all in a perfect line, neatly following the hedgerow on the southern, sun-receiving side. 'Planted,' he murmured to himself.

'Sorry, sir?' The first dog handler had clearly heard Webster.

'The trees.' Webster pointed to the line of young oak trees. 'I was really muttering happily away to myself but I don't at all mind sharing them with you – my humble and lowly observations, I mean . . .' Webster paused for a moment. 'The trees, these young oak trees, have they been planted as if someone wished to leave something behind him . . . or her? Ten oaks all in a row . . . like pretty maids, each with room to grow, all equally spaced, all south of the hedgerow, as you see, and receiving lots of lovely sun so that in a hundred years' time someone will walk down that lane,' Webster pointed to the road upon which the police vehicles were parked, 'and they will say, "someone planted those trees for us to enjoy today, and planted them a long time ago knowing they were never going to live to see them in all their wonderful mature splendour".'

'I see. That wouldn't have occurred to me.' The dog handler ran his eye along the line of oak trees. 'I would never have seen that, sir.'

'It probably wouldn't have occurred to me either,' Webster replied with a grin, 'that is, if I hadn't once tried to dig a hole beside an established tree . . . a very big mistake. What happened is that my elderly relative then had to agree to have the fish pond she wanted put in the middle of her lawn and not under the shade of the beech tree as she had planned. I just couldn't dig through the root plate, you see.'

'Yes, sir.'

'Nevertheless, the trees will help us date the grave, if it is one.' Another bead of sweat ran heavily down Webster's forehead. 'Amazing creatures.' He smiled at the dogs, 'Really amazing.'

'The dogs, sir?' The first dog handler nodded approvingly. 'Yes, it is truly astounding what they can do. You know, sir, I wouldn't swap my place in the Dog Branch for any other field of police work. I mean, sir, if I have to be in uniform then this is the place I'd want to be.'

'Good for you. I do like it when I meet a man who's happy in his work.' Webster reached into the pocket of his lightweight summer jacket, retrieved his mobile phone and selected the number for Micklegate Bar Police Station. He asked to be put through to Chief Inspector Hennessey upon his call being answered. 'It's far too early to say whether or not the remains are human, sir,' Webster explained. 'It could easily be a dead sheep, but both of the dogs have picked up the scent of rotting flesh and they have done so right at the map reference in question.' Webster paused as he listened. Then he continued, 'Yes, sir, understood.' He switched off his mobile phone and waved to the sergeant and the constables to approach and, as he did so, he made the motion of a man digging with a spade.

'We have a scent,' Webster explained as the sergeant approached, followed by six white-shirted male constables, each one carrying a long-handled spade. 'It's a bit of an exposed place to bury a body, as you can see.' Webster looked around, as did the grizzled-faced sergeant. 'Rooftops of two villages can be clearly seen,' he said.

'Yes, sir, very exposed, as you say,' the sergeant responded with a gravelly voice.

'But we'll have to dig anyway; the dogs have a scent.'

'Understood, sir,' the sergeant replied. 'Where?'

'Just here . . .' Webster dug his shoe heel into the area of soil which had excited the dogs.

'Very good, sir.' The sergeant turned and addressed the constables who had remained silent and who, having followed the hedgerows rather than walking through the crop, had by then formed a straight line. 'Right, lads,' he called, 'there's work for us to do. First two, please.'

The first two constables instantly stepped forward and began to dig strongly and determinedly at the sun-baked soil in the area indicated by Webster, who had by then walked away and was standing beside the dog handlers, thus allowing the two constables room to work. Webster watched with interest as the two young men settled down into a steady rhythm, chipping away at the hardened soil. The first two constables were replaced by the next two men in line when, after thirty minutes of hard labour, they had dug a hole Webster guessed to be one-and-a-half-feet deep. After in excess of ninety minutes of digging the first two constables were once again working with their shirts wet with perspiration. One of the constables stood and announced, 'There's something here, sir. We've definitely got something.'

Webster stepped forward and glanced keenly and curiously into the hole. He saw that the 'something' was a skull . . . a human skull. 'Well, that's not a sheep,' he said for want of anything to say. 'That is definitely not a sheep.' Then he turned to the sergeant and said, 'Can you please dig the soil away from the rest of the top of the skeleton so as to expose it, but do not dig beneath it until the pathologist gives the go-ahead?'

'Yes, sir.' The sergeant turned to the constables and loudly barked clear instructions.

For a second time that day Webster took his mobile phone from his jacket pocket and contacted DCI Hennessey.

'Male.' Dr Louise D'Acre looked down at the skeleton which had by then been fully exposed by careful, very careful, removal of the soil which had covered it. 'That's all I can tell you for now. Probably northern European, possibly Asian, but the deceased is definitely a male of our species.' She also noted how the roots of the nearest oak tree had closely entwined round the skeleton rather than pushing through it. She and DCI Hennessey stood side by side within the white inflatable tent which had been erected over the shallow grave. The skeleton, they observed, had been laid on its right-hand side and its legs had been folded in a near foetal position. 'Adult male,' she further explained. 'I note clear trauma to the skull. Do you see it, Chief Inspector?'

'Yes, ma'am.' Hennessey saw the linear facture on the top

of the skull. 'That would have caused quite a headache, I think.'

'It would also have caused instant death,' Dr D'Acre replied solemnly. 'At least I can say that it has that sort of potential. There might be more trauma on the hidden side to be considered, but that blow to the head alone . . . well, I have known less to cause death, can I put it like that?'

'Understood.' Hennessey gave a slight nod of his head. 'Can I ask you, Doctor D'Acre, how old do you think he is? I mean, how old was he at the time he died? That would be very useful in helping us to identify him.'

'Over twenty-five years is all I can say at the moment because the skull has fully knitted together, as you can see, but once I start the post-mortem I will be able to extract a tooth, which will enable me to make an accurate determination of his age at death to within twelve months.' Dr D'Acre paused. 'As you see, he has achieved the fifth stage of decomposition. That is to say that he is now almost totally skeletal. He's certainly been down there a good number of years. This soil hereabouts is rich in beasties the human eye cannot see and the moisture . . . but he has a few sinews left . . . He's been down there for less than seventy years . . . much less.'

'So work for us?' Hennessey smiled briefly. 'No rest for the wicked.'

'Oh, yes, Chief Inspector.' Louise D'Acre turned to Hennessey and smiled gently but briefly. 'It is work for you, I fear. Have you taken all the photographs you need?'

'Almost.'

'Very well. I'll begin to take soil samples, but other than that I have seen all I need to see here. I'll supervise the lifting of the skeleton and its placing into a body bag, once you have confirmed that all photographs have been taken. Who will lift the skeleton? Do you know?'

'Whoever,' Hennessey's eye developed a wicked gleam, 'or whichever two constables have the least experience. Whoever has the least years of service.'

Dr D'Acre smiled. 'Yes . . . that is a good philosophy. The "deep end" approach.'

'I'll talk to them first, of course.' Hennessey grinned. 'I'll remind them that they did not join the police force to escort little old ladies across the road.'

'They certainly didn't.' Louise D'Acre nodded briefly. 'So to confirm, I'll remain here until the skeleton is in the body bag. Then I'd like to check the soil underneath the skeleton, because there is the possibility that there might be something of interest to us there. I assume you'll dig down a little further until you are certain you have reached consolidated soil?'

'Of course, ma'am.' Hennessey wiped a bead of sweat from his brow.

'I don't see any non-degradable items like buttons or zip fasteners,' Dr D'Acre observed.

'Nor do I,' Hennessey replied.

'That will probably mean he was buried naked,' Dr D'Acre commented. 'That's usually the case with young women, not men, because there is often a sexual component to the murder of women that isn't present in the murder of men, but whatever.' She paused briefly. 'I assume you'll be witnessing the post-mortem for the police, Chief Inspector?'

'Yes, ma'am,' Hennessey replied. 'I will.'

'Good.' Dr D'Acre turned to leave the tent. 'I can very easily start the post-mortem today; there is still plenty of time. I am not particularly constrained by time, but Eric is . . . I have to bear that in mind.'

'Eric?' Hennessey sounded puzzled. 'Sorry . . . Eric?'

'Eric Filey, one of the pathology laboratory assistants. He usually works with me. He's a good man . . . a good young man and we are very lucky to have him, very lucky indeed. He'll willingly work overtime should I have to ask him to but I don't want to put upon him. I want to keep him on side so I won't risk antagonizing him. I must be careful not to exploit his good nature.'

'Oh, I fully understand, and Eric . . . Of course, how could I forget about Eric?' Hennessey stepped aside so as to allow Dr D'Acre to exit the tent. 'Man management is all about diplomacy.'

'I'll step outside for a moment to let the SOCO officers take the last of their photographs and to allow them space to photograph the exhumation.' Dr D'Acre moved thankfully out into the breathable air of the field and once again found herself pondering the fortune awaiting the person who invents an air-conditioning system which can be installed in inflatable tents for the use of the police. She, like Reginald Webster, found herself enjoying the rural setting to which her duties on that day had brought her and she was very pleased to be able to exchange the all-pervading smell of formaldehyde for the pleasing fresh country air. As she walked from the tent her eye was caught by a hawk – a sparrow hawk, she thought – hovering above an adjacent field, and she watched as the bird dived purposefully, disappeared from view amongst the wheat and then rose with a small object in its talons. The field mouse dies so that the hawk might live; life goes on. She noticed movement on the road and saw a farmer with a battered, mud-splattered, green canvas-topped Land Rover slow down as he passed the scene of the police activity. Dr D'Acre then realized it would be the talk of the pubs in Warthill and Gate Helmsley that evening and probably for a few more evenings to come. Gossip, she pondered, that just might cause a felon to have a sleepless night, as the news of the skeleton being found would be made public. Dr D'Acre knew that all such talk could be useful to the police; local gossip and wide publicity has all been known to make a felon trip himself up, or even, indeed, to walk into a police station desperately wishing to ease a terrible conscience which has been haunting him, or her, for years. But in this case it was clear to her that the wretched man with a hole in his skull was never intended to be found.

The skeleton, once delicately raised to ground level, was gently laid on to the black heavy-duty plastic body bag by the two ashen-faced young constables, which was then closed and zipped shut, placed on a stretcher and carried solemnly to the black, windowless mortuary van which had been summoned and, upon arriving, had parked behind the police minibus. Dr D'Acre returned to the tent and looked into the hole and, observing no further human remains or other items of signifi-cance, she then vacated the tent and approached DCI Hennessey. 'Nothing more for me to do here, sir,' she spoke quietly. 'I'll proceed to the York District Hospital and await the arrival of the skeleton.'

'Very well, ma'am. I have a press release to prepare and then to issue, and I will join you immediately after that has been done. I am sure I will not be much delayed.'

Dr D'Acre carefully studied the skeleton which lay upon the first of five stainless-steel tables which stood in a row in the pathology laboratory of the York District Hospital. It had been found on its side and in a foetal position, and was by then lying face-up with its arms by its sides and legs extended. Also present in the laboratory that afternoon were Eric Filey and DCI Hennessey, both of whom stood at a respectful distance from the dissecting table – Hennessey against the wall and Filey on the further side of the laboratory, against the bench which ran the length of the laboratory and beneath which were drawers containing instruments and other items which might be required by the pathologist. Dr D'Acre, Filey and Hennessey were each dressed in identical disposable green coveralls, complete with cap and foot covering. As on all previous occasions when George Hennessey had observed a post-mortem for the police, he once again found the air of the pathology laboratory heavy with the smell of bleach and industrial grade disinfectant. It permitted no natural light but instead was illuminated by a series of filament bulbs shielded by opaque Perspex screens, which prevented epileptic fit-inducing shimmer to reach the eyes of any person in the room.

Dr D'Acre pulled down the anglepoise arm which was bolted to the ceiling, so that the microphone at the tip of the arm was level with her mouth. 'Today's date and the next serial number, please, Judith.' She spoke for the clear benefit of the tape which would later, Hennessey knew, be transcribed by an audio typist who evidently knew which information to type and which to omit. Dr D'Acre then turned slowly to Eric Filey and said, 'This might mean late working for you, Eric. I hope you don't mind?'

'Not at all, ma'am,' Filey responded with a ready smile and Hennessey noted he pronounced ma'am in the correct manner so as to rhyme with 'calm' and not in the incorrect manner so as to rhyme with 'lamb'.

'Good man, thank you, I appreciate it.' Dr D'Acre paused

for a few seconds before she continued. 'The subject is a
skeletal male adult, over the age of twenty-five years, because
the complete knitting of the skull sutures is noted. At first
glance his teeth appear to be complete and so he will probably
have been no older than his early middle years when he died.'
Again Dr D'Acre paused and turned to Eric Filey. 'Can you
please hand me the tape measure, Eric?' And then added,
'Many thanks,' as Filey handed a yellow metal and retractable
one over. 'If you could help me, Eric?'

Eric Filey promptly stepped forward and took hold of the
end of the tape measure, holding it at the feet, while Dr D'Acre
extended it towards the skull. 'So,' she announced, 'five feet
eight inches tall or about 173 centimetres in Euro speak. He
was not a tall man in life, but neither was he particularly short.
He was just of average height for the north of England where
folk, it has been observed, tend to be a little shorter than their
southern counterparts.' Again, she paused. 'In terms of racial
extraction he is northern European or Asian, though I think
he is too heavily boned to be Asian. The skulls of both groups
can be somewhat difficult to distinguish but, having said that,
the Asian skulls have a tendency to be more finely made than
the Northern European skulls.' Dr D'Acre forced open the jaw
of the skeleton. 'All the teeth are present,' she confirmed, 'and
British dentistry is noted . . . so likely a UK citizen . . . in
fact, he certainly will be a UK citizen.'

'So there will be a missing persons report in respect of
him?' Hennessey commented.

'Yes, I would think so. Almost certainly so.' Dr D'Acre
continued to examine the teeth. 'He didn't look after his teeth
– we have fillings a-plenty, though at least that tells us he
wasn't a derelict, a down-and-out whom nobody would miss,
but then we knew that because as a general rule down-and-outs
don't get buried in shallow graves.'

'They certainly don't,' Hennessey growled. 'And the deeper
the "shallow" grave the more important the victim. That is
also as a general rule.'

'I'll extract one of the teeth and cut it into a cross-section
as I indicated I would do earlier today. That will give his age
at death to within twelve months . . . but . . . all his teeth,

looking after them . . . I can tell you that he will have been
nearer the beginning of his life than the end, a man with
something behind him but also with plans for his future . . .
that sort of age.'

'I see,' Hennessey replied.

'So let us turn to why we are also here, to determine the
cause of death if we can. Noted is damage to the skull, a blow
by a blunt object sufficient to be fatal but not in itself guaranteed to be fatal. No other injuries. Oh . . . hello, what have
we here?'

'Something?' Hennessey responded.

'Yes, yes, we very well might have – on the right-hand side
of the ribcage there is something, I think. Can you hand me
a magnifying glass, please, Eric?'

Once again Eric Filey responded with a promptness and an
eagerness which impressed Hennessey, placing a rectangular-
shaped magnifying lens in Dr D'Acre's hand. She held the
magnifying glass six inches from the ribcage and said, 'Would
you care to come and have a look at this, Chief Inspector . . .
it is quite interesting. Possibly.'

Hennessey advanced confidently across the linoleum-
covered floor of the laboratory until he stood shoulder to
shoulder with Dr D'Acre, who handed him the magnifying
glass. 'Just here.' She pointed to the right side of the ribcage
of the skeleton with her slender first finger.

'I can't . . .' Hennessey struggled. 'Where?'

'A little nick . . . a small V-shaped groove in the upper
rib . . .'

'Oh, yes, heavens, you know, I freely confess I wouldn't
have seen that . . .' Hennessey spoke softly.

'But you're not a pathologist.' Dr D'Acre smiled. 'I am,
and I am expected to notice such things, but I can't think what
could have caused it, though.'

'A knife?' Hennessey handed the magnifying glass back to
Dr D'Acre.

'No . . . it's been forced in upright; a knife would slide on
its side between the ribs, but this is not a knife.' Dr D'Acre
turned to Eric Filey. 'Eric . . . come and look at this, and tell
us what you think.'

Eric Filey strode across to the dissecting table and took hold of the magnifying glass. 'Just a few millimetres deep,' he observed. 'I've never seen an injury like this, ma'am, but, you know, I think I have a tool at home which would probably cause such a wound.'

'Oh?'

'Yes, ma'am,' Eric Filey continued, 'it's a file . . . it is V-shaped in cross-section, or rather it's triangular in cross-section with three sides and with a different texture on each side. It's about ten inches long and has a blunt tip, but the tip could easily be filed down into quite a murderous point.'

'I think I know the type of file,' Hennessey growled. 'I have indeed seen the like.'

'Yes, I too think I have seen the sort of file about which you speak,' Dr D'Acre murmured, 'and if that sort of file was used with a pointed end . . . and if it was as long as your file, Eric, then it would easily be of sufficient length to reach the heart. So the blow to the head disabled the man, and the thrust into the ribcage with a long file which is thin and triangular in cross-section finished him off. It would have stopped the heart in an instant.'

'Then he was buried in a shallow grave with trees planted on top of him.' Hennessey sighed. 'He deserves justice.'

The woman sat content in the living room of her home and glanced out of the window at the full array of bloom that was her back garden. She had just listened with interest to the hourly news bulletin broadcast on the local radio and she had heard about the discovery of a body near the village of Gate Helmsley, the report saying only that the remains were those of an adult male and adding that the police were appealing for anyone with information to come forward.

The woman allowed herself a brief smile. 'Well, they have got themselves there,' she said to herself. 'They have got there . . . so far so good.' She stood calmly, switched off the radio and then walked into her kitchen; she had her husband's evening meal to prepare.

*     *     *

'So,' Dr D'Acre said, 'let us now return to the issue of identification.' She drummed her slender fingers on the stainless-steel table. 'I'll have the skull photographed, front and side – that will be sufficient for a computer-generated image of his probable appearance. The process takes just a few minutes now; it used to take weeks by slowly building up layers of plasticine on a cast of the skull.' She looked again upon the length of the skeleton. 'I see nothing at all that might help you identify him in terms of significant appearance; there is no damage to one of his legs that would cause him to walk with a limp, for example. One of his arms, say, is not shorter than the other. He had fully formed hands and feet. So . . . unless toxicology comes back with reports of arsenic or other heavy poisons, which in this day and age is unlikely, I think we have a gentleman in his early middle years who was smashed over the head with a blunt object and then had a thin metal object, possibly a file, as we said, thrust powerfully between his ribs and reaching his heart. It would definitely have killed him if the blow to the head did not.'

'How long ago do you think he was killed?' Hennessey asked.

'You should know better than to ask that question by now, Mr Hennessey,' Dr D'Acre smiled reproachfully, 'but I confess I did like the other CID officer's . . .'

'DC Webster?'

'Yes. I did like his observation about the oak tree roots, how they had wrapped round the skeleton rather than pushing through it . . . and the trees themselves seem to be about ten years old. It means that the body was buried, more or less, within about three years, at the same time the trees were planted. If the body had been completely skeletal when the trees were planted the roots would have grown between the ribs, but when the roots reached the body they came across an impenetrable substance and grew round it. So we discovered a skeleton embraced by tree roots. He was buried close to the time that the trees were planted, minus two or three years, and the trees did indeed seem to be about ten years old.'

'Thank you.' Hennessey nodded. 'That gives us a very useful time window to work with, and a likely cause of death and also sufficient information to trawl through our missing persons files looking for a possible match. That's easily good enough to be going on with.'

'Thank you for working late, Eric.' Dr D'Acre turned to Eric Filey.

Filey inclined his head and said, 'Six forty-five, ma'am – that's not late,' and by doing so, once again demonstrated a generosity of spirit which Hennessey had also observed during previous post-mortems. Hennessey had liked the young man upon meeting him and had, over the years, continued to do so.

'We'll get back to you with the deceased's DNA profile as soon as we can; if you can trace a living blood relative that will confirm his identity.' Dr D'Acre returned her attention to George Hennessey.

'Thank you,' Hennessey replied. 'As you say, that will settle the issue of his identity very nicely.'

'It should be with you tomorrow, along with the facial reconstruction,' Dr D'Acre added.

George Hennessey left the low rise, slab-sided sixties building that was the York District Hospital and walked across the car park in the mild early evening air towards Wiggington Road. As he walked his eyes were drawn to a highly polished red and white Riley, circa 1947, and once again he found himself pondering the large size of the car with its graceful lines and yet, by the standards of motor cars built in the early twenty-first century, it had a very cramped interior into which passengers had to step up into, rather than lower themselves down into. Ah, but, he further pondered, great compensation was to be derived from the vehicle – the rich leather upholstery, the solid wooden dashboard, the long bonnet, the envious glances of other motorists and pedestrians, the strong camaraderie of the jolly fellow owners at the Riley Owners Club musters, and even now the car was still a comfortable ride despite the low roof and the cramped leg space. Although it would and did take the salary of a doctor to buy and run one, and he knew that Louise D'Acre had inherited it, lovingly cared for it, and intended to bequeath it to her son.

Hennessey continued to stroll into York, joined the walls at Lendal Bridge and walked weaving amid the tourists to Micklegate Bar where he carefully descended the steep stone steps down to street level. He crossed the street when the traffic lights stopped all vehicular traffic thus allowing foot passengers thirty seconds to make their way across the road, and entered Micklegate Bar Police Station. He signed as being 'in' at the enquiry desk and walked up the stairs to the first floor and to the CID corridor. He walked into the detective constables' room, collected the file on the Gate Helmsley skeleton from the top of Webster's desk and took it to his office. He read Webster's recording, noting that he had made a comment about the age of the oak trees and the manner in which the roots had seemed to wrap around the skeleton, thus giving some indication of the time the body had been buried. Hennessey then added Dr D'Acre's preliminary post-mortem findings as had been verbally given to him, then placed the file in his filing cabinet. He reached for his panama and as he did so he glanced at his watch: 8.10 p.m. He would be home reasonably early for once.


Wednesday, 31 May, 13.40 hours

George Hennessey, relaxed and fully satiated after lunch at the Starre Inne, reputed to be York's oldest hostelry, sat back in his chair in his office at Micklegate Bar Police Station and scanned the newly arrived report which had been faxed to him from Dr D'Acre at the York District Hospital. He picked out the salient points as he read: the toxicity test on the skeleton found near Gate Helmsley had proved negative, as, in fact, had been expected. DNA had been extracted from the marrow in the long bones and a profile had been created should any blood relative be found, thus enabling a conclusive identification to be made. A cross-section of one of the teeth suggested that the deceased was approximately forty-seven years old when he died. The cause of death, he read, was likely to be a combination of both the blow to the head and a long-bladed instrument entering the right of the ribcage at a slightly upward angle. Individually Dr D'Acre wrote, either might be fatal, but the combination of both injuries definitely would have been, especially if the blade had reached and had entered the aorta. Hennessey laid the report upon his desk top just as his phone warbled. He let it ring three times before leisurely extending his hand and picking up the handset. 'DCI Hennessey,' he answered.

'It's the switchboard here, sir.' The voice was female, young and sounded nervous. Hennessey heard an evident desire to please in the shaking voice; he also detected an enthusiasm behind the nervousness.

'Yes, switchboard,' he replied, calmly but authoritatively.

'There is a caller on the line, sir, a lady caller,' the switchboard operator explained. 'She says that she is calling in response to the e-fit which appeared in the morning edition of the local paper, sir.'

'Well, well, that is indeed a rapid response.' Hennessey groped for his notepad with his free hand and drew it towards him, then took his pen from his jacket pocket and held it poised over the notepad, which was firmly in his left hand, the pen in his right, and compressed the telephone handset against his right ear, in a practised manner, with his right shoulder. 'Very well, thank you. Can you put the caller through, please?'

'Hello . . .' the voice seemed meek, hesitant. 'Hello . . . hello . . .'

'Yes, madam,' Hennessey replied warmly. 'I understand that you are phoning in response to the e-fit which was printed in this morning's newspaper. Is that so?'

'Yes, yes I am . . .' the voice continued to sound nervous and hesitant. 'I think it may be my husband . . . he vanished some time ago. In fact, I know it's him.'

'I see.' Hennessey spoke softly, hoping thereby to encourage the woman's confidence. 'Very well.'

'I am certain,' the woman continued. 'I am confident that that is a picture of my husband. It is him . . . after all this time. It is him.'

'Your husband?' Hennessey repeated. 'I see.'

'Yes . . . his name is . . . was . . . James Wenlock.'

'James Wenlock,' Hennessey repeated as he wrote the name on his notepad.

'Yes, spelled exactly as it sounds . . . spelled like the place in Shropshire, you know . . . Wenlock Edge.'

'Yes . . . yes.' Hennessey wrote in his notepad.

'You know it?' The woman remained hesitant.

'Well . . . I know the location only by courtesy of the poem by AE Houseman, *On Wenlock Edge*,' Hennessey explained, 'so I have the correct spelling.'

'Yes, that's it,' the woman became more confident, 'spelled as in the poem, *On Wenlock Edge*. James, my husband, disappeared about ten years ago, at about just this time of year, in fact. He vanished as if into thin air . . .' the voice became excited, 'ten years ago . . . now his picture's in the paper . . . his e-fit or whatever it's called, but it's him, it's him.'

'All right,' Hennessey spoke in a calm voice, 'so long as you're sure, this is very good.'

'Yes, the e-fit has given him hair while in fact James was almost totally bald . . . his nose was much smaller than the nose shown in the e-fit . . . but the face, the cheekbones, his pointy little jaw, the high forehead, the overall thinness of his face . . . I tell you, sir, it's him all right . . .'

'Good . . . well, thank you for calling, Mrs Wenlock,' Hennessey replied. 'I assume it is Mrs Wenlock?'

'Yes, it is Mrs Wenlock; I have not reverted to my maiden name, nor remarried. It's still Mrs Wenlock, it always will be. Never will change it.'

'Very well. What is your address, please, Mrs Wenlock?'

Mrs Wenlock gave an address in Selby and added, 'Is that all right? I mean, is it all right to call the police in York? It was the number printed in the newspaper.'

'It's all right, Mrs Wenlock – it is the correct number that you phoned. The Vale of York police cover Selby.' Hennessey allowed his calming smile to be heard down the phone line for the benefit of the anxious and excited Mrs Wenlock. 'It's all our area, or our patch, as we say, so no worries there. Can I ask if you'll be at home this afternoon? I'd like to arrange for two of my officers to visit you to take a statement from you . . . and also to ask you a few questions?'

'Oh, yes, I was going out – there is something I want to do, but for this I will stay at home . . . for James I will stay at home, of course I will. Heavens . . . it's been a long ten years, so yes, yes, I'll wait for the police.'

'I assume you reported your husband as a mis per?' Hennessey asked.

'Mis per?'

'Sorry, police speak, I meant a missing person,' Hennessey explained.

'Oh, yes, yes I did, but to the Wetherby police, not the York police.' Mrs Wenlock was by then calming, quite rapidly.

'That's all right. We'll have the report here. After the person has been reported missing for more than forty-eight hours the information is sent here, to this police station to be placed in our archives.' Hennessey continued to talk in a relaxed and an assured manner. 'How old was Mr Wenlock when he disappeared?'

'Forty-six,' Mrs Wenlock replied. 'We were already planning to take a cruise for his fiftieth birthday . . . we had all the brochures and were poring over them.'

'I see. I am sorry to hear that.' Hennessey scribbled on his notepad. 'That really is quite tragic. It must have been quite a loss to you . . . really quite a blow.'

'It was at the time, it was a massive blow . . . but now these days it's the not knowing which gnaws away at me,' Mrs Wenlock explained. 'The horrible not knowing. It's awful.'

'Yes, it would do. I can understand that. Well, hopefully this might be the beginning of the end of it all for you; you might at least get some closure now,' Hennessey replied. 'Thank you for calling us, Mrs Wenlock . . . two of my officers will be with you very shortly.'

'Thank you, sir,' Mrs Wenlock replied with a soft but strong voice now fully calmed. 'Thank you very much.'

'No . . . it is really for us to thank you, ma'am,' Hennessey assured her. 'Yours was a very prompt response. Thank you.' He gently replaced the handset then picked it up again and dialled a four-figure internal number. 'Collator?' he asked when his phone call was rapidly answered.

'Yes, sir.' The male voice was crisp, alert, reassuringly efficient sounding.

'Can you please dig out a missing persons file in the name of James Wenlock, aged forty-six when he disappeared about ten years ago? He had a home address in Selby,' Hennessey asked.

'Got it, sir,' replied the crisp, alert voice. 'Wenlock, James, forty-six, home address in Selby. I'm on it. Leave it with me.'

'Good man,' Hennessey again let his smile be heard down the phone. 'Send it up to me as soon as you have retrieved it from the archives.'

'Yes, sir. It will be with you asap.'

Once again Hennessey replaced the handset of his telephone, then picked it up but thought better of using it. Picking up his notebook, he stood and walked down the CID corridor to the detective constables' room, and for a few seconds stood motionless on the threshold. He noted both Reginald Webster and Carmen Pharoah to be present. Carmen Pharoah was sitting at her desk writing; Webster, by contrast, Hennessey observed, was standing at the window looking out at the townscape behind Micklegate Bar Police Station, hands in his trouser pockets.

'Not too busy, I see, Reg.' Hennessey quietly announced his presence. Webster spun round, white-faced. 'Oh, sorry, sir. Really just this very second I stood up, a loud bang, like an explosion . . . and being a copper . . .'

'That's true, sir,' Carmen Pharoah added, 'it was really quite an explosion. We were both startled by it; it's strange you didn't hear it.'

'Yes, yes . . . all right.' Hennessey held up his hand. 'Well, one of you write this address down, please.' Hennessey then read out Mrs Wenlock's address in Selby.

'I have it, sir,' Carmen Pharoah replied, having written on her own notepad. 'That's quite a well-to-do area of Selby, I believe.'

'Well, I dare say you'll find out if you're right or not.' Hennessey closed his notebook. 'I'd like you two to visit her. She, Mrs Wenlock, has just phoned claiming to recognize the e-fit printed in today's paper as being that of her husband, her missing husband. One James Wenlock, Esquire.'

'Really?' Webster took his jacket off the back of his chair. 'That was timely.'

'So she claims, and she sounded very earnest. I'd like you two to visit her, asap – see what you see, find what you find.'

'Yes, sir.' Carmen Pharoah stood and reached for her light-weight summer jacket. 'Movement already, that can't be bad . . . can't be bad at all.'

'Obtain a sample of his or his familial DNA if you can,' Hennessey said as he turned and left the room. 'That would clinch the issue of identification very neatly.'

'Yes, sir,' Webster responded promptly as he put his jacket on.

Reginald Webster and Carmen Pharoah glanced at each other when Hennessey had left the room. Pharoah inclined her head reproachfully and Webster shrugged and then grinned. 'Thanks,' he said quietly, 'I owe you one.'

She returned the grin. 'Well, we work with liars and con men all the time; their well-honed skill tends to rub off on one. But I confess I was wondering when you were going to return to your desk, roof tops and backyards and new buildings on the skyline indeed. What on earth was it that held your fascination for so long?'

'Well, nothing really,' Webster conceded as he picked up his notepad. 'The world outside just suddenly became more interesting than the monthly statistical returns for the merry month of May just gone. All right, let's go and visit a lady in beautiful Selby; see what we see, as the boss says . . . and find what we find.'

Upon returning to his office Hennessey saw that, in the brief period of his absence, the missing persons file in respect of James Wenlock, forty-six, late of Selby, had been placed on his desk and had been done so with due deference, in the middle of his desk facing him, rather than left as if dropped haphazardly. He sat in his chair, picked up the file and opened it. He saw instantly that the photograph in the file did indeed resemble the e-fit published in that morning's newspaper, and was of a man with a smaller nose than that shown on the e-fit, but other than that, Mrs Wenlock was, he strongly suspected – indeed, believed – going to be proven correct. Her husband, or the remains of, at least, had now been found. Mr Wenlock's occupation, Hennessey read, was given as that of accountant. Other than that there was no more information in the file. The police had evidently done all they could at the time: they had taken note of the name of the missing person, the address, next of kin, put a photograph in the file and noted the date that James Wenlock was reported missing, knowing that the missing person would turn up alive and well within twenty-four hours, as most missing persons did, or else their body would either be found or it wouldn't. Only in exceptional circumstances, where there was clear evidence of foul play, would the police search for an adult missing person and, as Hennessey saw, this clearly had not been one such occasion. James Wenlock had quite simply vanished.

Mrs Wenlock's house revealed itself to be, as Carmen Pharoah had suggested, in a prestigious area of Selby. It stood set back from the main road leading westward out of the town. A well-tended sunken lawn of perhaps thirty feet in depth separated the house from the roadway. The lawn was bounded on both sides by thick and neatly kept shrubs; beyond the line of shrubs to the left, as an observer would view the house, there was a stone-paved drive, at the top of which was a brick built garage affording accommodation for just one car, and which stood separate from the house. The house itself was inter-war vintage, probably built in the late thirties, Webster guessed. A front door stood between two large bay windows with windows above those on the ground floor and also above the door. The house was, by then, built of faded red brick under a steeply sloping black-tiled roof which evidently, thought Webster, as he and Carmen Pharoah viewed the house, afforded much attic space. The house would, he further thought, greatly please his father-in-law, who had endlessly advised him not to consider buying any property built after the end of the Second World War. 'Take it from me, Reginald – they just don't build them any more – not properly anyway. They throw them together these days.' He had gone on to disappoint his father-in-law by buying a new-built house on the edge of a village. It was all very well for his father-in-law to have given that advice, he had argued, but let him try buying an inter-war house in the area of a town, any town, where he and his wife would want to live and do so on a detective constable's salary.

He and Carmen Pharoah walked slowly but purposefully from where they had parked their car at the kerb in front of the lawn of Mrs Wenlock's house, side by side up the driveway, at the top of which they turned to their right and walked past the first bayed window to the front door. The door, like the rest of the wood of the house, the window frames and the garage door, had been painted a loud canary yellow. The battery operated bell, when pressed, they discovered, rang the Westminster chimes.

'A burglar deterrent?' Carmen Pharoah glanced at Reginald Webster. 'What do you think?'

'Sorry?' Webster, listening with interest to the plethora of sound, the birdsong, a railway locomotive's two-tone horn in the far distance and the low rumble of traffic from the road beyond the lawn, was caught off-guard by Pharoah's questions.

'The colour of the house,' Pharoah explained, 'the yellow painted wood and the drainpipe too . . . it's not at all to my taste.'

'Nor mine,' Webster agreed.

'But it might deter a burglar?' she suggested.

'You think?' Webster raised his eyebrows.

'Well, yes . . . colours have different effects on people and yellow is a colour you shy away from.'

'Really?' Webster was intrigued.

'Yes, I believe so.' Carmen Pharoah turned and pondered the large amount of work that had clearly gone into maintaining the garden. 'All things being equal – all other things, I mean – a burglar would be less attracted to a house painted yellow than he would to a house painted black, for example, which is a colour which folk apparently find attractive and welcoming despite its association with funerals. The burglar would probably not be conscious of being attracted or repelled by a colour but I bet the influence would be felt on a subconscious level.'

'Maybe . . .' Webster also pondered the garden. 'I confess I didn't know that . . . about colours, I mean.'

'Oh, yes . . . for example, haven't you noticed how all the fast-food eateries lure you in with a bright red sign on the outside of the building, and yet once you are in and seated you are assaulted with the colour yellow glaring at you from every angle? The red pulls you in, you see, and then, once they have your money, the yellow hastens you on your weary way.' Carmen Pharoah raised her eyebrows. 'It's quite true. Believe me. There's thinking and pre-meditation behind the red and the yellow in these places.'

'My eyes,' Reginald Webster inclined his head in gratitude, 'have been opened, widely so.'

Any further discussion about the influence of colours upon the human psyche between our two heroes, was, dear reader, prevented by the opening of the front door. It was swung open, widely so, in a confident manner by a slender, middle-aged lady who was dressed in a yellow blouse which was the same shade as the colour of her house, a white three-quarter-length skirt, light shaded nylons and yellow shoes with small, sensible heels. She wore her hair short cropped. She had rings upon her fingers and bracelets, and a small watch upon her wrist. 'The police?' she asked. Her face was narrow with high cheek-bones, her voice soft and pleasing.

'Yes, ma'am.' Webster took his ID from his jacket pocket and showed it to her. Carmen Pharoah did likewise. 'You are Mrs Wenlock?'

'Yes, yes, I am, and I am, of course, expecting you. I spoke with your Mr Hennessey earlier today. He indicated that two of his officers would be calling on me directly.' Mrs Wenlock's voice, as well as being soft and pleasing, Webster noted, could, he thought, also be accurately described as mellifluous.

'Yes.' Webster replaced his ID in his jacket pocket. 'Mr Hennessey is our boss, and we are part of his team. We are the two officers he spoke of.'

'I see.' Mrs Wenlock stepped nimbly aside. 'Well, do please come in.'

The door opened on to a wide hallway with a dark brown-coloured carpet and highly polished wooden panelling, and smelled strongly of a mixture of carpet cleaner and wood polish. A black telephone stood on a low wooden table beyond the door, and a wide carpeted stairway rose up to the upper floor of the house. China plates gripped in metal braces and attached to the wall panelling provided tasteful decoration.

'If you could please go into the rear sitting room,' Mrs Wenlock closed the front door, 'second door on the right, or the parlour as my late father would have referred to it, God rest his soul.'

Webster, followed closely by Carmen Pharoah, walked quietly down the hall, pushed upon the second door on the right, as directed, and entered a large living room, gently decorated with a light blue fitted carpet and cream-coloured coverings over the armchairs and settee. Full bookshelves lined the wall opposite the door; the window looked out upon what Webster thought was a disappointingly modest rear garden though it was as well tended as the front garden. A small television set stood in the corner of the room, beneath which was a silver-coloured hi-fi system and a CD player.

'I put the dogs outside, which is why I was a little delayed in answering the door,' Mrs Wenlock explained as she entered the room. 'If you can't see them it's because they will have found some shade for themselves. Two black Labradors . . . like all brown and black dogs they do not do well in the heat. I knew you'd be the police so I knew I'd be safe, but I'm exceedingly grateful for their presence, during the night especially.'

'You live alone?' Carmen Pharoah 'read' the room: all age and social class appropriate, she thought, and felt, thusly, reassured.

'Yes, yes I do.' Mrs Wenlock sank gracefully into an armchair and, with a clearly practised gesture of her right arm and open palm, invited Webster and Pharoah also to take a seat. Reginald Webster sat in the remaining armchair, whilst Carmen Pharoah contented herself with the centre of the settee. 'I have two sons,' Mrs Wenlock continued. 'Both went to university and both didn't come back, as is often the way of it, and so for the greater part of each year, these days, I am alone in the house, but I am visited at Christmas and my birthday and also on one or two other occasions. The boys were much closer to James, my husband, than they were to me, so because of that the "old woman" is visited out of a sense of duty only – just token visits, with limited access to my grandchildren. Very limited access. I am held to blame for my husband's disappearance, you see.'

'You are blamed?' Carmen Pharoah sat forward. 'Why . . . in what sense are you to blame, or held to blame?'

'Why . . . why indeed . . . well, I suppose it's because our marriage had its ups and downs,' Mrs Wenlock glanced up at the ceiling, 'and I dare say that if I am to be at all honest it had more downs than ups . . . rows . . . such awful rows and such awful arguments . . . you can imagine it, I am sure . . . and the boys, my two dear sons, said I drove James away and they said that he just walked away into the wilderness and stumbled into a river somewhere, and his body was never found . . . or it remains still to be found. If I hadn't been such a shrew of a woman then he just wouldn't have left this house looking for peace, which is all he ever wanted. Just a peaceful home. If I hadn't been such a harridan . . . if . . . if . . . if. You know, they even found a copy of the Saint James' Bible – the Authorized version, and pushed it under my nose opened at the Book of Proverbs and pointed to the proverb "It is better to live alone in a hovel than to share a mansion with a difficult woman". They were making their point, and I felt it was a waste of my limited time to point out that the whole of the Authorized version has a misogynistic quality, and that in the New International version the word "woman" has been replaced by the word "person", but I did anyway, I told them so – I even showed them – but it did no good, no good at all. They said, "Woman or person, it's the same in this house – once we were up and grown he went away seeking peace . . ." So there you are, I am to blame, and that's the long and the short of it.' Mrs Wenlock forced a smile. 'But I have my dogs, Terry and Toni. They recognize their names and they have different personalities, though I treat them the same. I am always very careful to do that, always very careful.'

'So are you to blame,' Carmen Pharoah asked, 'or are your sons being wholly unfair? Are they seeking a scapegoat?'

'I really don't know. I always thought that James gave as good as he got. He could stand up for himself and I walked out once . . . Came back a few days later . . .' Mrs Wenlock glanced out of the window. 'So I don't know . . . Perhaps they are being a little unfair.'

'So . . . what,' Pharoah asked, 'do you know of his disappearance?'

'Very little.' Mrs Wenlock's reply was prompt and, thought Webster, suddenly a little sharp-tongued. 'All I know is that one evening he did not come home. Simple as that. One night his car's headlights did not sweep across our bedroom window as I dutifully lay in bed awaiting his return. He had, I recall, been keeping many late nights just prior to his disappearance and he'd often return with his breath reeking of alcohol. It was as if he would drink to avoid coming home and then he stupidly risks everything by driving his car while under the influence. You know, I dare say that I should have been a better wife . . . a man needs a good, warm woman to come home to and it was the case that I was always icy when he returned, but that is how our marriage had become. I really should have done better, much, much better. James was an excellent provider. I mean, will you just look at this house – who could complain about living here? A five-bedroom detached house in a lovely, quiet, civilized town. If you live in a town which has a tourist industry then you have landed on your feet. You know, the small wood beyond our back lawn there is also part of this property. The house, this house, occupies a plot of one acre of ground, only one third of which is cultivated as a garden; the wood is left to nature but it belongs to this house.' Mrs Wenlock paused. 'James did us really proud . . . and if I did drive him away and he went walking on the moors and fell down a ravine . . . oh . . . that possibility I have been living with . . .'

'Well,' Reginald Webster spoke, 'if the remains which have been found are those of your husband then he did not fall into a ravine. He was in fact a victim of foul play.'

'Foul play?' Mrs Wenlock gasped. 'You mean murder? You mean that he was murdered?'

'It appears so . . . in fact,' Reginald Webster quietly explained, 'the skeleton in question has injuries, and the shallow grave . . . it is clearly the remains of a murder victim but whether the skeleton is the remains of Mr Wenlock, your husband, remains to be established.'

'Oh . . . I see . . . but the e-fit . . .' Mrs Wenlock appealed to Webster then looked at Carmen Pharoah.

'The e-fit is merely an approximation of the likely deceased's appearance,' Webster explained. 'It is not proof of identity.'

'What am I going to tell the boys?' Mrs Wenlock wailed. 'Now they'll say I definitely sent him to his death . . .'

'Do you have anything which might contain your husband's DNA?' Pharoah asked, rapidly beginning to tire of what she strongly suspected was wallowing self-pity on the part of Mrs Wenlock.

'DNA?' Mrs Wenlock asked. 'Like what they talk about on television?'

'Yes,' Pharoah explained. 'A strand of his hair, a piece of fabric with a sweat stain on it . . . his perspiration, I mean.'

'I don't think that I can, sorry,' Mrs Wenlock said apologetically. 'I keep a clean house; I am very particular about keeping a clean house, most particular.'

'Yes,' Pharoah smiled, 'we can see that. In fact, you would not believe some of the houses we have to visit.'

'I can imagine . . . This house is kept this way as a reaction to the house I grew up in . . . it was the sort of household I think you are alluding to.'

'I see,' Pharoah replied. 'I fully understand you.'

'Mrs Wenlock,' Reginald Webster interrupted, 'can I ask you a bit of a delicate question?'

'Of course.' Mrs Wenlock turned to him.

'Your two sons,' Webster replied. 'Your two boys?'

'Yes? What of them?'

'They were James Wenlock's children?'

'Yes,' Mrs Wenlock frowned. 'Who else's could they be?'

'So they were not adopted,' Webster confirmed. 'Adopted or fostered, or children from a previous relationship?'

'No, no and no,' Mrs Wenlock replied firmly, sitting forwards as she did so. 'They are both our natural children.'

'Good, that will help us. You see, if you cannot provide something containing Mr Wenlock's DNA we can obtain DNA from your sons – with their permission, of course. It is called familial DNA and will enable us to establish whether the remains are those of your husband or not.'

'Oh . . . I see.' Mrs Wenlock relaxed her attitude and sat back in her chair. 'I am sure that they will be only too pleased to help you, and they both live locally.'

'Good, that will be very useful,' Carmen Pharoah replied. Then she asked, 'We understand that your husband was an accountant?'

'Yes, yes he was,' Mrs Wenlock replied with a clear note of pride in her voice. 'He worked for Russell Square.'

'In London?' Pharoah could not contain her surprise. 'In Bloomsbury? *That* Russell Square? *The* Russell Square . . . ?'

'No, no . . .' Mrs Wenlock stammered. 'Well, yes, *the* Russell Square in central London as you say, in fact I know of no other town or city in the UK which also has a Russell Square, but the Russell Square in question is the name of the firm of accountants which employed my husband . . . Russell Square Chartered Accountants, Saint Leonard's Place, York. I dare say their address had to be Saint Leonard's Place, among all the solicitors. It was, and still is, a very large firm of accountants. He . . . James, my husband, went to work and returned from work. I know nothing of what went on in the between time. I know nothing of the world of accounting. I am not learned like he was . . . We met through a hiking club . . . When I was employed I was a nursing auxiliary. Nothing grand at all. Very modest, but as a nursing auxiliary I learned how to keep things clean. I learned the value of hygiene.'

'A nurse is learned.' Carmen Pharoah smiled. 'Nothing to feel demeaned about there. Nurses are valued.'

'A theatre nurse who assists in operations is learned, but I was only an auxiliary. Nursing auxiliaries help patients to the toilet and empty the bedpans of those patients who can't go to the toilet, that sort of thing. I did not return to work upon marriage.' Mrs Wenlock sighed. 'I did not want to go back to that. But I learned about hygiene and I kept a clean home for my family to grow up in.'

'I see. So what is your income . . . if I may ask?' Pharoah queried.

'You may ask, of course you may ask, it is your job after all.' Mrs Wenlock paused. 'I am living off the money James left me, and he did leave me reasonably well provided for. He left cash in the bank, he left stocks and shares. I inherited it all when, after two years from his reported disappearance, he was deemed to be deceased. I can't claim on his life insurance policy, of course – the insurance company need a death certificate before they will pay up. I was, and am, helped by the fact that the mortgage was paid off before James vanished. That was a mighty comfort but I still have to watch the pennies. I buy my clothes from charity shops and I have not had a holiday since he disappeared. My garden is tended by a kindly gentleman who is a fellow parishioner at Saint Luke's. He will not accept any money for his labour, just a home-cooked meal when he is here . . . He is a widower, you see.'

'I see.'

'So that's how I survive. The image might seem impressive but my outgoings are few and the dependency upon charity in one form or another is great.' Mrs Wenlock sighed again, deeply so. 'The money which we were putting aside for the cruise to celebrate his fiftieth birthday was used to buy food for myself over the years.'

'So things were not all bad between you?' Carmen Pharoah suggested. 'A cruise . . . that can't be bad . . . can't be bad at all.'

'If I am honest, it was more for form's sake really.' Mrs Wenlock shook her head slowly. 'For appearances' sake. So rather than tell the world that there were difficulties between us . . . that things were stressed to breaking point, we decided to put on a show to celebrate that milestone in a man's life, to do something to give the right impression, but the money we had earmarked for the cruise has kept me in baked beans and tinned chilli con carne for the last few years. You know, I only really cook a proper meal when Eric Lucas calls to tend the garden.'

'Can I . . . can we,' Reginald Webster brought the interview back on track, 'ask if your husband had any enemies? That is, any enemies that you knew of?'

'Enemies? James?' Mrs Wenlock gasped. 'None . . . if he did I didn't hear of any . . . no, I am sure . . . none, no enemies.

He was a professional man. He wasn't a businessman or a gangster; those sorts of people have enemies . . . not mild-mannered accountants. Mind you, even if he did I doubt very much that he'd tell me. We just didn't have that level of communication – not at the time he vanished anyway. You know, we'd just sit here each evening in total silence . . . not saying anything at all.' Again, she shook her head. 'I should have been a better wife. I really should have. If I did drive him into the hands of someone who murdered him . . . Oh,' Mrs Wenlock looked suddenly alert, 'would you like his toothbrush?'

'His . . . toothbrush?' Carmen Pharoah queried. 'Your husband's toothbrush, you mean?'

'Yes . . . for the DNA you have just mentioned. For some odd and strange reason I kept it; it's just about the one thing I didn't throw away. He had bad gums . . . gum disease and, you see, they would bleed freely each time he brushed his teeth . . .'

'Sounds ideal,' Pharoah replied, glancing at Reginald Webster who nodded his agreement. 'That sounds just the thing. And if DNA can't be extracted from it we can always ask your two sons to cooperate. So yes, thank you. It will be useful. Very useful indeed.'

Reginald Webster returned home after recording the visit he and Carmen Pharoah had made to Mrs James Wenlock, while Pharoah had arranged the conveyance of James Wenlock's bloodstained toothbrush to the forensic science laboratory at Wetherby for their attention. He drove leisurely, returning to Selby, though not to the prestigious home of Mrs Wenlock but his much more modest home on a modern housing estate which surrounded an ancient village on the edge of the town. As he approached the house he sounded the car's horn, giving the agreed and long-established sign of two short beeps. Doing so was a violation of traffic laws, he knew that, as did his neighbours, but none complained for they all knew the reason. He halted his car at the kerb outside his home just as Joyce opened the door and allowed Terry, their long-haired Alsatian out of the house, who bounded up to him with his tail wagging in greeting. He patted the dog and then strode up to the house, talking to his wife as he approached so that she could gauge the shortening distance between them. He embraced her and kissed her gently on the lips. 'Sorry I'm late,' he said. 'Sorry, sorry, sorry.'

Joyce Webster lifted the glass covering the face of her watch and 'read' the time with her fingertips. 'Not late at all,' she replied. 'I have prepared a salad for us.'

'Lovely,' Reginald Webster replied, knowing how his wife enjoyed summer, that being the only time of the year when she could prepare a meal for her husband because he forbade her to even attempt to prepare hot food. 'A salad sounds perfect. I'll likely be busy over the next few days.' He slipped off his jacket and hung it in the wardrobe which stood in the hallway.

'Big case?' Joyce Webster led the way to the dining kitchen.

'New . . . and yes, big enough. Dare say you'll hear about it – the boss seems keen to use the press as much as he can.'

Later that mellow summer evening as he took Terry for a walk, Reginald Webster once again found himself pondering what he always saw as his wife's indomitable courage. She had tragically lost her sight in a car accident when she was just twenty years of age and at university studying fine art, of all things, and nonetheless was forever feeling herself fortunate to have survived because her three companions had been fatally injured. Her fortitude and her optimism was, he thought, inspirational.

In northern France Antoine Chadid sat silently in the living room of his house and read and reread the letter he had received from his brother Jules that day, in which Jules outlined his travelling plans once his present contract of employment had come to its end. His mind turned unbidden to his boyhood and the summers spent with Jules concealed in their hide photographing birds with the camera and its telephoto lens. Sometimes in acts of impish behaviour they would also photo- graph human activity . . . the two young lovers lying in the meadow . . . the middle-aged couple arguing . . . the drunken man being carried into a vehicle with UK number plates, and then driven away by two despairing women.

It was Wednesday, 22.10 hours.

# TWO

Thursday, 1 June, 09.20 hours – 22.50 hours

*In which James Wenlock's private life unfolds, a woman tells her tale and Carmen Pharoah is at home to the gracious reader.*

George Hennessey leaned leisurely back in his chair and cupped his fleshly and slightly liver-spotted hands round the mug of hot tea which he was holding. 'Just can't think without this lovely stuff,' he commented, lifting the tea to his lips and, finding it to be still too hot to drink, lowered it again. 'So,' he said, 'we can begin to assume that the identity of the person in the shallow grave at Gate Helmsley is that of James Wenlock. The DNA test will be a match, a positive identification. In my old copper's waters I can feel the certainty very strongly: the man's age, the similarity of the e-fit, the local nature of Mr Wenlock's address and his place of employment, the man's height . . . everything so far dovetails neatly with the information given in the mis-per report, and so we have quite a mystery on our hands, a murder most foul to solve.'

'It does seem so, sir.' Somerled Yellich held his own mug of tea in one hand and the opened case file in the other. 'I've read Carmen's recording and she paints a clear picture of Mr Ordinary, an accountant, with a settled though apparently none too happy marriage by all accounts.'

'By one account, Somerled, and only by one account.' Hennessey began to sip his mug of tea. 'So far we only have Mrs Wenlock's view of her marriage.'

Somerled Yellich opened the palm of his hand in acknowledgement of Hennessey's point, and then continued, 'He had two children, now up and away . . . and he had an appropriate standard of living given his reported position in life, an accountant, no less. Was that the impression you two got?'

'Yes, Sarge.' Carmen Pharoah sat upright in her chair. 'Yes . . . I . . . we detected nothing at all that could be seen as suspicious, nothing untoward or out of place, just a widowed lady living alone with two black Labradors, which we didn't see, and she was intent on blaming herself for everything. I dare say it was better than blaming other people for everything but I thought that it did get a little tedious after a while. She was . . . is, very self-absorbed, wouldn't you say, Reg? She is very "me, me, me" . . . ?'

'Yes, definitely.' Reginald Webster also clasped his mug of tea with both hands. 'I would go along fully with that. Nothing to cause suspicion about the house and a woman who thinks it really is all about her but who is not suspicious in herself.'

'Two adult children,' Hennessey commented. 'Do we have any suspicions there? I mean to say that if we were to follow the book of rules we'd look at the in-laws before we'd look at the outlaws.'

'Well . . . sir,' Carmen Pharoah was first to respond, 'Mrs Wenlock didn't hide the fact that the marriage was less than perfect, but she did say that the boys were closer to their father than they were to her and she claimed that they blamed her for his disappearance but, as you say, we have only her word for that. I would think that a visit to the two sons might be . . . how shall I put it? Illuminating?'

'Which is what I was thinking,' Hennessey replied softly. 'Do we perchance know where each of her sons lives?'

'No . . . sorry, sir.' Pharoah looked embarrassed and glanced at Webster. 'I'm sorry, we should have . . .'

'No matter,' Hennessey held up his hand, 'a simple phone call to the good Mrs Wenlock will be sufficient to obtain their addresses. Can you do that please, Carmen? And then you and Reg can visit the sons. I want you two to stay teamed up on this one; you seem to be working well together.'

'Yes, skipper,' Webster responded alertly.

'So, an accountant,' Hennessey continued, 'and those four postcards of Scarborough which started it all, that is a mystery within a mystery. Somebody wanted James Wenlock's body to be found, someone with a conscience perhaps? We might never know . . . but anyway, the sender of the cards is of interest but not a priority.' Hennessey gulped his tea, then reached forward and lifted up the copy of the *Yellow Pages* which lay on his desk top and turned to 'Accountants'. 'Yes . . .' he said, 'here we are . . . Russell Square, Chartered Accountants and with an address in Saint Leonard's Place, just where Mrs Wenlock said they'd be and just where any self-respecting firm of accountants would indeed locate themselves. So, Somerled . . . a visit for you and Thompson to undertake.'

'Yes, sir,' Yellich again replied promptly.

'I can report,' Hennessey advised, 'that the forensic science laboratory came back with a negative result in respect of the postcards; there were no latents at all and the postage stamps were of the modern self-adhesive type so no DNA could be obtained from any saliva, as would be the case if the stamps had been licked. The postcards themselves unfortunately did not have a barcode on the reverse, which might otherwise have helped us pin down a retail outlet. Some postcards do . . . but these did not, so the sender was either lucky or he or she knew what they were doing when they selected the cards.' Hennessey paused. 'Right . . . so we all know what we are doing?'

'Yes, skipper,' Somerled Yellich replied. 'Understood.'

'Yes, boss,' Webster echoed. 'Clear as daylight.'

'Good, and also remember it is essential that you let me or anyone else in the team know if you deviate from your assigned visits.' Hennessey leaned forward. 'I must know – we must know – where each other is at all times.'

'Understood.' Reginald Webster replied for the whole team. 'That's also as clear as daylight.'

'James Wenlock.' The man's face initially, briefly, beamed with pleasure and warmth then very quickly turned into a scowl. 'Yes . . . yes, he was employed here, he was one of the team . . . ' Clarence Bellingham had revealed himself to be a portly man when he'd received Somerled Yellich and Thompson Ventnor in his office. He had a full, round face and, Yellich thought, for an accountant, was somewhat flamboyantly dressed in a plum-coloured suit, a blue shirt and a loud yellow bow tie. His office walls were lined with leather-bound books, save for the fourth wall in which the door was set and which was reserved for the display of prints of famous paintings. Bellingham, Yellich noted as he recognized Vermeer's, Bruegel's, Frabritius's and de Hooch's work, clearly favoured the Dutch and Flemish schools. The man himself sat behind a heavy-looking, highly polished wooden desk. Ventnor and Yellich sat in leather armchairs in front of him. The carpet was deep-piled and dark brown in colour. The room smelled richly of furniture polish and the view from the widow overlooked St Leonard's Place and the theatre. 'Yes, James, or "Jimmy", but we at Russell Square frown on nicknames really. So, James Wenlock was with us for about . . . how long? About . . . yes, about fifteen years, I believe, and then he vanished. It was all very odd. A real mystery. He was a certified accountant, a lower status than a chartered accountant like me,' Bellingham added, a little smugly in Yellich's view. 'I am a chartered accountant as are, of course, all the partners in Russell Square. The salaried staff are certified accountants but they do sterling work, really they are the backbone of our service.'

'I see.' Somerled Yellich sat forward. 'Would you say, Mr Bellingham, that so far as you can recall, James Wenlock was happy and content whilst he was employed at Russell Square?'

'I would say so,' Bellingham replied cautiously. 'He wasn't a management problem in any way, which is often the sign of a malcontent in employment. He was with us for quite a number of years, as I said. He qualified on the job rather than by attending university and obtaining his charter. All certified accountants do that, you see. They qualify by taking a series of professional body exams whilst working.'

'He came up through tools, as it were?' Yellich asked.

'Yes, you could say that . . . he came up through the tools. Somerled,' Bellingham beamed, 'S-o-r-e-l-y? That is an unusual name.'

'Gaelic,' Yellich replied and told Bellingham the correct spelling of his name.

'Yes . . . I thought it must have been. I have a very distant

relative with that name and I have never known how it was
spelled, until now. So, it's S-o-m-e-r-l-e-d. How interesting.
You know, as I child I would invent puns on his name such
as, "he is sorely missed" and "my cousin sorely injured
himself", though I kept it all to myself. I sensed it would not
go down very well with my straight-laced parents . . . but it
did amuse me. I'm sorry, I digress . . .'

'No matter, sir, no matter. So, can I ask, is there anything
that you might think relevant to Mr Wenlock's disappearance
and to his murder?'

'His murder!' Bellingham paled. 'He was murdered?'

'Yes, I am sorry to say. The skeleton found at Gate Helmsley
. . . you may have heard about it in the news.'

'That was James Wenlock?' Bellingham gasped. 'I saw the
news reports . . . yes, I saw them . . . my . . . that was . . . is
James Wenlock?'

'Yes, I'm afraid to say we are all but one hundred per cent
certain, just awaiting the DNA test results as we speak, but
everything points to the remains as being those of James
Wenlock.' Yellich spoke solemnly. 'We have notified his family.
We are certain enough of the identity of the skeleton to do
that.'

'Well I never.' Bellingham glanced to his left and out of
his office window towards the cream-coloured walls of the
theatre, then turned to the officers. 'This really is going to
take some absorbing . . . for all of us who remember him . . .
my heavens.'

'So . . .' Yellich pressed, 'if you can, can you tell us what
Mr Wenlock was like as an employee?'

'He seemed to be conscientious, I would have said.'
Bellingham looked at his desk top. 'We certainly never had
any form of complaint about him or his work, not that I can
recall either from colleagues or clients. He seemed to be a
good, steady worker.' Bellingham nodded. 'Yes, I can say that
– he was a good, steady worker.'

'I see . . . and as a person, as a personality, how did he
impress?' Yellich asked.

'Ah, well, as I said . . . a reliable worker, no complaints
there, but as a person . . .' Bellingham paused, looked upwards

and seemed to Yellich to consult the ornate plasterwork on the ceiling. 'Well, I don't wish to speak ill of the dead and to be fair, I didn't know him well, but quite frankly and only so far as I recall, I always found him to be a little smug. Yes, I think I am prepared to say that, a little self-satisfied.'

'Smug?' Yellich echoed.

'Yes, I would think that is accurate,' Bellingham confirmed. 'Self-satisfied, holding himself aloof; a little more deference to the senior partners would not have gone unnoticed and unappreciated. I think it is fair to say that his attitude could be described as one of "hubris". He always struck me that he carried himself like the chartered accountant he wasn't, instead of carrying himself like the more lowly certified accountant he actually was. And . . . and . . . it might be relevant to your inquiry that he did seem to be very well off, financially speaking. He must have had private means over and above the salary we paid him . . . but then most accountants do.'

'Really?' Yellich raised his eyebrows. 'What do you mean, sir?'

'Oh, yes, you appreciate that our world is the world of finance. When an accountant is at lunch he is invariably also reading the stocks and shares pages in the newspaper and he or she will be almost guaranteed to have a nice little portfolio of gilt-edged securities plus a few pounds risked in recently floated companies. So it wasn't particularly strange that James Wenlock lived in the size of house he lived in and drove the sort of cars I recall he favoured . . . top of the range Audis, for example. I merely assumed that he had made a few shrewd investments and I thought no more about it. Either that or he had got himself into the buy-to-let market and was renting out terraced properties near the railway station to university students. I confess that that is also a very nice source of income, very nice indeed.'

'I see,' Yellich replied. 'That might be worth our looking into, but Mr Wenlock never spoke of his investments?'

'Not to me, but then he wouldn't have done so anyway. This is a large company,' Bellingham explained. 'We have ten chartered accountants and thirty-five certified accountants, and there is little contact between the two. That's the way we like

it . . . but . . . let me think for a moment. You know, you'd
better . . . or you'd be better, rather, talking to Nigel March.
I always used to see them in each other's company.'

'Nigel March?' Yellich repeated, as it committing the name
to memory.

'Yes . . . March . . . exactly the same spelling as the month,
and also of the small market town of Cambridgeshire.'
Bellingham smiled. 'You know, I always thought that March
is a kind of non-month; it is neither winter nor spring in
March and you'll probably find Nigel March to be like that,
a kind of non-personality, as if living up to his name. I have
never found much to get hold of in terms of his character –
not much there at all really. I have always thought that Nigel
March is a bit like "me robot" – he has a perfunctory attitude
to his work, so he does his job and holds his job down.
He keeps his head above water . . . you can't take that from
the man . . . but he's a bit pedantic . . . quite perfunctory. He
goes through the motions but doesn't give much of himself
as he gets through his working day. But he'll be able to tell
you more about James Wenlock than I probably can.'

'Where is he?' Yellich asked. 'We would like to talk to him.'

'He'll likely be at his desk. If not there then he'll be in the
building somewhere.' Bellingham smiled again.

'Thank you; we'll go and have a chat with him.' Yellich
paused and then added, 'What do you know of James Wenlock's
home life?'

'Again, it's not something he and I ever talked about. My
home life wasn't exactly happy and I used to stay late to
avoid going back, but you know, these days I can't wait to
get home.'

'Oh,' Yellich replied warmly, 'you and your wife were able
to settle your differences?'

'We did that all right, we settled it all very well. We got
divorced.' Clarence Bellingham chuckled at his own joke.
'These days I love the journey home because I have found
that going home to an empty house is also going home to a
tranquil house. My heavens, I should have got divorced years
and years ago. All those long years of arguments and all that
horrible silent tension . . . all that could have been avoided

. . . but so far as I could observe, James Wenlock never showed any sort of reluctance to go home at the end of the working day, none at all. He would just tidy his desk, walk out of the building to the car park we use, get into his Audi and he'd purr away, chrome wheels, tinted windscreen, all that Flash Harry number . . . His was a real poser's car, which we didn't approve of, but we had no control over his choice of car or all the add-on goodies it boasted. We didn't like the boy-racer image – not as an accountant with this firm,' Bellingham grimaced, 'but we couldn't do anything about it.'

'It certainly isn't the image that springs to my mind when I think of an accountant and his choice of car,' Yellich replied.

'No . . . and as I said, it was not an image that the partners of Russell Square were wholly in favour of, but we had no control over that aspect of his life.' Bellingham spoke thoughtfully and softly. 'And, as I also said, he was efficient at his job . . . quite a good team player as well. He seemed to be a popular member of staff.'

'I see. Well, thank you, Mr Bellingham.' Yellich stood, as did Ventnor. 'So, we'll go and find your Mr March . . . if we may?'

'Yes, I am sure we can allow you the use of one of our interview rooms. They might be found to be a little small – each one has four easy chairs around a low table – and perhaps a little cramped but I am sure they'll suffice. We have four such rooms; there is almost always at least one that is vacant at any one time so that will give you privacy.' Bellingham reached for the phone which sat on his desk and picked up the handset. 'Carol . . . can you connect me with Nigel March, please? Thank you.' He cupped his hand over the phone. 'I'll take you to the interview room. I'm going to ask March to meet us there. I'll introduce you to him, then I'll leave you in peace and privacy.'

'This . . .' Tony Wenlock sat heavily in an armchair in the living room of his house, 'this is a sobering time for our family, very sobering. I have had to take some time off work . . . hate to do that . . . it looks bad.'

'Yes, I . . . we can imagine.' Carmen Pharoah sat opposite

Tony Wenlock in the second armchair. 'It can't be an easy time.' She paused. 'Can we ask, what is the nature of your employment, sir?'

'Surprisingly, you might think, I am an accountant.' Tony Wenlock forced a smile. 'Like father like son, but I went to university and I have a charter. I did that because I felt that it was what my father would have wanted. In the end I didn't want to fall far from the tree. I was seventeen when he disappeared . . . I was planning to read maths at university but then decided on accountancy when Dad vanished. I did that out of respect to my father.'

'That is quite a sensitive age,' Carmen Pharoah observed. 'Seventeen is a very difficult age to lose your father.'

'Yes, and it was all the more difficult because we didn't know what had happened to him. That was the horrible part. All sorts of things run through your mind.' Tony Wenlock wore a neatly trimmed beard and had, it seemed to Pharoah, good muscle tone, as if he was no stranger to the inside of a gymnasium. 'You think, "Did he run away? Did he run from us? Were we to blame for him leaving like he did?" It's the not knowing that really reaches you. In a sense if we had had a grave to visit then that would have been preferable because at least then we would have known what had happened to him.' Tony Wenlock was dressed in a blue T-shirt and faded blue denim jeans, and he had moccasin slippers on his feet. His home was of the Victorian era, sparsely furnished with rugs on varnished floorboards rather than fitted carpets. A pile of children's toys had been allowed to accumulate in the bay of the window. All were made of chunky plastic and brightly coloured. 'But no age is good for that to happen: seven, seventeen, twenty-seven. No age. My brother was just fourteen and he took it particularly badly. I suddenly found myself having to be the strong one, the head of the household, pulling through and holding the family together.'

'Good for you.' Carmen Pharoah smiled approvingly, then asked, 'Mrs Wenlock – that is, your mother – told us that you and your brother blamed her for your father's disappearance?'

'Oh, she would, that's just the sort of thing that she would say and it doesn't surprise me that she told you that.' Tony Wenlock sighed heavily. 'She's a very difficult woman. She really is bad news. She might have presented well to the police but you can take it from me she is an attention-seeking, self-pitying game player and has probably built our resentment of her up into something which is a lot greater than it actually is. She continually holds herself up as though she is blamed for all the family ills, and yes, I do permit her only limited access to my children but not because I blame her for Father's disappearance. She is a very unhealthy personality. She is not a good influence on the children. She is very manipulative.'

'I see,' Reginald Webster growled.

'Their marriage wasn't as bad as she will have had you believe,' Tony Wenlock continued. 'It worked and they never got anywhere near a divorce. It was never, ever as extreme or as desperate as that. We, that is, my brother and I, might have said something about her driving him away, but if we did say that it was said in the heat of the moment by two confused teenagers whose emotions were suddenly all over the place. We never really blamed her at all for his disappearance. We always assumed some form of misadventure had befallen him because we knew he'd never leave his family . . . he just wouldn't . . . not Dad. Not the old dad we knew. We never assumed that he'd been murdered . . . heavens, no. We always thought his body would be lying somewhere, hidden from view, waiting to be discovered by chance, as indeed such things do happen from time to time.'

'Indeed they do.' Carmen Pharoah nodded her agreement.

'So . . . you can say . . . and we learn that it was not a blissfully happy home, but it was a more successful family, a more healthy family than Mrs Wenlock portrays and certainly far from murderous?' Webster asked.

'Yes . . . yes,' Tony Wenlock nodded slightly, 'you can say that, especially it being far from murderous. The culprit, whoever he or she is, is some person or persons unknown, wholly outside the family. You can definitely say that.'

'Very well, that helps.' Reginald Webster sat forward. 'So, if you can tell us what you can recall about your father at the time of his disappearance . . . his mood, his attitude, any changes in his day-to-day life, anything of significance, even the slightest significance, that you might remember.'

'I remember the time very well – who wouldn't?' Tony Wenlock put his hand to his forehead. 'He was working long hours and often came home quite tired, that I recall well. He didn't normally work late, you see. He was a creature of habit. For many years he'd return at six p.m. and then go up to the Fleece.'

'The Fleece?' Pharoah queried.

'The Golden Fleece pub in Selby, in the centre of the town. Dad had a penchant for a rum and coke or two each evening, to my – our – mother's displeasure, but she accepted it. He'd return at about eight p.m., we'd eat as a family and then he'd amble off to bed at about ten p.m. for an early night. That was the established pattern for many, many years until about twelve months before he died, when he began to come home late each evening and noticeably without the smell of alcohol on his breath. He told us; or rather he told our mother, that he was suddenly under a lot of pressure with an important client to look after. Doing a good job of the account would help his career, so he said – well, so he apparently said. It was a large account, he told Mother, which was in a dreadful mess and with HM Inland Revenue looking for blood. He had to rescue what he could and save as much of the client's scalp as he could. No tax reportedly had been paid for years, but equally, many claims against tax had been made. So he came home late, with that as his story, ate alone and went up to sleep always looking utterly exhausted. That was the way it was for ten, perhaps twelve months before he disappeared.'

'All right, that's a different image.' Reginald Webster wrote in his notepad. 'Did he, do you know, have any enemies – any that you know of?'

'None that I or we ever knew of.' Tony Wenlock relaxed back in his chair. 'I mean, he never seemed to be frightened of anything. He was never afraid to go out of the house in the evening, even in the dark nights, nor was he at all afraid to leave the house in the mornings.'

'Very well.' Webster again wrote in his notepad. 'I am sorry if we seem to be clutching at straws but it is early days yet.'

'I am equally sorry if I am not being of much assistance.' Tony Wenlock shrugged his shoulders in a gesture of helplessness. 'Now we have another issue to live with – that our father was murdered.' Wenlock paused. 'You know, I feel confident enough to say that if it was murder it is probably, highly likely, in fact, to be a case of mistaken identity, or a random attack by a lunatic who was out looking for a victim and any man would do. He had no enemies and who on earth would want to kill a harmless accountant?' Tony Wenlock shrugged. 'Accountants . . . we are like librarians – a harmless bunch of souls, we really are . . . adding up columns of figures all day. Who are we a threat towards?'

Carmen Pharoah smiled. 'Well, I am sure it's more involved than that but I take your point, sir.' Then she continued, 'Can we ask if your family, that is to say your father's family, benefited in any way from his disappearance?'

'No, they didn't; in fact, it made things more difficult. Quite a lot more difficult, I can tell you,' Tony Wenlock grimaced. 'The house was fully paid off so that was a blessing. We kept the roof over our heads, and Father had left a nice little portfolio of stocks and shares which kept us going, but we grew to depend on charity shops for clothing and kitchenware. Holidays . . . ? We couldn't even dream about going on holiday . . .'

'Yes, so Mrs Wenlock indicated,' Reginald Webster commented.

'So we were certainly not so destitute that Mother had to go out and find a job; we continued to eat and my brother and I were able to continue with our studies without having to find work,' Tony Wenlock continued. 'But the insurance company wouldn't pay out on his life insurance policy without the requisite death certificate. You know, I dare say we can make that claim now, that is, once the DNA test confirms his identity. That will be a useful bit of money for the family.'

'So . . . no hardship but equally no benefit either,' Carmen Pharoah said. 'Just the emotional trauma for you to cope with?'

'Yes, that's a good way of putting it – no hardship but no benefit either.' Tony Wenlock nodded. 'Now we'll have a funeral to arrange, and that will finally bring some closure for us.'

'Did your father have friends?' Reginald Webster asked.

'I assume so,' Tony Wenlock replied indignantly. 'He wasn't a recluse.'

'I mean . . . sorry . . . I mean did he have any friends with whom he was particularly close . . . or any brothers or sisters?' Webster clarified.

'No and no.' Tony Wenlock sat forward. 'He had his drinking mates up at the Fleece but I don't think he had any really close friends. If he needed someone he'd very likely turn to Mother, come to think of it, and he was an only child, so he had no brothers or sisters to be of assistance in times of need.'

'So,' Pharoah said, 'it would be fair to say that your father's life revolved around his home, his work and his friends in the Fleece, so far as you are aware . . . or were aware?'

'Yes.' Tony Wenlock nodded in agreement. 'So far as I was aware.'

'Do you know the names of any of his drinking friends?' Reginald Webster's eye was caught by a blue and red high-sided vehicle travelling at speed along the road in front of Tony Wenlock's house.

'No . . . sorry,' Wenlock replied, 'and the old publican retired to Spain some years ago. The Fleece is now run by a fairly young husband and wife team, but I think that some of the older patrons will remember Dad. I am sure they might be able and willing to assist you.'

Nigel March, certified accountant, looked uncomfortable, or so thought Somerled Yellich, and he duly commented upon it.

'Well . . .' March sat upright in the chair and clasped his thin hands in front of him, resting his elbows on his knees, 'that's probably because I am feeling quite uncomfortable. I confess that I have not felt quite so uncomfortable for a very long time . . . for many, many a long year.' He spoke willingly to Yellich and Ventnor but did so in a near monotone, and Yellich clearly and immediately saw what Clarence Bellingham had meant when he described Nigel March as being 'me robot' and wholly perfunctory. Pedantic might, Yellich thought, also be a word which would accurately describe the man. Despite acknowledging his emotional discomfort, he impressed Yellich and Ventnor as a man who went through the motions without actually engaging in life.

'So why are you feeling so uncomfortable?' Yellich asked quietly and then glanced quickly around the room. It was, he found, pleasantly furnished with prints of rural Yorkshire hanging on the wall as decorations. It had a window which, like that of Clarence Bellingham's office, looked out across St Leonard's Place, though it did so from two floors lower in the building. At that moment part of the window was partially open, allowing fresh air to ingress but also allowing the ingress of the sounds of the traffic in the street below.

'Well, I mean . . . wouldn't you?' March was dressed soberly and probably appropriately for an accountant in a dull grey suit with an inexpensive brown tie over a white shirt. He wore a wristwatch but no wedding ring. His feet were encased in unseasonal and heavy-looking highly polished black shoes. He was, Yellich guessed, in his mid-fifties.

'Only if I had something to hide,' Yellich replied promptly. 'Have you got something to hide, Mr March?'

'No . . . nothing, nothing at all,' March replied equally promptly. 'Nothing that the police would be interested in, anyway.'

'We'll take your word for that.' Yellich smiled. 'So . . . please tell us about James Wenlock. All that you know about him.'

'Yes, I understand that you believe him to have been murdered?' March spoke flatly.

'Yes . . . yes, we do,' Yellich replied. 'We still have to confirm his identity but all indications are that the skeleton we found is that of Mr Wenlock . . . his earthly remains.'

'James . . . he just vanished,' March began. 'Just vanished.'

'So we understand. We are told that you knew Mr Wenlock quite well?' Yellich asked.

'Yes,' March continued to speak in a monotone but seemed to be growing less fearful, 'I knew him.'

'Well?' Yellich pressed. 'Did you know him well?'

'A bit. We liked each other as colleagues but we didn't go out together for a drink in the evening after work like some men do in here. I never visited his house and he never visited mine. But we got on well in the office during the working day.'

'I see, so just a couple of colleagues who liked each other?' Yellich confirmed.

'Yes.' March nodded. 'That is about the long and the short of it.'

'Just in the office?' Yellich asked.

'No, not just in here, not just in the office – we'd go out for lunch together on occasions, take a pub lunch or go to a café.'

'Not unusual,' Ventnor commented.

'Not at all,' March explained. 'You see, if you didn't return smelling of alcohol or fall over between the desks the partners didn't mind. Alcohol isn't an issue with me. I was brought up a Methodist . . . I don't drink at all. James would occasionally wash his haddock and chips down with a pint of beer; even then it was low alcohol beer, so it wasn't a problem – the going out at lunch, I mean, and we only did it once or twice a week. We never fell asleep in the afternoon.'

'I see. So what can you tell us about James Wenlock around the time he disappeared?' Yellich asked.

'I can certainly tell you that he wasn't a happy man,' March replied in a matter-of-fact manner, 'I can tell you that.'

'Really?' Yellich raised his eyebrows.

'Yes,' March continued, 'he was not at all happy at home. In fact, he was very unhappy; he said quite often that the spark had long since left his marriage.'

'That is interesting.' Yellich glanced to his left at Ventnor, who nodded in agreement. 'Most interesting.'

'I can also tell you that he was seeing someone outside his marriage as I believe some people do if they have an unhappy home life.'

'He was having an extra-marital affair!' Yellich could not contain his interest. 'He had a lady friend?'

'He once told me,' March explained, 'that he told his wife he was having to work late on a big account which was in a mess, masses of unpaid tax going back years . . .'

'But in fact . . .' Yellich probed.

'But in fact he left Russell Square each day as early as he

could and drove away in his Audi with its alloy wheels and its tinted windscreen; he was going to meet up with his lady friend.'

'And he told you this?' Yellich asked. 'I mean, what he had said to his wife?'

'Yes . . .' March looked down at the carpet. 'He told me because he asked me to lie for him. He asked me to alibi him . . . I mean, he asked me to provide an alibi. He wanted me to say that I was with him, to say that we were together one evening when in fact we were not.'

'Did you?' Yellich asked. 'Did you provide the alibi?'

'No.' March shook his head sluggishly. 'No, I told him that I would not do that. I told him that apart from anything else I would not make a convincing liar . . . even at the best of times . . . I suppose it's the old guilt thing which comes from a Methodist background. I understand that there exist folk who can hold eye contact and lie through their teeth but I am not one of them.'

'Well . . . good for you,' Yellich replied, and did so with a ready smile. 'Good for you on that score, Mr March.'

'Yes . . .' March looked at Yellich. 'I wouldn't at all want to be that sort of person. I really do think that it would be a most unhealthy frame of mind. I definitely wouldn't be able to fake a pass at a lie detector test.'

'Again, good for you. In fact,' Yellich relaxed in his chair, 'the only person that could lie and still pass a lie detector test is a psychopath. The Americans can keep the wretched machines.'

'I never thought of it like that.' March shrugged.

'Please carry on,' Yellich continued. 'James Wenlock . . .'

'Oh, yes.' March shuffled in his chair. 'James had apparently set this girl, or woman, up in a little flat. He called it "a little love nest". It was only a rented bedsit . . . inexpensive rent and he was well able to afford it.'

'Yes, so it seems . . . the house, the Audi . . .' Ventnor growled.

'Yes, you know, it's funny you mention the Audi.' March turned slowly to Ventnor. 'That was a bit of a mystery . . .'

'Oh,' Yellich queried, 'in what sense?'

'A car like that and a house like that on a certified account-ant's salary,' March explained. 'A cheap bedsit is one thing, but buying and running an Audi, and a top of the range model at that – well, he had to have had a separate source of income.'

'We know he had a portfolio of stocks and shares,' Yellich commented. 'That might explain it.'

'Yes, but even allowing for that . . . I thought he was prob-ably moonlighting, you know – I thought he was taking private clients. Some accountants do that but it seems that James was in a kind of mid-life crisis.' March continued to speak in his near monotone. 'I have read about men refusing to surrender to middle age and going out and buying sports cars and taking young mistresses. It won't happen to me, though.'

'No?' Yellich smiled. 'You think not?'

'Apparently not, because people who know me tell me that I was born middle-aged. They tell me I left school and then waited for my generation to catch up with me.' March shrugged. 'If that's so I won't have a mid-life crisis, will I?'

'Probably not, if that is the case,' Yellich replied. 'It is a bit of an unfair thing to say, though.'

'If enough people tell you or you're told something often enough, you come to believe it,' March complained. 'I was apparently stuck in my ways by the time I was seventeen.'

'I am sure you were nothing of the kind . . . but James Wenlock?' Yellich pressed the man.

'Oh, yes, James. Well, like I said, he would leave Russell Square as early as possible at the end of each working day. He'd drive off to visit his young lady and then return home and tell his lady wife that he'd been working late on the very important account which was in a dreadful mess. So,' March continued, 'one day, at one of our pub lunches, he confided in me that he was frightened of this lady's husband.'

'She was married?' Yellich gasped. 'He was having an affair with a married woman?'

'She must have been married if he was frightened of her husband,' March replied.

'Of course, but I assumed she was single for some reason

. . . probably your reference to middle-aged men taking young mistresses,' Yellich stammered, 'but please continue.'

'I also think that they were both in the same boat,' March explained. 'Both trapped in loveless marriages, both feeling their youth slipping away, both frightened of old age, both seeking some sort of youthful passion and thrill and excitement . . . and then they found each other. I'm no white-coated psychologist but that's how I saw it.'

'All right. Now,' Yellich spoke softly, 'her husband begins to interest me. If James Wenlock became frightened of her husband, the husband must have found out about the affair, or she confessed to him.'

'He found out about it,' March explained flatly. 'I don't know how, not for definite, but he did and he was, and probably still is, a large, powerfully built man. I think he was a man who was prone to violence . . . and James, he was an average-sized pen pusher . . . I think he had very good reason to be afraid. Any fights between them would have been one sided, a very one-sided affair indeed. I wouldn't have liked to witness it. I do not like violence. I care not at all for it.'

'Yes . . . again, good for you, Mr March,' Yellich replied. 'And you don't know how the lady's husband found out about the affair?'

'I think that she managed to get a message to James, from her hospital bed, which might explain things.'

'Her hospital bed?'

'Oh, yes, I told you her husband was violent.' March shrugged. 'He put her in hospital when he somehow found out about the affair between her and James. James was suddenly scared stiff that he was to be next on her husband's "to do" list. His wife apparently asked a nurse to smuggle a letter out for her. She wrote a quick note and addressed it to the bedsit he had rented, their little "love nest". He must have found it when he went there to see her.'

'She had to smuggle it out of hospital, you say?' Yellich queried.

'It appears so,' March explained. 'The husband was apparently a very controlling gentleman – James told me that. When he visited he would check the drawer by her bed for writing materials. She was to have no communication with anyone apart from him, her husband, but she became pals with a nurse who wrote a letter for her. She dictated it and told James what had happened, and the nurse put it in an envelope, stuck a stamp on it and posted it.'

'I see.' Yellich stroked his chin. 'Did you see the note?'

'No.' March shook his head slowly. 'He told me that he had found it, like I said, waiting for him when he went round to the bedsit. He told me he tore it up out of fear and then he gave up the rental on the bedsit. He believed, or assumed, that the bruiser knew his identity, that he had battered that information out of his wife, and James was anxious to cover his tracks. It was around then that he vanished off the face of the earth.'

Yellich paused, then said, 'And you didn't come forward with that information, Mr March?'

'I did,' March pleaded. 'Well, at least, I thought about it, of course I thought about it, but by then he was already passed over.'

'And you knew that!' Yellich raised his voice.

'In my heart of hearts I knew that . . . no body was found . . . so what good would it have done?'

'It would have enabled us to solve a murder and saved your colleague's family ten years of anguish – that's what good it would have done!' Yellich spoke angrily.

'But there was no body,' Nigel March pleaded. 'You can't have a murder inquiry without a body.'

'That's not true. It's difficult but not impossible.' Yellich took a deep breath as he tried to calm himself. 'That's not the point anyway; you withheld evidence, Mr March.'

'No . . .' March raised a long, bony finger. 'I beg to differ. I concede that I might have withheld suspicion but I did not withhold any evidence at all. If his body had been found then I would definitely have come forward. Now it seems that his body has been found, and what am I doing now but giving information?'

Yellich sighed. 'Do you know his name – the husband, I mean? Do you know the name of Mr Wenlock's lover's husband?'

'No.'

'What about her name?' Yellich pressed, still fighting to control the anger that he felt towards Nigel March.

'Muriel.' March smiled triumphantly. 'Her name was Muriel.'

'That's a great help, Mr March.' Yellich could not disguise the sarcasm of his answer. 'A great help.'

'Bond,' March added. 'Her name was Muriel Bond.'

'Address?' Yellich snapped. 'Do you know where she lives?'

'I don't know,' March replied, 'but she was hospitalized into York District Hospital, I can tell you that, and they'll have records going back ten years to about the time that James Wenlock went missing.'

The man angrily paced up and down the living room of his house and then stopped as he stood in front of the window, which looked out on to his back garden. 'So how on earth did they manage to find him?'

'A fox?' his wife suggested, sitting in her chair by the fireplace. 'Or a badger . . . ?'

'Not after ten years.' The man spoke in a controlled but yet still angry voice. 'No . . . a fox or badger would have dug him up when he was a fresh corpse, so who would dig a hole there at random? No one. They knew where to dig so they had to have been tipped off. Who'd do that?'

'I really don't know, darling,' the woman replied meekly. 'But you have fully covered every angle; there's nothing to tie you to him. So keep calm, let it all blow over.'

'You're right . . . I must, we must keep calm . . . Did you do what I told you to do?'

'Yes, I did just exactly as you said. Do you think I want to lose a husband?' The woman forced a smile. 'Especially such a wealthy one?'

The man smiled. 'Yes, you're right. It will blow over. They can't link me to him. It'll all be ancient history this time next week – you'll see.'

'So, how did you find me?' Muriel Bond revealed herself to be a small, slight of frame and, Yellich thought, a finely made

woman. Her voice seemed calm but Yellich saw great fear in
her eyes.

'A simple criminal records check – we do that as a matter
of course when a name comes our way.' Yellich spoke calmly.
'But we only need a little information. Don't be fearful, we
are only interested in what you might be able to tell us.'

'No more charges?' Muriel Bond replied with clear hope
in her voice.

'None . . . not from us anyway.' Yellich smiled, hoping to
calm the woman. 'We just want a little chat.'

The agents' room at Skerne Women's Prison was bleak and
functional. Metal chairs at a metal table, tiled walls painted
clinical white. A slab of thick opaque glass set high in the
wall allowed natural light into the room but the illumination
was provided by a filament bulb set in the ceiling. Muriel
Bond wore a thick blue cotton shirt, faded denim jeans, white
socks and tennis shoes. All jewellery had been confiscated but
she had self-inflicted tattoos on her arms for decoration. She
was forty-two years old but Ventnor, sitting beside Yellich
across the table from her, thought she looked older – much
older. She had deep wrinkles and a cold attitude. She had
evidently been hardened by her husband, hardened by prison,
hardened by life. Yellich, for his part, thought she had 'victim'
written all over her.

'Well,' she spoke in a thin, whiny voice, 'a girl has to make
ends meet, doesn't she? I am long past being able to sell
myself on the street, so all I could do was go on shoplifting
expeditions, wasn't it?'

'A few expeditions, we believe?' Yellich replied. 'You seem
quite skilled.'

'Yes, a few. I was only caught a few times. But most times
I got away with it, and I made good money . . . sell it all for
half the marked price,' Muriel Bond explained. 'So I don't
blame the York magistrates – they gave me second chance
after second chance and then finally I went down on the tenth
conviction, but it's better than a fine. See, you got to pay a
fine, but here there's no rent and no food to pay for. I stopped
myself from smiling when the chief beak said, "six months",
and pretended to be upset, but inside I was grinning like a

Cheshire cat. I'll be at it again when I get out . . . but here
. . . all this clean water, all this food, all the free time, a gym
to play in, a library which has magazines . . . I like it in here.'

'All right, so you're a door revolver.' Yellich sighed.
'Anyway, we're here to ask for your help. Heavens, it was the
police who got you on your way here, so we can ask a favour
in return.'

'Oh.' Muriel Bond gave a brief smile. 'Since you put it like
that.'

'Yes.' Yellich sat forward. 'We'd like to know about James
Wenlock.'

'You know, I thought that'd be what you wanted to know
about.' Muriel Bond nodded. 'I saw the news, I read the papers
. . . I knew that's why you called on little me. I am going to
go there . . . it's on my bucket list.'

'Where?' Yellich asked. 'Where are you going to go before
you kick it?'

'Wenlock Edge,' Muriel Bond replied flatly. 'James said
he'd take me there and then he vanished, he did. Now his body
has been found I think I will go there and light a candle for
him.'

'It would be a better thing to do than spend your time
shoplifting,' Ventnor snarled.

'Oh . . . I'll have to go lifting to raise the bus fare,
sweetie . . .' Muriel Bond winked at Ventnor. 'Old Muriel
can't raise the money no other way.'

'So,' Yellich continued, as Ventnor sat back, deflated by her
reply, 'you'll know that your husband threatened him.'

'He did . . . and it's ex-hubby, if you don't mind. I got out
of that mess eventually . . . after he put me in hospital – it
was then that I left. I'd had a few black eyes and a sore face
and bruised ribs, but that's marriage, isn't it? You expect that,
but when he found out about James, well, I woke up in hospital
all plastered up like an Egyptian mummy and I still have no
memory of the attack. That's why he got away with it – because
I had no memory of it and there were no witnesses; he made
sure of that. I was apparently found by the roadside. He took
me out of the house, going for a drive, he said . . . he just
wanted to get me out of the house and into a field . . . after

dusk. A motorist found me by the roadside and called an ambulance. They thought I was the victim of a hit and run, then they realized the injuries didn't match up to a hit and run – more like an assault. But I didn't remember anything, like I said, and in a field at night, there's not many witnesses, darlin' . . . not a lot of eyes. Despite what they say about the woods having ears and the fields having eyes . . . there were no eyes in that field that old night – not when Muriel was getting her hiding. He was a trawlerman on the Hull trawlers. A hard man.'

'Was?' Yellich queried.

'Yes, darlin', was.' Muriel Bond leaned back in her chair, clearly beginning to relax in the officers' presence. 'The fishing's gone now. He was on the last of the trawlers. You know, I felt safe with him at first . . . I felt I was being totally protected. He was a large man and it was that that made me feel safe but when he turned on me . . . and his fist was as big as my face . . . then I felt the opposite. Sometimes he'd punch me just because he felt like it or just out of spite. He was that sort of man, Shane Bond. So that was my lot until James Wenlock came into my life like a ray of sunshine . . . a rescuer . . . but he wouldn't leave his wife. Me, though, I would have left Shane like a shot.'

'Shane?' Yellich asked. 'Your ex-husband, Shane Bond?'

'Yes, darlin', Shane Bond.' Muriel Bond smiled. 'What a silly name; it makes him sound like a cowboy, doesn't it? Shane Bond . . . tall in the saddle with his Colt 45s and his Winchester repeating rifle.'

'Can I ask,' Yellich said, 'how long you and James Wenlock were involved with each other?'

'Just a few months, darlin'. Over the spring and the following summer, so not very long . . .' Muriel Bond glanced up at the ceiling. 'No . . . no . . . longer than that, from the winter into the summer, maybe, but it was definitely less than a year. We met at a singles bar – I might be a bit of a mess now, darlin', but I could pull in those days. Caesars Nightclub. Do you know it?'

'No,' Yellich and Ventnor both replied in unison.

'Lucky you two.' Muriel Bond smiled. 'It's where all the

lost and the desperately lonely go and it's there that we met. James . . . James . . .' She sighed. 'He was just what I was looking for; he was just the opposite of Shane. Shane was large and muscular; James was small and slight. Shane had a rasping voice; James had a smooth, soft voice like a television news-caster. Shane was all beer and cigarettes; James was a little wine and no smoking at all. Shane was football; James was art galleries and museums. Shane was rock music from his youth; James was classical music. Shane would boast about the times he'd been drunk and the fights he'd been in; James wanted to know me as a person. I was on the edge of Shane's life but I felt at the centre of James's. James was like a ray of sunlight into my dark little world and he made me feel so very special; he made me feel as though I really mattered. James rented a flat for us, a little self-contained flat in a large house . . . it was what was originally the downstairs living room of a large old house, but we had a double bed and a little cooker and a TV, a couple of easy chairs and it had a solid lock on the door. We'd meet there, we would . . . but James kept the keys . . . I couldn't keep them in case Shane found them. We were careful like that – really very discreet, but sometimes we'd go out for the day. Once, one day in the summer, we went to the coast. James made an excuse not to be at work . . .' Muriel Bond's voice tailed off and she looked downwards to her left.

'Something?' Yellich asked gently. 'You're remembering something?'

'Yes . . . yes . . .' Muriel Bond took a deep breath. 'Yes, you see, it was at the coast that day that we were rumbled and it was the end for us. Shane was at sea; we went to Bridlington and we were walking along the promenade at Brid when we met a neighbour and his wife. I mean, one of my neighbours . . . not one of James's neighbours.'

'Oh, no . . .' Yellich sighed, 'I think I know where you are going.'

'Oh, yes, darlin'.' Muriel Bond forced a smile. 'Oh, yes . . . oh, yes . . .' She took a deep breath. 'Well, what can I say? I knew it was the end. We just glanced at each other, me and my neighbour, as we walked past each other, two couples arm in arm, but a really evil gleam crossed her eyes. Really

evil. He looked uncomfortable but his wife looked like a little
girl on Christmas morning opening up her presents under the
Christmas tree. I told James that she'd find some way of telling
Shane. I knew that her man wouldn't say anything but I also
knew that she would . . . evil cow that she is, downright evil.
I knew she'd let Shane know somehow; it would be anonymous
but she'd do it. We didn't know what to do but Shane wasn't
due back for a few weeks – he was deep-sea fishing in the
White Sea – so we carried on seeing each other. I was never
worried for James but I knew Shane would have it in for me.
I always thought that Shane would keep it between me and
him so as to keep the police out of it. I just didn't know how
angry he'd get with me, and I never thought he'd go after
James at all, never thought that . . . never did think that, so
help me I didn't. Murder him and then bury him. I never
thought he'd do that.'

'So,' Yellich asked, 'what happened?'

'Well . . . it was just as I thought; in fact, it was worse than I
thought: the neighbour played a sly trick,' Muriel Bond explained.
'Shane had been back for about three weeks and nothing was
said. He was getting ready to go to sea again and I was beginning to think that I had got away with it and the neighbour
wasn't going to say anything after all. I even sent James a
letter to the bedsit telling him we could pick things up again
when Shane went to Hull to join his ship, but the neighbour,
the cow, was just playing a waiting game, I reckon, holding
off until she knew that I was beginning to think I had got
away with it. Then Shane gets the anonymous letter I'd been
dreading printed so as to disguise any handwriting, telling him
all about me and my "fancy man" and enclosing a photograph
of us with our backs to the camera. She must have turned
round and taken the snapshot when we were walking away
from her but it was me all right, wearing a very distinctive
jacket I had then, purple with a fawn patch on the back. I
don't mean a repair make-do-and-mend patch but a designer
patch. So then Shane keeps it to himself and tells me that we
are going for a drive. We drive out into the country and he
parks up in a narrow lane by a field and shows me the letter
and the photograph, then he takes me into the field and plays

football with my body . . . all the time wanting to know who the "fancy man" is. After that I don't remember anything – it's all blank. It's still all a blank. Shane got arrested for assault but got away with it . . . no witnesses . . . no trace of my blood on his clothing. He'd changed his clothes by the time the cops arrested him. He had probably burnt the ones he was wearing in the field.'

'Will we know your ex-husband?' Yellich asked.

'Oh, yes, he's got a record. He's got convictions for violence. Anyway,' Muriel Bond continued, 'I never heard no more from James. I just assumed he'd gone back to his wife and was keeping his head down because he knew a mad mountain of a trawlerman was looking for him. It never occurred to me that Shane had murdered James. Not once did that occur to me.'

'You know that's what happened?' Ventnor pressed.

'No . . . no, I don't . . . Shane never said anything, it's just that's what I assume. The murder, well, that I can understand, but not the burial part.' Muriel Bond held eye contact with Ventnor. 'The Shane Bond I know, or knew, would have left James's body lying in the open somewhere waiting to be found . . . so long as no one saw anything and there were no witnesses . . . that's all Shane would be worried about. He wouldn't go to the trouble of burying someone he'd killed. Mind you, he had the van; he had all the tools he would need to dig a deep hole kept in his allotment shed . . . a pick . . . a spade . . . so I don't know. It's just what I think must have happened.'

'So what . . . yes, so I gave her a bit of a slap, so what? She was fishing for it.' Shane Bond sneered at the question. He was, Yellich and Ventnor found, a tall, muscular man, as Muriel Bond had described him as being, with the biting salt sea air seemingly engraved in his ragged, jagged facial features. He had, thought Yellich, very small pupils, which seemed to pierce rather than look. 'I mean, you tell me, what marriage doesn't have that bit? Which wife never gets what's coming to her now and again? It's what makes any marriage work, isn't it?'

'It didn't seem to make your marriage work, Shane,' Somerled Yellich observed coldly.

'It didn't exactly destroy it either,' Bond retorted savagely. 'She left, didn't she? I didn't chuck her out. She could have stayed but she left. Her choice.'

Shane Bond's house and home was a small, soot-black terraced house in Holgate behind the railway station. Like all the other houses in Holgate, it had just two rooms downstairs and a kitchen. Upstairs were two bedrooms and a bathroom. There was a small backyard enclosed by a high wall and a cobbled stone-surfaced alley running parallel to the houses beyond the wall. The room in which Shane Bond talked to Yellich and Ventnor was small and cramped. Newspapers were strewn over the floor and a large television set dominated the room.

'The particular incident of violence we are interested in,' Yellich continued, 'is the one which took place in a field outside York, after you found out about your wife and her lover, a man called James Wenlock. You were tipped off . . . we believe . . . you received a letter notifying you about the affair and containing a photograph of Mrs Bond and Mr Wenlock together in Bridlington?'

'Yeah, never found out who did me that favour.' Bond coughed deeply. 'So she's having fun with her fancy man in Bridlington while I'm at sea . . . wearing the jacket I bought her and she swaps me for that man, a short little bloke like an office worker. So yes, I battered the information out of her. She told me his name and that he lived in Selby and drove a white Audi with tinted windows. That's all I needed. But I wasn't putting nothing on paper. What I just said – well, I didn't say it, if you see what I mean. You can't prove it and I won't sign a statement admitting it . . . but I got the information I wanted.'

'Then you went looking for him?' Yellich clarified.

'No, though I was tempted. I've got a reputation to protect.' Shane Bond seemed surprised at Yellich's question. 'I didn't want to be laughed at by the other trawlermen. Even though I lived in York, the Hull trawlermen would eventually have found out about my old lady playing away from home and they would have expected me to do something about it. I was going to, but decided to leave it in the end. I knew you lot would come after me if anything happened to him.'

'But you knew enough to find him?'

'Yes . . . she told me enough,' Bond admitted. 'She didn't want to but eventually she saw sense and she told me.'

'So you went looking look for him?' Yellich pressed. 'You did that.'

'No, I just told you,' Bond insisted, but his reply seemed evasive to the officers. Too evasive; too evasive by half. He suddenly became a man with something to hide. 'I didn't go looking for him.'

'You had reason enough to want to harm him,' Yellich observed.

'Maybe I did.' Bond shrugged his muscular shoulders. 'So what?'

'Well, motive makes us very interested,' Yellich explained, 'and if a man has the means and the opportunity as well, then we are very, very interested.'

'Very, very interested,' Ventnor echoed. 'Very, very curious.'

'Look . . .' Bond edged forward in his seat, 'he was sleeping with my wife . . . so yes . . . OK, I admit it . . . I was angry. What man wouldn't be angry?'

'Did you threaten him?' Yellich asked.

'Listen . . . I don't make threats, I don't threaten anyone . . . I make promises. If I say I am going to work someone over, I work them over. And I do a good job as well.'

'Yes, it seems so . . . we've read your record. You're a real hard man, aren't you, Shane?' Yellich held eye contact with the man. 'As hard as they come.'

'You need to be if you're going to survive on the trawlers,' Shane Bond growled. 'It's how it is.'

'You're not working now?'

'The work's dried up.' Shane Bond looked at the floor. 'The Spanish, the French – they took it all. There's no cod now. It's all dried up.'

'Unfortunate turn of phrase for a fisherman.' Yellich smiled. 'So what do you do now?'

'A few odd jobs,' Bond explained. 'Just about retiring now but I couldn't ever settle on the land. I was at sea all my life. I left school when I was fifteen – I didn't wait until the end of term, I just walked out of school the day I turned fifteen and straight on to my first trawler. I went to the Icelandic waters and didn't return for two months.'

'You just walked on to a ship? Just like that?' Yellich asked, surprised.

'The *Holderness Princess*. It was one of the firsts in life I never forgot. No mariner ever forgets his first ship and mine was the old *Holderness Princess*. My father was on the trawlers and he got me started.' Bond paused and took a deep breath. 'You know the *Princess* delayed sailing for two days until my fifteenth birthday – couldn't take me before then without breaking the law, though some of the old hands had gone to sea at thirteen, so they told me, but after forty years at sea I couldn't settle shore side. If nothing else, I couldn't cope with the hours. Even now I still sleep as if I was at sea. You know the watch system – four hours on, four off?'

'All right.' Yellich held up his hand. 'You are certain that you didn't trace your ex-wife's boyfriend?'

'No . . . I told you.'

'You've got previous for violence,' Yellich argued. 'A lot of it, in fact.'

'It's a useful way of settling things,' Bond replied defensively.

'One of your convictions interests us,' Yellich continued.

'Oh, yes?' Bond once more became defensive. 'Which would that be?'

'We are particularly interested in the conviction for violence in Selby,' Yellich replied firmly. 'For attacking a man in the car park of the Golden Fleece pub. You attacked him just as he was getting into his car.'

'A white car with tinted windows,' Thompson Ventnor added. 'That man, that car.'

'So what?' Bond snarled.

'You left your prints all over the car,' Yellich continued, 'and all over the wooden club you used to batter him with.'

'So?' Bond shrugged again and looked down at the carpet. 'So . . . ?'

'But he wasn't your wife's lover. He was a gentleman called Farrell – Roy Farrell – and he ran a white BMW with tinted windows which could easily be mistaken for an Audi at night

. . . especially by an angry trawlerman looking for a guy in a white car with tinted windows who drinks at the Fleece in Selby. It's easy to see the reason why you thought he was your wife's lover.'

'I never said that he was. He was just a bloke and I went inside for eighteen months for that. I served time for that.'

'Oh, yes, we know.' Yellich smiled again. 'Like I said, we read your list of previous convictions. And you still say you didn't go looking for your wife's lover?'

'I forget things these days. I didn't remember that until you mentioned it,' Bond added.

'How convenient for you,' Yellich commented as he took another quick scan of the room. It was all very functional. 'But your victim, he'll remember it, and he'll remember you shouting that you'd kill him if he ever went near your wife again . . . and the other people in the car park who witnessed it all will also remember you saying that. It puts you well in the frame, all right.'

Once again Shane Bond shrugged. 'But I never done no murder, never did.'

'Well, it means that you did go looking for James Wenlock, despite what you say, and shortly afterwards you found him. A week after you assaulted that gentleman in the car park of the Fleece, James Wenlock was reported to the police as a missing person.'

'James Wenlock?' Shane Bond queried. 'Who is that?'

'Your ex-wife's boyfriend,' Yellich spoke angrily. 'Come on, Shane, stop playing games . . . he was your ex-wife's boyfriend. He is now deceased. His remains have been found. Get your coat. You're coming with us.'

'You're arresting me?' Bond sounded alarmed. 'I done nothing.'

'Yes.' Yellich stood and stepped forward and placed his hand on Shane Bond's shoulder. 'Shane Bond,' he said clearly, 'I am arresting you in connection with the murder of James Wenlock. You do not have to say anything but it will harm your defence if you do not mention, when questioned, anything you may later rely on in court.'

\* \* \*

Carmen Pharoah drove out of York under a vast blue sky following roads through fields of golden wheat to Roy Farrell's house in Cawood. The house, she found, was at the edge of the village with flat fields behind it and what she thought to be an interesting-looking church adjacent to it. When she arrived Roy Farrell was weeding the flower bed beside his front lawn. 'Miss Pharoah?' he said as she approached.

'Yes.' Pharoah showed her identity card.

Farrell stood. 'Thank you for the phone call. I appreciated the notice.'

'We don't like to call unannounced unless we have to arrest someone,' Carmen Pharoah explained warmly, 'and it does save us a journey if the person in question is not at home.'

'So, the assault.' Farrell drove the garden fork he was holding into the soil and let it remain there so as to give his undivided attention to Carmen Pharoah. He saw a slender woman, tall, in her twenties, he guessed, elegantly dressed in a three-quarter-length skirt and sensible shoes, a white blouse and a red jacket, with a cavernous handbag hanging from her right shoulder. 'I still have a plastic plate in my skull and it'll go with me to my grave.'

'Plastic.' Pharoah smiled. 'I thought they used steel?'

'They did use stainless steel at one time, so I was told, but the steel would expand and contract with the heat and the cold and cause dreadful discomfort so they switched to plastic. It's just as good and doesn't expand or contract so much.'

'I see.' Pharoah glanced at Farrell's home – 'inter-war', she noted. 'So do you recall the attack?'

'Yes, very well,' Farrell grimaced. 'My brain function was not affected, thank goodness. No impairment there. I was very lucky.'

'Indeed. Can you tell me what happened?'

'I can . . . all I recall, anyway, and that's pretty much all of it,' Farrell explained. 'But why the sudden interest after all this time?'

'It . . . well . . .' Pharoah hesitated. 'All I can say is that it has come to have a bearing on another investigation.'

'Understood. Well, the attack made me recall quite a lot of that evening, which I doubt that I would normally remember, such as the topics of conversation I had with my friends in the Fleece just before it happened, almost word for word. I recall leaving the pub at about ten p.m. and walking across the car park to my car.'

'Being a white vehicle with tinted windows?' Pharoah clarified.

'Yes, a BMW. Nice car. Anyway, just as I put the key in the car door I was felled by a massive blow to the back of my head. I fell, was then kicked in the face . . . I was still conscious and looked up to see him standing over me holding a knife.'

'A knife?' Pharoah queried. 'Are you certain it was a knife?'

'Well, it was something like a knife. If it wasn't a knife it definitely had a long blade . . . not shiny, quite dull, and I knew that he was going to stab me with it.' Farrell paused. 'Then he shouted, "I always kill people who mess with my wife", except that, being a trawlerman, as I later found out he was, what he said was liberally sprinkled with earthy Anglo-Saxon words.'

'I can imagine.' Carmen Pharoah smiled. 'I have heard the like.'

'I am sure you have in your line of work.' Farrell breathed deeply. 'Anyway, I was saved by a group of men coming out of the Fleece before he could carry out his intention. I remember a lot of shouting, then I passed out and came to in hospital. Apparently he made a run for it and drove off in his little van and two of the guys from the group who had saved me followed him in a much faster car . . . until he was forced to stop at a set of traffic lights and they took a note of the registration number of his van, then let him drive on. He was traced by the number plates. He'd put his paw prints all over my car and my blood was on the toecaps of his boots . . . there were many credible witnesses. Anyway, he very sensibly pleaded to a reduced charge of assault, collected three years and came out after eighteen months. Apparently he mistook my white BMW with its tinted windows for a white Audi with tinted windows. They would, in fact, look similar at night, especially to a man who doesn't know cars. It was the old mistaken identity number. I was just in the wrong place at the wrong time.'

'That's a very forgiving attitude.'

'Possibly, but it helps me to understand why it happened.'

'Can I take a statement from you please, Mr Farrell?' Pharoah asked.

'Yes, of course.' Farrell nodded. 'Of course. I am sure my lady wife can rustle up a tray of tea and scones for us but I very much doubt that I can add anything to the statement I gave to the police ten years ago.'

'Possibly, but we need clarification and emphasis. The blade he was holding was dull, not shiny as a knife would probably be, and also the part where you say he said he was going to murder you because he believed that you were having an affair with his wife . . . details like that,' Pharoah explained.

'I see . . . well, of course,' Farrell indicated his house and the open front door. 'Shall we go inside . . . get out of this heat?'

After tea and scones and his statement had been taken, Carmen Pharoah returned to Micklegate Bar Police Station in York and added her recording of the visit to Roy Farrell's house to the rapidly expanding file of the murder of James Wenlock, and placed Farrell's statement in the file. It was by then 5.00 p.m. She signed 'out' and returned home to her flat in Bootham, where she showered and changed into a pair of tight, figure-hugging jeans and a blue T-shirt before setting out again. She intended to retire to bed at 10.30 p.m. that evening so as to be fully refreshed when she reported for duty at 8.30 a.m. the following day.

The city was at that moment too thronged with tourists to enable her to explore the ancient streets and the medieval passageways which was how she had come to enjoy her free time, so instead she took a bus out to the village of Sutton-on-the-Forest and walked the six miles back to York along the straight as a die B1363, enjoying the flat rural landscape of the Vale of York under a vast blue sky as she did so.

As she walked her thoughts turned invariably to the events which had brought her from London to York . . . that car . . . that wretched car . . . the drunken man at the wheel. Her husband, an accountant, and she a detective constable, both employed by the Metropolitan Police and both having absorbed her father-in-law's advice: 'You're black – that means you have to be ten times better just to be as good'. The knock at the door, hesitant yet at the same time insistent. She wondering why her husband hadn't used his key, her senior colleagues on the doorstep in the rain breaking the news as gently as they could. Their promises to 'throw the book at him' meant so little, so, so little . . . so meaningless. She had sold her house, which had been their home, in Leytonstone and moved north because she felt she had to pay a penalty, so north it was, where it was colder in the winter and the summers were shorter, and here she would remain until she felt she had paid her debt. In full.

Having returned to her flat, she showered again and climbed into bed listening to the sounds of the night, the click of women's heels on the pavement below her window, the 'hee-haw' of locomotives arriving or leaving the railway station, or just the low, endless rumble of a goods train as it slowly passed through the station without stopping. She lay still and listened until sleep embraced her.

It was Thursday, 22.50 hours.

# THREE

*In which a charge of two murders is read, a fifth postcard is received and Hennessey and Yellich and Ventnor are severely at home to the most urbane reader.*

'Twice in two days.' Muriel Bond smelled faintly of body odour; her weekly shower was clearly imminent, observed Thompson Ventnor. 'So me,' she said, 'I can't be all that bad, can I?'

'We are very glad you see it like that, Muriel.' Somerled Yellich smiled as he and Ventnor sat opposite her in the agent's room. 'No . . . you are not all bad.'

'Well, that's me, darlin', happy to help, always happy to help. You got me in here so I owe you a favour.' She folded her arms in front of her and sat back in her chair, smiling at Yellich and Ventnor across the surface of the metal table which stood between them. 'But it also gets me away from sewing mail bags.'

'You don't do that any more, Muriel, you know that,' Yellich grinned, 'and it only ever happened in men's prisons.'

'Well . . . if I wasn't here I'd only be on work detail, like picking up litter in the public park as part of my pre-release training. Like when I am back out there am I really going to spend my free time picking up other people's litter . . . I don't think so.'

'You don't want to be out there in the fresh air?' Yellich asked. 'It's quite stuffy in here.'

Muriel Bond shook her head. 'It's too hot today. I prefer to stay in here out of the sun, and yes, it's good to get out in the fresh air but you see all the things you miss . . . it's not all bad, but then you have to come back in here, and folk out there stare at you, they know who you are . . . If you ask me, it's like being on a chain gang with invisible chains. So pre-release training has its downside, darlin'.'

'But you're cooperating with it? If you want to get out you'll cooperate. You don't want to be in here any longer than you have to, despite all the free food and rent-free living.'

'Oh, yes, I wouldn't mess up my chances of parole. I'm not so sad that I can't survive on the outside. I just don't like having to do so. It's hard work. One girl did . . . she messed up, smuggled half a bottle of vodka in here with her.'

'How did she manage that?'

'One of her mates planted it in the park where she knew the girl would be working; put the vodka into a mineral water bottle so it looked like water . . . in fact, vodka is Russian for "water", so I believe. Anyway, she picked it up and put it in her bag and the screw didn't check it on her return. She drank it that evening, half a bottle . . . neat . . . and she got silly with the drink in her and the screws smelled the alcohol on her breath so her parole was put back for six months. Silly cow. But me, little me, I am out of here asap.'

'Good for you.' Somerled Yellich rested his forearms on the table top, 'Will you be returning though? What do you think?'

'Oh, probably. I mean, knowing my Donald Duck, certainly . . . and if I get fed up of struggling I'll let myself get caught. So it's a question of how long I can stay out but I'll be back one day . . . got to keep covering my tracks until I want free food again.'

'Not going straight?' Ventnor asked.

'Unemployable, that's me, darlin', I can't survive on the dole. If I want to eat I have to shoplift, like I told you yesterday – I have to steal. Mind you, I have decided to learn to dip the skips outside supermarkets. They throw good food away just because it's reached its sell-by date. It's a real waste.'

'That's better than shoplifting,' Yellich commented. 'Technically it's still stealing but we turn a blind eye.'

'There are also soup kitchens too,' Ventnor offered. 'Churches and charities do soup kitchens . . . free food for the hungry.'

'Aye, I could do that, couldn't I?' Muriel Bond pursed her lips. 'I am not too proud to do that.'

'All right.' Somerled Yellich shifted in his chair. 'I hope you do stay out, Muriel, at least for as long as possible . . . but let's cut to the chase. We have arrested your husband.'

'Ex,' Muriel Bond corrected Yellich. 'My ex-husband, if you please, sir.'

'Sorry.' Yellich nodded. 'Your ex-husband. We have just arrested your ex-husband for the murder of James Wenlock.'

'Silly man,' Muriel Bond glanced to her left, 'the silly, silly man . . . but at least that means he won't be on the outside when I am let out. That's a relief. I won't have to worry about running into him.'

'Yes . . . yes.' Yellich nodded. 'I dare say it will be something you won't have to worry about, but he wrapped himself up very tightly in a pack of lies about not seeking James Wenlock or assaulting anyone and then he was proven to have attempted to kill someone he believed was James Wenlock for "messing with his wife", and tried to kill him in exactly the same way that James Wenlock was then subsequently murdered, with a dull blade. It's all there – means, motive and the opportunity. As neat as neat can be.'

'Aye . . . I remember him going down for that. He was lucky not to have been charged with attempted murder.' Muriel Bond spoke with barely concealed anger. 'He was trying to kill that guy in the pub car park, and he would have done if those other guys hadn't pitched in and stopped it.'

'Our feelings too,' Yellich replied. 'We also thought that he was lucky but it does seem that there was a forty-eight-hour window between that assault and his arrest, during which he found and murdered James Wenlock.'

'I see.'

'But, Muriel,' Yellich continued, 'the reason why we have called on you is that when he attacked the man in the car park of the Fleece in Selby he was heard to say, "I always kill people who mess with my wife".'

'He said that?' Muriel Bond replied with some surprise. 'Is that what he said?'

'Yes,' Yellich confirmed. 'Now it might have been hot air,

heat of the moment stuff, and he equally might just have been putting the frighteners on the man he thought was James Wenlock . . .'

'Oh,' Muriel Bond paled, 'you know, gentlemen, I can see where you are going with this.'

'Yes.' Yellich nodded solemnly. 'It is because he said that we cannot now overlook the possibility that there might be earlier victims of your ex-husband, earlier murders we have not linked to your ex-husband and which remain unsolved.'

'Oh . . . yes . . . I see . . . I thought that's where you were going,' Muriel Bond sighed, 'but really I can't help you . . . I'm really sorry.'

'So you didn't have any other extra-marital affairs with another man or men? Man or men who also disappeared?' Yellich asked. 'You must tell us if you did.'

Muriel Bond shook her head vigorously. 'No darlin', I did not, I promise . . . hand to God I never. Honest to God I didn't. The only man I ever played away from home with was James Wenlock.'

'So,' Yellich sat back and sighed with relief, 'it was just hot air after all. I dare say that's something.'

'Oh, I dunno about that, darlin',' Muriel Bond held eye contact with Yellich, 'I can only speak for myself. I am wife number two. I am the second Mrs Shane Bond.'

'Number two wife!' Yellich remained still as Thompson Ventnor leaned forward.

'He was married before he was married to me,' Muriel Bond explained, 'and that's only his two legal marriages that I know about. He's had a few common-law marriages with women he would refer to as his wife – they never had no proper piece of paper but they lived together as man and wife and he has quite a few children of various ages living between York and Hull. So I can only speak for myself . . . so sorry, darlin'.'

'Oh . . . just when we thought it was getting easy,' Yellich groaned. 'What can you tell us about his other, legal wife?'

'Gloria? Well, I can tell you that he thought she was a much better catch than little old me.' Muriel Bond shook her head. 'I never measured up to her in any way, so he kept telling me.

She was older than me so she'll be a real old bird now. Gloria, like I said. Gloria Bond. They divorced.'

'Do you know where we can find her?' Ventnor asked, still leaning forward in his chair.

'Don't ask me, darlin'.' Muriel Bond shrugged her shoulders. 'She'll be in the wind somewhere; you'll find her in the wind.'

'You must know something,' Ventnor urged.

'Do you want to win parole?' Yellich asked. 'You sound as though you do.'

'Yes, darlin', as you say, it's stuffy in here.' Muriel Bond clasped her fleshy hands together. 'I do want my parole and I'm working for it. You can get fed up with prison grub, even if it is free.'

'Well, in that case, Muriel,' Yellich spoke sternly, 'stop playing games. You help us and we can put a word in for you.'

'You can do that?' Muriel Bond looked at Yellich.

'Yes,' Yellich nodded, 'we do it all the time and our word counts for something. You're in for shoplifting, and if you gave information which helped solve a murder inquiry, that will pretty well guarantee your parole at the first hearing.'

'My first hearing!' Muriel Bond gasped. 'That never happens. Not ever. No one gets their parole at the first hearing. It's the rule. I know that. Don't make promises you can't deliver on.'

'It's a rule which can be interpreted and it has been known to happen if the person has been particularly cooperative in respect of an important case,' Yellich explained. 'So we can deliver . . . not guaranteed, but we can put in a heavyweight word for you.'

'Such as this one – this case,' Ventnor added. 'I mean, you're already on pre-release training, so any help you give us will grease the wheels. You'll be out by Christmas.'

'Hope not, darlin'. I want to be inside over Christmas. If I'm out I'll be alone in my little damp bedsit. In here we get turkey and all the trimmings and a lovely carol service in the chapel. But spring . . .' Muriel Bond smiled at the thought, 'yes, a spring parole – that would be good. Come out as the crocuses are appearing, stroll along the river bank looking at the new flowers and the blossom . . . summer and winter in here, then out with spring. All this for a few woollen pullovers.'

'A few woolly pullies.' Yellich smiled. 'We understand that it was more in the manner of distributing a lorry load of stolen clothing.'

'Whatever.' Muriel Bond shrugged. 'Whatever, darlin', whatever you say.'

'So, come on Muriel,' Yellich urged, 'you scratch our back and we'll scratch yours.'

'Well . . . as I said . . . Gloria, she's in the wind . . . in the wind, darlin',' Muriel Bond smiled vacantly. 'She's out there somewhere.'

'Muriel,' Yellich growled, 'come on, this is serious.'

'Well, she is in the wind like I keep telling you, but you'll know her sons, David and Goliath.'

Yellich sighed. 'Look, Muriel, as well as scratching your back we can also make things difficult for you. We can prosecute you for wasting police time. How about another couple of years in here for you? Do you fancy that?'

'I am serious – I'm as serious as a heart attack,' Muriel Bond protested. 'I am helping you. Listen to me, will you? David is the real name of one of her sons and he's quite small, but his older brother takes after his father – he's massively built. His real name is Patrick but they're both well known to the police, both have got criminal records, both have a lot of track, and they're known round York as David and Goliath, except they don't fight each other.' Muriel Bond smiled broadly. 'You see, I am helping you, but old Gloria, she never ever stays still – one address, then another, then another. She just can't seem to settle anywhere. So any address you'll have for her will be well out of date. She's in the wind, darlin', but you'll know where her boys are, especially Patrick, because he's inside right now, doing bird at Full Sutton, so I hear, and him, Patrick, he'll know where his mother, Gloria is.'

Yellich nodded. 'Well, thanks, Muriel. We'll check that he's there and if he is we'll pay him a visit . . . and if this helps us, then, like I said, we'll help you.'

'But not before Christmas, darlin',' Muriel Bond pleaded.

'I don't want to be out before Christmas, not if it can be helped.'

Driving away from the prison with its dull grey medium-rise walls and the light blue flag of Her Majesty's Prison Service hanging limply from the white-painted flagpole above the main gate, Thompson Ventnor commented, 'You know, Sarge, I feel a bit sorry for her.'

'Oh?' Yellich brought the car slowly to a halt at the end of the prison approach road before driving it on to the public highway. 'What do you mean? No one asked her to fence a lorry load of stolen clothing; she's a volunteer in a sense.'

'Yes, I know, but if she's doing pre-release training now it means she's been earmarked for parole in the autumn, a couple of months from now.'

'Ah, yes, I see what you mean.' Yellich observed the vehicles on the public highway, searching for a gap that he could exploit in order to join the traffic stream. 'In fact, I thought exactly the same but also thought the better of commenting, as you also clearly did. So, come the twenty-fifth of December it will be a damp bedsit and beans on toast for Christmas dinner for our Muriel.'

'Unless she's back in there,' Ventnor used his thumb to indicate the prison behind them, 'and I tell you I wouldn't bet on which one it will be.'

'Even odds, I'd say.' Yellich moved forwards and placed the car neatly in a gap in the traffic stream between two heavy goods vehicles. 'Even odds.'

'It's not much to show for sixty years, is it?' the woman said apologetically, looking up at Yellich and Ventnor from the old armchair in which she sat.

'We've seen worse, Gloria,' Yellich replied gently. 'Believe me, we've seen much, much worse.'

'But not that much worse, and not after sixty summers and sixty winters.' Gloria Bond forced a grin which broke across her grime-encrusted face. She brushed her grey, heavily matted hair back over her scalp. 'I bet you're both thinking what a right old dump this is. I mean, look, I'm not proud but this is the way it has turned out for me.' She pointed to the floor which was strewn with domestic refuse and half-eaten pizzas still in their cartons. The window panes were unwashed and half covered by threadbare curtains.

'Take it from me, Gloria,' Yellich reassured her, 'we still have seen much worse.'

'But I'm clean now, no more drugs for me.' She showed Yellich and Ventnor her forearms. 'No more booze either, just tobacco and even then it's just roll-ups. I pick my tobacco out of dog ends that folk leave in those ashtrays outside pubs or from off the pavement. I can get three or four good smokes a day doing that, and that's on top of the tobacco I buy. That's all I can afford anyway – just tobacco. I tell you, the pension goes nowhere.' Gloria Bond spoke with a harsh, rasping voice. 'I'd ask you to sit down but all the chairs are damp. I've got diverticulitis . . . I have no bladder control to speak of; it just dribbles out of me.'

Somerled Yellich thought, yes, we can smell your problem, especially on a hot day like this, but said instead, 'It's all right, Gloria, we're happy standing. We've called on you because we need a little information. We hope you'll be able to help us.'

'I'm not ratting out my sons,' she replied defensively. 'They're both good boys. They get a bit hot-headed at times but they're both good boys.'

'It's all right, Gloria,' Yellich placated her with a raised palm, 'we want some information about Shane Bond, your ex-husband.'

'Him!' Gloria Bond almost spat the word. 'Him! I'll rat him out all I can, that's one rat that well needs ratting on. You see, this is what all that poison does to a woman. All that booze.' She patted her distended stomach. 'Do you know that men used to fancy me? Can you believe that? I could turn heads when I was a teenager . . . now look at me. I mean, I was well fancied, then I married a rat and it all went downhill from there. But my boys are good.'

'Sorry, Gloria,' Yellich continued to speak softly, 'it's a rough old ride you've had over the years, but we need a little information. Look, this is a bit of a cheeky question . . .'

'Oh . . . pet . . .' Gloria Bond smiled and in doing so she

revealed a set of coal-black teeth. 'Cheeky I can handle. I can handle cheeky, all right . . . ask away.'

'All right.' Yellich smiled. 'We'll take you up on that. So, going back in the day, when you were married to Shane.'

'Yes . . .' Gloria Bond sounded curious, hesitant and cautious.

'Did you ever play away from home with another man . . . possibly while Shane was at sea?'

'Play away?' Gloria Bond queried.

'Have an affair . . . with another man, while Shane was heaving large quantities of cod fish out of the White Sea? Not often, just once or twice?'

'Yes . . . yes . . . I don't mind admitting it, pet,' Gloria Bond smiled. 'I mean, that rat would drive anyone away from him. But it wasn't once or twice, it was just the once . . . just the once I had a bit of the old extra-marital.'

'Did Shane find out?'

'Yes.' Gloria Bond suddenly looked to be feeling uncomfortable.

'What happened when he did find out?' Yellich asked as gently as he could.

Gloria Bond looked to her left, then to her right and then to her left again. 'I knew it would come out. I knew it couldn't stay buried forever.'

'What couldn't stay buried, Gloria?' Yellich pressed.

'You know . . . that's why you've come here, isn't it? After all this time?'

'The murder,' Yellich chanced, 'yes, we know about it, but we don't know the whole story. If you want to help yourself and if you want to make sure Shane stays locked up, you'll tell us all you know.' Beside him he felt Ventnor tense up.

'Shane . . . he's got a temper . . . he's . . . he's what's that word? Possessive . . . he's possessive . . . he wants his things. He wants it all his own way. I'm sorry I kept quiet. I kept it from David and Goliath . . . I mean, from David and Patrick. Sorry, that's a family joke, you see . . .'

'Yes . . . yes,' Yellich once again held up an open palm. 'It's all right, we know the joke.'

'So you've found the body?'

'Yes,' Yellich replied gently, 'we've found it. It'll be on the news soon but we need you to tell us all you can. You must decide whether to work for yourself or against yourself.'

'The boys needed their father,' Gloria Bond pleaded. 'I did it for them – I only did it for them, David and Patrick; they needed a father, even if it was a swine like Shane. I thought it was still better than no father at all and I needed him to control them . . . I couldn't control them and David was getting like his father, wild, violent, bad temper. He's got a chip on his shoulder about being small. It makes him violent. He's doing time now; he went down for manslaughter. He was lucky it wasn't murder . . . what he did to that bloke.'

'Yes, we know, it's how we traced you, Gloria; you're his next of kin. We phoned the prison and they gave us your address.'

'So I'm just a phone call away.' Gloria Bond sighed. 'Keeping on the move to stay hidden and all the time I am just a phone call away.'

'Look, we can't chat here.' Yellich glanced around the room. 'Let us take you into York, have a chat in our interview suite . . . comfy chairs . . .'

'You'll have to disinfect them afterwards or let me go to the toilet every five minutes.'

'Either way,' Ventnor smiled, 'you'll be our guest. We'll take good care of you.'

'Toilet would be better,' Gloria Bond suggested. 'Better for both of us.'

'As you wish.' Yellich smiled. 'We'll lay on coffee or tea if you'd prefer and possibly a bite to eat. You look a little hungry.'

'Had a bit of pizza yesterday.' She pointed to the half-eaten pizza on the carpet. 'That's all that's left of it. Don't eat much these days. Hardly eat at all.'

'So a cup of tea and a sandwich?' Yellich suggested.

'Tea sounds good. I've been drinking tap water since I ran out of tea bags.'

'You can have as much tea as you like, Gloria.'

'All right,' Gloria Bond struggled to her feet, 'let me get a dry pair of jeans on.'

Forty-five minutes later, Gloria Bond, Somerled Yellich and Thompson Ventnor sat in the interview suite at Micklegate Bar Police Station. Gloria Bond, fortified with a mug of tea and a round of chicken and lettuce sandwiches from the police canteen, became more animated and very willing to talk to the officers.

'Marriage, you know . . . if you ask me the person who invented marriage should be put up against a wall and shot. I really mean that. Shot. Well, I wed Shane and it all went wrong from there. He was always drinking. When he wasn't at sea he was out till all hours drinking with his mates. A woman needs more than three-month-old magazines and a TV set for company, especially when she's newly wed . . . so yes, I met a man. Henry, he was called Henry, a nice, gentle man, not anything like Shane.'

'Henry?' Yellich wrote on his notepad.

'Henry Hall.' Gloria smiled as if at a good memory. 'He was a council worker . . . a gardener . . . he pushed a lawnmower for the council, he kept the lawn nice and fresh cut and he kept the flower beds weeded. Just a gentle soul, close to nature. He didn't deserve to be murdered by a gorilla like Shane Bond. No . . . no . . . I tell you, calling Shane a gorilla is unkind to gorillas.'

'Yes.' Yellich smiled. 'I understand that gorillas are quite gentle creatures despite their size, but do please carry on. What happened to Henry?'

'Well, you know what happened if you found his body.' Gloria drank her tea.

'Yes, yes,' Yellich held a straight face, 'but we don't know how he got there . . . not the details . . . there are a few gaps we need to fill in.'

'Shane found out about us – the boys told him, can you believe that?' Gloria shook her head and looked at the floor. 'My own sons ratted me out to my husband. Mind you, they were still young at the time. Shane took them out and being as bad a lot as he is, even to his own children, David said, "You're not as nice as mum's friend. He's a nice man", or something like that. Henry was good with the boys, you see, really a natural father; he always got the best out of them. He could always do that. He seemed to be able to make them want to behave just like he could make plants grow – he could bring out the best in difficult children. Children just liked him and he liked them, but not in a bad way. I don't mean like that. So when Shane and the boys came home that day I got a slap, and I mean a trawlerman's slap, and when I came to I got another slap, and when I'd been awake for an hour or two I'd get another slap which knocked me out again. So what could I do? I couldn't go to the police or the hospital. I was trapped in the house, so eventually I told Shane about Henry. A week later . . .'

'A week?' Yellich sighed. 'You mean Shane waited for a week before he went looking for Henry Hall and you didn't warn Henry?'

'I was trapped in the house,' Gloria Bond pleaded.

'Sent him a letter, even a postcard?' Yellich despaired.

'I never did learn to read and write, pet,' Gloria explained matter-of-factly. 'Never did.'

A silence fell on the room. It was broken eventually by Yellich, who asked what Shane Bond had done in that week.

'He bought a motor . . . a small van . . . a white one. Then he made me go with him to show him where Henry lived. You see, I had told him that Henry lived alone, all by himself, and so we went to where he lived, to his house one day . . . well, it was one night really. Anyway, I walked up the path to his little house and I knocked on the door and he says, "Who is it?" and I say, "It's me, Gloria" and he opens the door and smiles because he is pleased to see me, and then Shane, who was standing at the side of the door out of sight, pushes past me and bundles Henry back down his hallway into his house. Henry is as white as a sheet just before Shane planted one on him and busted his nose . . . there was blood everywhere. It was all quick and quiet; the neighbours never heard anything. So Shane punched Henry and kept on punching him until he was out cold, and then he carried him like he weighed nothing out to the street where he had parked the van and I shut Henry's front door and followed Shane like he told me to. I always did what I was told by Shane. Always did. I was a good wife like that. I was always good at doing what I was told.'

'Just carry on.' Yellich strained to control the anger he felt towards Gloria Bond. 'Henry Hall's body . . . what did you do then?'

'Yes, well, Shane put his body into the back of the van, and I thought he was going to dig a hole in a field and put Henry's body in it,' Gloria Bond explained. 'But he didn't. He drove out to a fishery instead.'

'Which one?' Ventnor asked.

'Oh, I don't know, pet,' Gloria Bond replied apologetically. 'I really couldn't tell you. Honest I couldn't. So, anyway, we get there and Shane drove through the gateway and along the track, with water on both sides, and he kept going right to the far side of the fishery like he knew where he was going, and pulled up beside a pile of rubble. He dragged Henry's body out of the van, took a spade from the back and brought it down hard on Henry's head a few times. He was making sure Henry was dead all right . . . poor old Henry. Then he picked Henry's body up again and put it on the side of the track, then took a knife and stabbed it into Henry's stomach . . . for some reason. I don't know why he did that because poor Henry was already dead . . . then we began to pile rocks on top of his body.'

'You helped him?' Yellich clarified. 'You helped Shane conceal Henry Hall's body?'

'Yes. On account of my sons, I told you. For their sake I had to. It was horrible.' Gloria Bond shuddered in her seat.

Somerled Yellich breathed deeply. 'Just carry on, Gloria, you're doing well.'

'So we buried the body. It was well covered with rocks by the time we had finished, then Shane takes the spade and starts digging the soil about the rubble and putting spadefuls of soil on the rubble which was over Henry's body, not to cover them with soil but because he wanted to make sure there was soil on the stones, for some reason. He seemed to know what he was doing but he didn't tell me. Then he threw the spade and the knife in the water and said to me, "You, girl, you keep your little mouth shut. Or else", and then he drew his finger across his throat like he was cutting it. "Don't tell anyone about this", he said, "not anyone". Then he said, "I mean, think what will happen to the boys if I go inside for life?" So I said, "All right, Shane, I won't breathe a word." Anyway, by then dawn was coming up fast and he said we'd better go because fishermen like to fish at dawn, for some reason. I don't mean fishermen like trawlermen, I mean fishermen who fish with a fishing rod. You see them by banks of rivers and lakes, just sitting there, not moving even when it's raining.'

'Anglers,' Yellich said. 'It's all right – we know what you mean.'

'Anglers,' Gloria Bond repeated. 'That's a new word for me . . . anglers. I'll try to remember that word. So we left the fishery and drove back to York.'

'What do you remember of the return journey, Gloria?'

'Not much. It was a good while ago now and old Gloria's memory lets her down a bit these days . . . it does . . . it's the booze, you see, but I did right for my boys.'

'All right, so no details of the return journey come to mind, no names of pubs, no significant buildings?' Yellich asked.

'No . . . sorry, pet.' Gloria Bond shook her head.

'So you said it was dawn – where was the sun as you returned home?'

'Right in my eyes, pet, I remember that. Shane pulled over because of the glare.'

'So you travelled eastwards to return to York?'

'I don't know, pet, but I remember the sun blinding us.' She paused. 'Anyway, I thought you said you'd found his body.'

'A little poetic licence, Gloria,' Yellich replied. 'We were stretching the truth a little, I'm afraid.'

'Poetic what?' Gloria Bond looked confused.

'Never mind, I'll explain later,' Yellich placated her. 'So the fishery was to the west of York?'

'Dunno, pet. Don't know where it was.'

'Well, it must have been if the sun was shining in your eyes as you drove home at dawn,' Yellich explained. He then asked, 'How long was the journey home, in terms of time, I mean?'

'Not long. It was not a long journey.' Gloria Bond looked vacantly around the interview suite. 'Not too long.'

'About?'

'About half an hour,' Gloria Bond replied, 'half an hour tops, as near as I can remember.'

'Good . . . that helps us.' Yellich and Ventnor stood. 'Just wait here, will you, please, Gloria?'

'Yes, pet, but are you going to drive me back home soon?' Gloria Bond whined.

'Not yet,' Yellich replied firmly. 'Just remain here, please.'

'We'll be right back,' Ventnor added as he and Yellich left the interview suite. 'We won't be very long.'

In the corridor outside, Thompson Ventnor turned to Somerled Yellich and said, 'So, a fishery about fifteen miles to the west of York? There can't be many.'

'Yes . . . not many at all,' Yellich pondered. 'Can you please get a map and see if one such is marked and I'll look out the missing persons file on one Henry Hall, Esquire. I don't think that there will be many of those either.'

Somerled Yellich spread the Ordnance Survey Map across Hennessey's desk. 'Thompson Ventnor has been able to identify only one candidate, sir,' he explained, 'and frankly I would go along with him . . . just here.' He put his fingertip on a small area of blue on the map fifteen miles to the west of York, close to a railway line. 'It's about a thirty-minute drive, but it's pretty well due west of York, as you can see.'

'Yes.' Hennessey looked at the map. 'The only likely fishery; it's the only fishery in the area, in fact, unless the actual one has been filled in and levelled for housing and this fishery shown here is an entirely new venture – the crime in question being, what did you say? Twenty years old?'

'Yes, sir.' Yellich stood up. 'That is a possibility; but we'll have to take that chance.'

'Yes, we have to.' Hennessey leaned back in his chair. 'What do you suggest?'

'Oh . . . well, I think I'll visit the fishery with a team of constables to move the pile of rubble one stone at a time in case it is the correct place. Then if we do find a corpse I'll whistle up for SOCO and a pathologist.'

'Very well. We'll also need divers if we are going to recover the murder weapon and the spade.' Hennessey paused. 'Do you require sniffer dogs?'

'I don't think so, sir,' Yellich replied. 'The body is reportedly concealed in a mound of rubble rather than being buried. I'll use the old mark one eyeball; it should be easy enough to identify the rocks – they're at the far end of the fishery, according to Gloria Bond.'

'Yes.' Hennessey nodded. 'Where is your informant?'

'Still in the interview suite, sir. We listened to what she told us but didn't take it down as a statement for her to sign as such.'

'No?' Hennessey raised an eyebrow. 'Why not, Somerled?'

'Well sir, I think we'll need an appropriate adult on this one,' Yellich replied calmly.

'Oh?' Hennessey nodded. 'I see . . . I see . . .'

'Yes, sir, you see, under the Police and Criminal Evidence Act I think she would be termed "vulnerable",' Yellich replied.

'Really?' Hennessey nodded.

'Yes, sir. I think she is at least educationally subnormal, or in today's speak she has "learning difficulties". She has also not helped her mental state by long-term alcohol and heroin abuse.'

'Heroin?' Hennessey expressed surprise. 'At her age?'

'Yes, sir. She is a sixty-year-old smackhead. Anyway, she confessed freely to her involvement in the murder of Henry Hall without her seeming to realize the implications of what she was saying, and so Thompson and I didn't, and in fact couldn't, make it an official statement on her part. We just listened to what she told us but what she said won't hold up in court. She'll have to be re-interviewed with a legal representative and an appropriate adult both being present.'

'I see,' Hennessey replied.

'I would also think it unlikely that the Crown Prosecution Service would proceed against her. She can argue that she was under duress, and overbearing intimidation on the part of Shane Bond. She is, I think, of such meagre mental capacity that she could well be deemed not guilty by reason of "diminished responsibility", but right now she is singing like a blackbird in spring time . . . so sweet and melodious it is a pity to shut her up.'

'Understood,' Hennessey replied, with a smile. 'We can act

on her information without compromising the investigation but I suggest you consult with the CPS before taking a formal statement and charging her.'

'Very good, sir.' Yellich nodded. 'I'm very happy with that approach.'

'Good, good.' Hennessey glanced out of his office window at the walls of the ancient city. 'You know, with a bit of luck we might be able to wrap this up today and charge Shane Bond with not one but two murders. That would be nice and neat.'

'Indeed, sir.' Yellich smiled. 'That would be neat, as you say, very neat indeed.'

'But we still need to find out more about Henry Hall. Can you give his mis-per file to Reginald and Carmen?'

'Yes, sir,' Yellich replied sharply. 'Will do.'

'Ask them to get background information on the gentleman. All they can.'

'Yes, sir.' Yellich nodded.

'Then if you and Thompson Ventnor stay teamed up on the visit to the fishery . . . see what you see, find what you find,' Hennessey added.

'Yes, sir.'

Carmen Pharoah settled back in her chair behind her desk, sipping a mug of coffee, and began to read the missing persons report on Henry Hall.

Henry Hall, she read with interest, was a single man at the time he was reported missing, and lived alone. He was reported as missing by a concerned neighbour who had not seen him for some days. He had been employed by the local authority as a gardener, as Gloria Bond had described, and he seemed to have been a man of quiet habits, liking nothing more than to walk up to his local pub, the Empress of India, after a day's work, leaving the pub at 8.00 p.m. to return directly home, before it got unpleasantly noisy and crowded. Henry Hall seemed to have been a quiet, harmless man who had disappeared, now believed to have been murdered at the age of forty-five years. After reading the report and noting the details, Pharoah rose from her chair and walked to George

Hennessey's office, knocked reverentially on the frame of the open doorway and entered. 'I would,' she announced, 'like to pay a visit to the Empress of India public house, sir. It's mentioned in Henry Hall's mis-per file as a favourite haunt of his. We might obtain more information about the gentleman by chatting to the publican and the regular patrons. Even if it is twenty years on.'

'Yes,' Hennessey nodded, 'as much background as possible on Shane Bond's first known victim will be useful. As you say, after such a length of time it's a bit of a long shot but they've paid off before. I think we'll keep Gloria with us for a while – the custody sergeant is ensuring that she has regular access to the ladies' toilets.' He paused. 'She has a certain medical condition, you see.'

'I see, sir.' Carmen Pharoah smiled. 'Like the one brought on by too much alcohol over the years?'

'Yes.' Hennessey returned the smile. 'Like that one. Are you happy to go by yourself to the Empress?'

'Oh, yes, sir. I'm going now about midday just to talk to the publican.'

'Very well, but if you go anywhere after that let me know. You know the drill – we must know where you are at all times,' Hennessey reminded her.

'Understood, sir.' Carmen Pharoah nodded. 'Fully understood.'

'Somerled Yellich and Thompson Ventnor are at the fishery at the moment,' Hennessey explained. 'If they find his body we'll have a clearer picture of what happened.'

'Yes, sir.' Carmen Pharoah turned smartly away and walked back to her office, to collect her jacket and handbag.

Somerled Yellich parked the car close by the entrance to Liskeard Fisheries and got out of car to talk to the gatekeeper, leaving Thompson Ventnor in the passenger seat. A white police minivan containing a sergeant and six constables halted behind Yellich's car.

'A strange name,' Yellich commented to the initially bemused and then worried-looking gatekeeper, 'I mean, Liskeard Fisheries . . . here in deepest Yorkshire, of all places.'

'Yes, I suppose it is a trifle strange.' The elderly gatekeeper kept a watchful eye on the police vehicles and seemed to Yellich to be growing increasingly wary and apprehensive, as if some long past felony he had committed was haunting him. 'The owner of the fisheries is a Cornishman. He named the business after his home town . . . so they told me when I started work here.'

'He's a long way from home.' Yellich glanced at the area beyond the gate: a half-a-dozen ponds, he thought, shrubs and a few anglers sitting motionless by them. Beyond the fishery was a long mound with a flat surface. A signal post told Yellich that a railway line ran atop the surface of the mound.

'Aye . . . too far away, he always says; he pines for Cornwall but he married a Yorkshire lass who wouldn't leave home, so it was that Mohammed came to the mountain, so to speak, or so I understand the case to be.' The gatekeeper shrugged as he sat in the booth at the entrance to Liskeard Fisheries. He seemed to Yellich to have found a peaceful, open-air, undemanding job to help eke out his state pension. He wore faded denim jeans and a green T-shirt, and Yellich noted a mottled green military-style combat jacket hanging from a hook in the booth behind the gatekeeper's head. A tabloid paper lay clumsily and untidily folded upon a shelf within it. 'So, how can I help you? Are you looking for stolen goods hidden in the water?' The gatekeeper laughed softly, 'Or a dead body or two? In fact, the members have complained that the fish have not been rising to the bait recently; maybe they're staying down because they are chewing on someone's flesh. Perhaps that's the reason, eh?'

'That's probably closer to the truth than you realize.' Yellich brushed a fly from his face. 'An awful lot closer.'

'Oh, yes?' The gatekeeper's eyes narrowed as he looked at Yellich.

'Yes.' Yellich nodded slightly whilst holding solemn eye contact with the old man. 'In fact, it could be much closer to a certainty but not in the water.'

'Buried?' The gatekeeper's jaw sagged slightly. 'Buried between the pools?'

'Maybe.' Yellich glanced at the rough track which led from the gate into the fishery. It was, he guessed, quite wide enough to accommodate a motor car or a small van and seemed to extend to the further side of the grounds. Between the ponds was rough scrubland dotted with bushes, but he could not, from where he stood, detect a mound of rubble. The anglers looked at him and the other policemen, though none moved unless it was to throw a handful of bait into the water. Above the scene the sky was an expansive, near-cloudless blue.

'So you won't be dragging the ponds?' the elderly game-keeper asked.

'We might have to send divers in,' Yellich replied. 'Why do you ask? Will dragging the ponds cause some sort of damage?'

'No, it won't cause any damage but it will upset the fish,' the gatekeeper explained. 'They'll stay well down after you have dragged the ponds. The fish have to be kept calm – they mustn't be alarmed and they graze for their food; trout do, anyway. I dare say piranhas hunt but we don't have them,' the man grinned, 'just trout and they're not pellet fed either, so you can eat them. We keep 'em alive by emptying bucket loads of maggots into the ponds . . . but not too many. We have to keep the edge on their appetite, or they won't take the anglers' bait.'

'Well, we will probably only need to search one pond, if at all,' Yellich explained. 'So tell me, there is no gate at the entrance. A permanent open entrance is a little unusual, isn't it?'

'Not needed, mate; we just need two posts to make the entrance and a wooden hut for me or the other gatekeepers to sit in while we check licences. There's nothing to steal, you see.'

'So someone could drive a vehicle into the fishery at night?' Yellich asked.

'Yes, if they have a mind to,' the gatekeeper replied. 'There's nobody to stop them – not at night, anyway.'

'Has that always been the case?' Yellich asked. 'Do you know?'

'Yes.' The man gave a brief nod of his head. 'I have been

a gatekeeper here for the last three years but I have lived around here all my life and I have never seen gates on the fishery.'

'That is interesting.' Yellich once again glanced around the grounds. 'Would you know where there is a pile of stones in the fishery, or a pile of rubble?'

'Like a pile of stones large enough to hide a human body?'

'Well . . . yes . . . in fact, yes, as large as that,' Yellich confirmed.

'Wait till I tell my old lass about this.' The gatekeeper began to grin. 'Just wait.'

'Rather you told me first,' Yellich growled as he brushed another fly from his face.

'All right, all right . . . the pile I am thinking of is between ponds three and six.' He raised his right arm pointing to the far side of the fishery.

'Three and six? Sorry,' Yellich forced a smile, 'we'll need directions. Ponds three and six don't mean anything to us. They don't seem to have signs indicating which number they are.'

'They don't – we just know which is the number of each pond.' The gatekeeper kept his hand raised. 'The ponds are numbered outwards from the entrance, three ponds on either side of the track.'

'Yes.' Yellich looked out over the fishery. 'All right, I see six ponds.'

'Well,' the gatekeeper explained, pointing to the ponds as he did so, 'from here down to the left side of the track is pond one, then two, then three . . . and from here down the right-hand side of the track is pond four, then five, then six.'

'Got you.' Yellich smiled his thanks. 'So ponds three and six are the two furthest ponds from the entrance here and the mound of stones you mention is between ponds three and six?'

'That's it, squire.' The gatekeeper beamed. 'You can't miss it . . . or them . . . the pile of stones is well overgrown, though; they've been here a long time going by the weeds growing on them. They were certainly here when I came – no one seems to know what to do with them so they just get left alone.'

'I see. So tell me,' Yellich asked, 'do you know how many

anglers are here at the moment? I see only about ten, but I imagine that there must be others hidden from view?'

'Yes, there are, squire, you imagine correctly, squire.' The gatekeeper glanced at a clipboard which hung on the wall to his left. 'There are twice that . . . there are twenty anglers at the moment, it being midweek, you see, squire. We're busier at the weekend, as you'd expect.'

'Indeed,' Yellich noted. 'Listen, I am sorry but I am going to have to ask you to clear the fishery. All anglers must pack their stuff up and leave. We'll ask them if you don't want to . . . and we'll need to speak to the owner.'

'I can let you have his phone number,' the gatekeeper replied. 'I'd also like the police to clear the fishery, if you don't mind. They'll move more quickly for you anyway. If I ask them they'll just grumble and drag their feet.'

'Understood.' Yellich again glanced at the fishery. 'As you say, it's probably better coming from us.'

A police constable saw the skull first. A human skull, grinning, it seemed. Once the fishery had been cleared of complaining but also curious anglers, who carried their rods and bait and keep nets and stools away, the police constables, helped by Yellich and Ventnor, began to lift the stones from the pile of rubble one at a time, carefully pulling them loose from the weeds which served to bind them together, and laid each dislodged stone in a new pile, creating a new mound of rubble parallel with the original one. The team worked in silence and methodically until a young constable stood up suddenly and exclaimed, 'Oh!' He then collected himself and said, 'Sergeant Yellich, here please, sir.'

Yellich walked three paces from where he was standing and viewed the skull. 'Very good, we have found what we are looking for,' he said, then addressed the team of constables. 'Keep removing the stones, one by one, until the whole skeleton is exposed, but do not touch it.' He spoke to Ventnor. 'I'm going to phone this in; I'm going to tell Mr Hennessey what we have found. I'll be requesting the attendance of SOCO and a pathologist.'

Ventnor nodded. 'Right, Sarge.'

\* \* \*

'Henry Hall? I haven't heard that name for a while.' The publican stood back from the bar and folded his muscular arms as he did so. He was tall and broad-chested, dressed in a blue shirt, blue tie and white slacks. 'Yes, I well remember Henry. Twenty years ago now, must be about that, but I remember him very well. Damn shame that.'

'Shame?' Carmen Pharoah repeated. 'What was a shame?'

'Well, the old boy going missing like that. I mean, something must have happened to him. I still keep wondering what it was. He wasn't a man to go off, not just like that. Not easy to do, anyway, not these days. You can't pawn the family silver and invent a new life for yourself in another part of the country, not these days you can't.'

'Did you know him well?' Pharoah glanced round the pub. It seemed to be neatly kept, well-polished, with just two elderly female patrons at that moment, sitting together, both with a schooner of port but not talking to each other. The television on the wall was turned on and was showing an ice hockey match, but the volume was, to Pharoah's great relief, on mute.

'He was a regular, an early bird,' the publican replied. 'He liked a pint after a hard day's gardening in the park. He was very quiet,' the publican glanced to his right, 'always well behaved, never caused any trouble and he knew what he liked. Yes . . . yes . . . a harmless, peaceable sort. He'd have a game of arrows with the other early evening regulars and a few pints of low-strength beer, then he'd leave about eight for an early night. He liked to get up early for "the best job in the world", as he would often describe his work. He spoke about that rich smell of turned soil, of delicate plants, being outdoors, and he liked being left alone to get on with his job. Then he goes missing . . . damned iffy if you ask me . . . damned iffy. So, has he turned up?'

'Possibly.' Carmen Pharoah diplomatically kept her cards close to her chest. 'What do you know of Henry Hall's social life?'

'You're standing on it.' The publican smiled. 'This, the Empress, was his social life . . . this pub, his job, his little council house . . . that was the sum of Henry Hall's world, so far as I could tell.'

'Did you notice anything strange about Mr Hall at around the time he disappeared?' Carmen Pharoah asked. 'Anything you thought to be a little odd or unusual?'

'I didn't.' The publican slowly shook his head. 'You see a lot from behind a bar but not everything. You should ask Bill Knight. If anyone knows anything it'll be old Bill Knight.'

'Bill Knight?'

'Bill Knight,' the publican explained, 'is a neighbour of Henry Hall's. Or he was, I should say.'

'Where can I find him?' Pharoah asked. 'A neighbour, you say, as in the next-door house?'

'If you like you can visit him at home, but he's behind you.' The publican raised a fleshy finger, indicating the area behind Pharoah.

She turned and saw a tall, thin man entering the pub. He seemed unkempt, with straggly, untidy hair, and wearing old, saggy clothing.

'This is old Bill Knight,' the publican explained. 'He's here for a pint. He'll take an hour to drink it, and then he'll go home until this time tomorrow.'

'It used to be a gravel quarry.' Phil Edwards was a rotund, bearded individual who spoke with a thick Cornish accent. He was, Yellich thought, very well presented but he was also casually dressed; wearing a yellow T-shirt and white slacks, he kept his arms folded as he leaned on the side of his highly polished black Mercedes Benz. Yellich estimated that he was in his late middle years, somewhere on the fifties/sixties cusp. 'The ponds are the remains of one huge gravel bed which was quarried out.'

'Deep?' Yellich queried. 'I mean, are they deep for fishing ponds?'

Phil Edwards chuckled. 'I was going to say, not compared to the Atlantic Ocean, but yes, they are deep enough for fish ponds – ten to fifteen feet. Nice depth for angling, but deep enough for gravel beds. It made me, financially speaking.' He turned. 'This little acre and a half made me.'

'Oh,' Yellich prompted the man to talk. 'Fisheries are a good business to be in?'

'Yes, they certainly are.' Edwards whistled. 'I shudder to think what a mess I would have made of my life if my lady wife had agreed to leave Yorkshire and come back to Cornwall with me. I reckon I would have done something small but nothing like I have done up here. You see, the ponds used to be a grassy area, like a meadow on the banks of the canal. There's a canal just this side of the railway embankment, and the meadow was soggy so didn't attract builders, who didn't want to build houses next to a canal and a railway anyway. They'd never sell them. The meadow came up for sale and it had a few caravans on it which people used for weekend geta-ways. It was quite remote then, this area. That housing estate,' he pointed to his left, 'wasn't here, just the village about a mile away on the other side of where the estate is now and the few isolated farmworkers' houses. Anyway, I took a big gamble and I bought the land thinking I could use the soggy ground to my advantage. I then made the caravan owners a fair offer for their vans. I told them to sell to me because if they didn't I would tow them off my land and leave them in the road.'

'That was fair?' Yellich growled. 'Sounds a bit cut-throat to me, Mr Edwards.'

'Of course it was fair.' Phil Edwards looked at Yellich in a despairing manner. 'It was wholly fair; you see, that way they at least got something for their vans. I could have served them with notices to remove their vans which, if they did not comply, would have then entitled me to tow them on to the road, leave them there and not give the owners a penny piece. They wouldn't have got anything because the council would have removed them from the public highway and then it would have scrapped them, so yes, very fair, very, very fair.' Edwards breathed deeply. 'They got something and I got a swamp. I had intended to hollow it out to about five feet deep and build a marina for narrow canal boats with some hard standing so the narrow boats could be lifted out of the water for mainten-ance. The plan was that I'd make money from canal boat owners from berthing fees and then I planned to acquire about six narrow boats and hire them out to holidaymakers. I had the planning permission and everything but I then fell lucky, didn't I?'

'I don't know,' Yellich replied. 'Did you?'

'Yes.' Edwards smiled contentedly. 'Yes, I did. So we did a few test bores to find out how deep the meadow went down and to see if there was bedrock beneath it. Anyway, we went down the eighteen inches and hit gravel . . . this whole area was gravel. I'd paid for a swamp and I'd bought a gravel bed.'

Somerled Yellich gasped. 'Fell lucky, as you say. I could do with luck like that in my life.'

'Yes, so then I was a millionaire overnight. I made my million.' Edwards smiled smugly. 'I excavated the gravel and sold it to the building trade. Anyway, once we had taken all the gravel out we were left with a massive hole in the ground which was too deep for a canal boat marina. Yachtsmen can cope with a good depth of water under their keel but not canal boat owners; three feet of water under their keel is all they need, and it's all they want. But then when I was deciding what to do, like offering the land to the council as a landfill site, I noticed how the hole was filling up with rainwater, and also how the water from the surrounding land was draining into it. So then I had an idea. You see, my old man was a keen trout fisherman, so I decided to create a fishery. I put some rubble in to divide the area into six ponds with a central road running the length of it, though the ponds are all inter-connected with hollow pipes about six feet below the surface. I then covered the dividing bits with soil and here I am, charging annual fees to permit a fisherman to fish for his supper. I keep the fishery well stocked and provide a little live food for the fish. So, a body has been found on my little acre and a half, in my little gold mine?'

'Yes, about twenty years buried, we think,' Yellich advised.

'Twenty years? I had not been long up and running by then . . . definitely the first few years of the fishery. Definitely.'

'Can I ask,' Yellich said, 'if you employed many men when you were building the fishery?'

'Yes, I dare say I did.' Edwards pursed his lips. 'Yes, I had quite a crew when we were dividing the large, original hole into the six ponds we have now, but it was all casual labour.'

'Do you remember any names?'

'I might if I had reason to do so . . . same as schoolteachers.

One of my customers is a retired schoolteacher; I was chatting to him one day and he told me that after thirty years' teaching he only remembers the good pupils and the bad ones – the rest, the majority, made no impression on him at all and have evaporated from his memory . . . it's a bit like that,' Edwards explained, continuing to lean on his Mercedes Benz with his massive arms folded. 'I remember the good workers and I remember the ones that caused trouble.'

'Shane Bond.' Yellich floated the name. 'Does that name ring any bells?'

'The trawlerman!' Edwards held eye contact with Yellich and then looked away. 'Yes, I remember him very well.' Edwards' jaw set firm. 'Yes, he was employed here. For some reason he couldn't go to sea at that time, he was injured . . . I recall that he had an injury to his back.' Edwards patted his lumbar region then folded his arms again. 'He had done something to his back which prevented him lifting heavy loads. He came here looking for work and I was able to set him on doing light duties. He could fill a wheelbarrow with rubble, one stone at a time, but he couldn't lift and push the barrow, work like that.'

'I see,' Yellich replied.

'And at lunchtime he was the team's gofer. He'd be the one to go and fetch the fish and chips from the chippy in the village. He wasn't a popular man . . . not Shane . . . even got into a fight with an Irishman who was built like the side of a house and collected the second prize. He walked off the site – I mean, he stormed off it – and returned with a knife to fillet the Irishman and took the second prize again. After that I paid him off – I let him go, I had to – he was bad news all round, and I never saw him again. I assume his back injury repaired itself and he went back to the trawlers where he belonged. I wasn't sorry to see him go.'

'He attacked someone with a knife?' Yellich clarified.

'Yes.' Edwards nodded. 'It would have been a murder if he had succeeded.'

'You didn't report it?' Yellich was surprised. 'A crime like that, even if it was only attempted . . . ?'

'No, no I didn't.' Edwards explained, 'You see, the crew

were all ex-cons who only worked for cash in hand. A few had warrants out on them. Men like that . . . well, they have their own way of sorting things out. No one was hurt except Bond, who got exactly what was coming to him, then he left and didn't return. So we handled it ourselves and kept the police out of it. I reckon if I had called the police when Shane Bond returned with the knife my workforce would have taken to the hills.' Edwards glanced into the middle distance. 'It made good sense to handle it like that, to keep a lid on it.'

'Fair enough, but it's quite interesting he picked up a knife,' Yellich pondered. Then he said, 'So Shane Bond knew the layout of this site?'

'Oh, yes.' Edwards nodded gently. 'He helped build it . . . he should know the layout of the fishery all right.'

'I mean, he knew his way around it?' Yellich clarified.

'Every inch, I would say,' Edwards replied. 'Every inch. He was with us towards the end of the project, you see.'

'And he'd know about the pile of rubble at the bottom end of the fishery?'

'I would think so,' Phil Edwards replied with a wide grin. 'He built it. What happened was that when we had built the road and separated the ponds there were a lot of stones lying about, so I asked light-work Shane to go over the site picking up rocks that were lying about here and there and put them in a pile at the end of the fishery. He used the wheelbarrow, him and his bad back, carrying just two or three stones in the barrow at a time. He could manage that sort of weight. It was about then, when pretty much all the loose stones had been collected, that he picked a fight with Big Mick Delaney from Donegal.'

The attention of both men was drawn to a red and white Riley circa 1947 which drove up to the fishery and halted behind the police minivan. It was followed by a white Ford carrying two men. A slender woman in her forties got out of the Riley carrying a brown Gladstone bag, and wound down the window of her car to allow the interior of the vehicle to 'breathe' in the sun. She then closed the car door gently and walked towards the entrance to the fishery. The men got out of the Ford and, by contrast, wound up the window of the car. They donned yellow 'high visibility' vests and also walked towards the fishery carrying square black suitcases.

'The lady is the pathologist,' Yellich told Edwards. 'The two men are SOCO.'

'SOCO?' Edwards asked, sounding to Yellich to be genuinely interested.

'Scene of crime officers – they take photographs of crime scenes.'

'Interesting,' Edwards mumbled. 'Police work fascinates me.'

'So Bond built the pile of rocks?' Yellich confirmed, turning to face Dr D'Acre as she approached.

'Yes, as I said.' Edwards stood in deference to Dr D'Acre. 'It is, was and still is, all his own work.'

'I'd like to take a statement from you to that effect and also a statement about the knife attack on the Irishman,' Yellich advised Edwards.

'Well, it was hardly an attack,' Phil Edwards explained. 'I mean, Shane Bond was seeing stars before he could do anything. Big Micky was about to drop a rock on his head but he was stopped by another boy who said, "We don't want the police here, Micky". So Big Micky left Shane Bond alive. But yes, I'll give the police a statement with pleasure.'

'Afternoon, ma'am,' Yellich addressed Dr D'Acre when she closed in on his personal space. 'I'll take you to the corpse.' Then he turned to Edwards. 'We'll have to take possession of the fishery until . . . well, certainly for the remainder of the day,' Yellich explained. 'And possibly tomorrow as well.'

'Fair enough.' Edwards nodded. 'Take all the time in the world. I think that I'll close the fishery for a week. It's the thing to do if a body has been on the site all the time. Yes, I'll shut it down for a week and then ask the minister to bless the site before I reopen it. I'll do that out of respect to the dead.'

'As you wish, sir,' Yellich replied with a smile. He thought Phil Edwards' attitude was gracious and sensitive. After early concerns about the man's attitude to the caravan owners, he had grown to like him.

*    *    *

'He's a worried man.' Bill Knight sipped his beer. 'Someone was looking for him, a large, well-built guy he was – I mean, the guy who was looking for Henry was large and well built.'

'Would you recognize this man again?' Carmen Pharoah asked.

'I might.' Bill Knight scanned the lounge of the Empress. 'I might,' he said again, looking downwards. 'But it's a while ago now. A good long while.'

'Did he say why he wanted to find Henry Hall?' Pharoah asked.

'No, but it wasn't to tell him he'd won the lottery, that's for sure.' Bill Knight put his glass of beer down on the table top. 'He was walking up and down the street, moving like a very angry man, looking at houses, and he stopped me and asked if I knew where Henry Hall lived. Of course I said "no", then I told Henry about him and Henry looked scared. I mean, he was really frightened. White . . . he went white. It was shortly after that he went missing. So why the police interest?'

'Let's just say there has been a development,' Pharoah replied. 'I'll have to take a statement from you and ask you to look at some photographs to see if you can identify the man in a line-up of people who are of similar appearance, allowing for them ageing.'

'Oh, yes, I've seen that on television.' Bill Knight again sipped his beer. 'Are we doing that now?'

'Yes. I'll drive you in and return you home.'

'Best finish my beer first.' Bill Knight took another sip. 'I won't be long, miss, I won't be long. Just let me sink this. I usually take my time but I can drink it in a jiffy if I have to.'

Four men sat in upright chairs, two on each side of a polished pinewood table which stood against the wall. The floor of the room was covered in hard-wearing Hessian matting; the walls were painted a uniform shade of grey. The illumination for the room was provided by a filament bulb set in the ceiling behind an opaque Perspex sheet. The tape recorder was installed in the wall at the side of the desk, the twin cassettes spun slowly and a red light glowed, thus giving a clear indication to all present in the room that the machine was switched on and each word, each sound, was being recorded.

'I am Detective Chief Inspector Hennessey,' Hennessey began. 'The place is interview room three at Micklegate Bar Police Station in the city of York, the date is Friday, the second of June, the time is 16.33 hours. I am now going to ask the other persons present in the room to identify themselves for the purposes of the tape.'

'Detective Sergeant Yellich of Micklegate Bar Police Station.'

'Grant Joyner, Solicitor, of Ellis Burden Woodland and Lake and Co., of Saint Leonard's Place, York, representing Mr Bond.'

Shane Bond paused and glanced at Grant Joyner, who nodded, prompting Bond to say, 'Shane Bond.' Bond spoke sullenly and looked downwards.

'I'll be frank with you, Shane,' Hennessey began, knowing Bond's sullenness meant that it was going to be a long and difficult interview with information and concessions having to be prised out of the man. Both Hennessey and Yellich knew that Bond would not be giving anything away or carelessly tripping himself up. 'The case against you is . . . well, it's open and shut.'

'Really?' Joyner peered at Hennessey over the rim of his spectacles. He was a young man, immaculately dressed in a dark blue pinstripe suit and a university tie. He reeked strongly of aftershave and proudly wore a wide gold wedding band. Grant Joyner was at least six feet tall, Hennessey guessed, and seemed to be muscular, as if, thought Hennessey, he was a skilled man in a particular sport of a strenuous nature.

'Well, yes . . .' Hennessey replied. 'Yes, we think so. Your wife, Shane, your first wife, Gloria, has made a full confession about her part in the murder of Henry Hall, from enticing him to open his door to helping you bundle the body into your van; she also admits to helping you bury the body under a pile of stones at the fishery which you knew were there because you built the mound when you were working ashore because of a bad back. You punctured the stomach to let the gases escape, you threw top soil on the mound of stones to encourage

the weeds to establish themselves and you had the motive
because she was being unfaithful to you. You found out and
beat the information out of her as to Henry Hall's address.
Then with that information you went looking for him at his
house and asked a neighbour, Mr Knight, where Henry Hall
lived. Mr Knight picked you out of the identity parade just
now as being the man who asked him where Henry Hall lived,
as if to make certain of the address. You also have, or at least
at the time had, a propensity for knives to settle scores. You
had a fight at the fishery with an Irishman – you lost, and
you returned later with a knife seeking your vengeance. You
lost again and the owner of the fishery gave you the sack there
and then.'

Bond looked at Joyner, who said in a soft-spoken and
cultured voice, 'It's a strong case, Mr Bond. It will be an
uphill battle to convince a jury to acquit you. Two witnesses
that will connect you to the murder of Mr Hall, a third witness
who will connect you to the pile of stones. The motive, to
want to harm Mr Hall for having an affair with your wife
while you were at sea . . . the knife attack on the Irishman at
the fishery . . . your later conviction for attempted manslaughter
in the car park, sundry and other previous convictions, and all
for acts of violence. It's not a hugely good place you're in.'

Shane Bond looked down at the floor, then he turned to
Joyner and, quite unexpectedly for the officers who had
anticipated a long and gruelling interview, he asked meekly,
'So what can I do? What is the best thing to do?'

'I'm afraid that there is not much you can do, Mr Bond,'
Joyner replied, and as he did so Hennessey believed that
he detected a trace of Welsh in the man's speaking voice. 'We
won't be able to negotiate a reduction of the charge to
manslaughter because of the strong element of premeditation
. . .' Joyner looked at Hennessey for clarification.

'No way,' Hennessey confirmed. 'The Crown Prosecution
Service will be charging Mr Bond with murder. I can guarantee
there won't be a reduced charge in return for a guilty plea.
Not in this case.'

'Will you be charging Mrs Bond with conspiracy to murder?'

'That decision is presently with CPS,' Hennessey replied

diplomatically, 'but she is prepared to give evidence in court against her ex-husband. He was and is a violent man and he was violent towards her. She has much ill-feeling towards your client.'

'Will she make a credible witness, do you think?' Joyner probed. 'Can she damage my client in the eyes of the jury?'

'Yes,' Hennessey replied, feeling a pang of guilt as he misled Joyner. Gloria Bond was an alcoholic, she was a recovered heroin addict, she was mentally challenged and she could not stand in the witness box for more than five minutes without having to be allowed to run to the ladies' toilets. It was really up to Joyner to make his own assessment of Mrs Bond, Hennessey believed, but he also believed that the mild-mannered Henry Hall, council gardener, deserved justice. So he added, 'Remember, she took us straight to the body – well, she didn't take us but she gave us perfect directions. Henry Hall's body was exactly where she said it would be and I feel sure that when we send divers down into the pond they'll find the spade and the murder weapon where she said Mr Bond, your client, threw them.'

Joyner sighed and took off his glasses. He rested his forehead on the fingertips of his right hand as his elbow rested on the table top. 'I'm sorry, Mr Bond,' he turned to Shane, 'I can't see a defence. I can't see a way out for you. It does indeed seem open and shut.'

'What is the best thing to do?' Bond asked. 'What can I do for the best?'

'Plead guilty and throw yourself at the mercy of the court.' Joyner looked at Bond as he spoke. 'You'll collect the nominal life sentence . . . but if you work your ticket and you don't rock the boat when you're inside,' Joyner advised. 'Well, then . . .'

'Yes, I know the score.' Bond nodded. 'I know how that ball bounces.'

'Don't just work towards an early parole but also work towards being classified from Category A to Category B or C. It's just the way of it,' Joyner further advised, 'because of their show of remorse and their total cooperation, murderers have in the past worked their way to open prisons which are . . .'

'Holiday camps,' Bond snarled. 'So I hear.'

'So I hear also,' Joyner replied. 'With a bit of luck and the right attitude you'll be out within ten years.'

Shane Bond buried his head in his hands and then after a pause he looked at Hennessey and said, 'All right, I did it, you've got me for Henry Hall's murder. It went down exactly like Gloria told you and also for that reason . . . she was playing away. I slapped the details out of her and went looking for Hall, but I couldn't find his house so I went back home and slapped her some more, and then I made her take me to his door. So show me . . . where do I sign?'

'You will note my client's cooperation?' Joyner insisted. 'It must be taken into consideration at his parole hearings.'

'Yes, yes, we'll write the statement for your lawyer here to read and if he agrees, you'll sign it,' Hennessey advised. 'And we will record your cooperation.'

'Do I get bail?' Bond asked. 'I have things to tidy up.'

'Not for murder, Shane, but look at it this way: your life sentence starts now, from the moment we charge you, not from the moment you are convicted at your trial, which could be eighteen months from now. It will be nearer six months most likely; it depends on the backlog of cases to be heard. So you're already on your way to your first parole hearing, already on your way to the Category B prison. Now . . .' Hennessey paused, 'one murder out of the way, let's talk about the other.'

'Other, what other? Murder?' Bond turned to Joyner. 'I didn't do no other murder.'

'The carbon copy, Shane,' Hennessey advised him. 'You murdered the lover of your first wife, one Henry Hall, and later, when your second wife was doing the same thing, carrying on with another man while you were at sea, you also murdered her lover, one James Wenlock.'

'I did not!'

'We can make a case that you did,' Hennessey pressed.

'Can you?' Joyner sat up. 'Can you really?'

'The pattern of offending,' Hennessey explained to Joyner, 'the choice of murder weapon, the attack on the man in the car park of the Golden Fleece pub in Selby when Mr Bond mistook him for the man who was seeing his second wife.

Your client's statement, "I always kill my wife's lovers" or
whatever he said – the actual words are recorded and I can
easily access them. The fact that Mr Wenlock disappeared
shortly after you attacked the wrong man in the car park of
the Fleece and the fact that Mr Wenlock's body, like Mr Hall's
body, was similarly buried as a form of concealment.'

'I did one . . . not the other,' Bond protested. 'I told you,
one but not the other.'

'You'll serve the sentences concurrently,' Yellich added.
'You won't serve two actual sentences.'

'Now you're coercing my client,' Joyner leaned back in his
chair, 'and quite frankly I can't see any actual evidence of my
client's guilt in the second murder you speak of. I mean, where
are your witnesses, for one thing? What forensic evidence
have you got . . . ?'

'We'll be putting it all before a jury; we'll let them decide,'
Hennessey replied. 'We'll be taking Mr Bond to the charge
bar now and we'll be charging him with the murder of Henry
Hall and with the murder of James Wenlock.'

'When they charge you,' Joyner turned to Bond, 'don't reply.
Don't say a word.'

'All right.' Bond nodded. 'Understood. But I never did
Wenlock. I never did that turn.'

George Hennessey drove home after he had supervised the
charging of Shane Bond with the murders of James Wenlock
and Henry Hall, and arranged his appearance before the York
Magistrates the following morning, wherein, dear reader, bail
requests would naturally be opposed, being Shane Bond's
second step towards his eventual appearance before York
Crown Court in a few months. Hennessey found to his relief
that he had missed the so-called 'rush hour' where traffic, in
his experience, did anything but rush, and so he enjoyed a
leisurely and peaceful drive out of York on the A19 to
Easingwold and his home, on the other side of the market
town in which he enjoyed living. He turned his car into the
driveway of his detached house on the Thirsk Road and the
subsequent crunching of the gravel alerted a dog within the
house to his master's return, which caused the animal to begin

barking with excitement. Hennessey let himself into his house and was greeted by the barking, tail wagging, jumping Oscar, whom Hennessey stroked and patted. He walked through the house, let himself out of the rear door and was followed by Oscar (who had free access to the fenced-off rear garden courtesy of a dog flap) and then returned to the kitchen and made himself a homecoming pot of Yorkshire tea. After the tea had infused he poured a mug of same, added a drop of milk, and then carried the mug outside and stood on the patio as Oscar criss-crossed the lawn as if searching for an interesting scent.

'We wrapped it up neatly in the end,' George Hennessey said, in such a way that an observer would think he was talking to himself, or was addressing the garden, or a fantasy person whom only he could see. 'One reported murder on Tuesday, as I told you, led to charges for two separate murders by the end of the week. Not a bad result. He'll collect two life sentences; we won't have any difficulty in getting convictions for both.' He sipped his tea. 'You know, I often wonder if the victims of murder know of the justice meted out on their behalf.'

The gentle and most gracious reader will, however, be saddened to learn that our hero speaking to, apparently, no one at all is not the symptom of a harmless eccentricity in a man in his late middle years; rather he is fully sane and his practice of telling the rear garden of his day is the consequence of a dreadful tragedy and the second significant loss in his life.

George Hennessey had been married for a just a few years when his wife Jennifer had collapsed in the centre of Easingwold one very hot summer's afternoon, just three months after the birth of their son, Charles. Passers-by had rushed to her aid, assuming that she had fainted in the heat, but upon examination no pulse could be found and an ambulance was summoned. At the hospital she was found to be deceased upon arrival, or 'Condition Purple' in ambulance crew terminology. The cause of death was deemed to be 'Sudden Death Syndrome', which is the nearest the medical profession has been able to come to explaining why it is that the life force suddenly leaves a person, without warning, and usually affects those in their twenties who are in perfect health and who are often doing nothing more strenuous than walking along the pavement in the middle of the day, as indeed Jennifer Hennessey had been doing. When Jennifer had been heavily pregnant with Charles and was unable, indeed not permitted, to exert herself, she had sat down one evening and drawn up a new design for their rear garden to replace the unimaginative simple expanse of lawn which they had inherited upon buying their house. The lawn, she deemed, should be divided in two, widthways, about halfway between the house and the end of the garden, by a privet hedge in which there was to be set a gateway. To the left of the garden, just beyond the hedge, a wooden shed would be erected, and the bulk of the remainder of the garden beyond the hedge would be given over to apple trees, both eating and cooking varieties. She planned for twenty trees. The final ten feet of the garden, she had deemed, would be allowed to remain as a wilderness, left to its own devices, save for a pond which would be created and frogs introduced. Jennifer Hennessey had, George recalled with fondness, a fascination with the creatures. He had always preferred toads, finding them more colourful and more adventurous: frogs, he had argued with Jennifer, would never stray from their water-course, but a toad will go walkabout.

After Jennifer's funeral, incongruously a summer affair, he returned to their house and scattered her remains over their rear garden, walking from the house, across the lawn, casting her ashes by hand from side to side. It had then, he decided, been his task to create the garden Jennifer had designed, and it had also become his custom to stand on the patio upon his return from work and tell Jennifer of his day. One summer's afternoon he told her of a new lady in his life, but assured her that his love for her had not and would not ever diminish, and upon his delivery he had felt himself embraced by a warmth which could not be explained by the sun's rays alone.

Upon telling Jennifer of the arrest and charging of Shane Bond, Hennessey turned and went back inside his house, leaving Oscar to return via the dog flap when it pleased him to do so. He listened to the local radio as he prepared his evening meal of salad, lean meat and boiled potatoes, and heard on the news bulletin, with no small measure of satisfaction, of the arrest and charging of Shane Bond for two counts of murder. Later on as his supper settled he read a detailed account of the retreat to Dunkirk in 1940 and the subsequent evacuation. He had not realized, until reading the book, that it had been such a bloody, hard-fought battle and the newly acquired book was a most welcome addition to his collection of military history. Later still, when the sun had set and the day had cooled, he took Oscar for their customary walk to the fields beyond the line of houses and man and dog returned three-quarters of an hour later. And even later, George Hennessey strolled casually into Easingwold for a pint of Brown and Mild at the Dove Inn, just one before last orders were called. On the walk back from Easingwold he glanced up at the cloudless sky and the myriad stars. He identified the Plough and saw again how one of the 'pointers' to the Pole Star was flickering. The star was dying but he had no imminent fear for the sailors; he knew the star would still be flickering when his grandchildren were elderly and consequently all mariners in the northern hemisphere would still be able to find their way home for some years to come.

It was Friday, 23.40 hours.


Saturday, 3 June, 10.15 hours

George Hennessey sat at his desk and sipped a mug of tea whilst reading the report which had been compiled in respect of the case against Shane Bond, who had that morning at a special sitting of the York Magistrates been denied bail and remanded in custody pending his trial at York Crown Court. He also read a memo from the forensic laboratory at Wetherby confirming the identity, by DNA match, of James Wenlock. He closed the file and as he did so a worried-looking Carmen Pharoah entered his office unusually without tapping on his door and sat down in one of the chairs in front of his desk, also unusually, without waiting to be invited to do so.

'There's no damage done, sir,' she blurted out, 'no damage has been done and the CPS would have seen it anyway . . .'

Hennessey held up his hand. 'Take a deep breath, Carmen . . . just calm down and tell me what we have missed. It sounds to me as though we have missed something.'

Carmen Pharoah took a deep breath, nodding slowly as she did so; she then consulted a piece of paper she was holding in her hands. 'It'll have to be checked. We should have seen much sooner than this but at least we've seen it before we got egg all over our faces . . .'

'Seen what, Carmen?' Hennessey spoke calmly. 'Seen what?'

'The dates, sir . . . oh, this would have been just so embarrassing.' Pharoah shook her head.

'What dates?' Hennessey's voice hardened. 'What have we missed?'

'The date of Shane Bond's attack on Roy Farrell.'

'He was . . . ?' Hennessey queried.

'The gentleman whom Shane Bond attacked in the car park of the Golden Fleece pub in Selby, having mistaken him for James Wenlock.'

'Ah, yes . . . whose identity is just confirmed, by the way.' Hennessey held up the memo received from the forensic science laboratory. 'No surprise there, but the confirmation is made. Sorry, do continue . . .'

'Well, sir, according to reports when Bond was arrested later that same night, he was charged with attempted murder, later to be allowed to plead to assault.'

'He was lucky,' Hennessey growled.

'Yes, sir . . . but he wasn't bailed,' Carmen Pharoah continued. 'He was remanded in custody, just as he was remanded in custody this morning.'

Hennessey's brows furrowed. 'I think I can see where you are going with this . . .'

'Yes . . . anyway . . . as you can probably guess, as you say, James Wenlock was reported missing three days later, which means that Shane Bond was in custody when James Wenlock was last known to be alive.'

'I'll have a look at the files myself but as you say, no damage has been done. If you're right we can amend the report to the CPS and they will drop the charge of murder in respect of James Wenlock . . . but the charge of murder in respect of Henry Hall still stands.'

'Yes, sir, that case is solid.' Pharoah sat back in the chair. 'At least that is solid.'

'It could not be more solid. He is going "G" to it, as my son would say.' Hennessey swept his liver-spotted hands through his silver grey hair. 'But thank you, Carmen. As you say, we would have been made to look prize idiots if we had proceeded against Bond in respect of the murder of James Wenlock.' He breathed deeply. 'What idiots we would have looked.'

'The CPS would have spotted it, sir,' Pharoah replied encouragingly. 'It wouldn't have got as far as open court.'

'You hope,' Hennessey grinned, 'but in my experience errors and oversights like that have a way of surviving against all the odds and make it from box to box to box, but at least we've stopped this one in its tracks . . . so well done you.'

'Thank you, sir.' Pharoah smiled at the compliment.

It was just then, as Hennessey would later recall, that the pale green phone on his desk warbled softly. He let it ring twice before he picked up the handset. 'DCI Hennessey,' he spoke efficiently, promptly, listened for a few moments and then he said, 'is she now? All right, I'll come down to the inquiry desk. Ask her to take a seat, please.' He replaced the phone. 'Well, well, well, that's a turn up for the books; Mrs Bartlem has paid a call on us.'

'The lady with the postcards?' Carmen Pharoah asked. 'That Mrs Bartlem?'

'Yes,' Hennessey stood, 'the one and the same. Would you care to accompany me? Let's you and I go down and see what she wants.'

What Mrs Bartlem wanted, it transpired, was to show Mr Hennessey a postcard. 'It came in today's post, to the drop-in centre,' Mrs Bartlem explained as she handed the postcard to Hennessey. 'We get an early delivery. We're at the beginning of our postman's walk.' Hennessey took the card and considered it. Like the previous postcards it showed a photograph of the harbour at Scarborough. He turned it over and saw that it had been posted locally the previous day. 'The report of Shane Bond's arrest for the murder of James Wenlock was first broadcast on the six p.m. news . . .' He spoke as much to himself as to Pharoah. 'The last collection is at seven-thirty p.m., so yes, there would have been time to do it. The person who sent it must have a number of these cards.' Hennessey handed it to Pharoah. The message on the reverse was type-written, as before. She read it aloud, 'Wrong man for James Wenlock. Check Wenlock's client list for right man.'

Somerled Yellich and Thompson Ventnor, having represented the police at the committal hearing of Shane Bond at the magistrates court, stepped side by side out of the staff entrance of Micklegate Bar Police Station and stood in bright, early afternoon sunlight. The two men paused as if enjoying the sun.

'Fancy a beer?' Ventnor asked.

'Can't, sorry,' Yellich replied warmly. 'I'm on guard duty this afternoon and evening, and I don't like drinking at lunch time anyway . . . you lose the afternoon.'

'Dare say you're right,' Ventnor felt in his pocket for his car keys, 'silly of me to ask really. I have things to do today as well. See you on Monday, Sarge.'

Somerled Yellich returned home and parked his car in front of his new-build house on an estate of similar houses in the expanded village of Huntingdon, to the north of York, and walked casually up the short drive to the front door. As he opened the door and entered his house Jeremy ran towards him with a squeal of delight. Yellich braced himself for the impact, and responded to his son's warm welcome with an equal display of warm emotion. He washed and changed into casual clothing and over lunch with Sara and Jeremy he commented favourably on Sara's haircut. 'Reminds me of the time I first set eyes on you at that party,' he smiled, 'so slender and in a pair of jeans and such short hair. I saw you from behind and thought it was a sixteen-year-old boy who had wangled himself an invitation and wondered who had let him get near the punch bowl.'

'I've filled out a little since then.' Sara Yellich put an extra helping of salad on to Jeremy's plate.

'Not by very much,' Yellich replied, 'not by very much at all. It is clear that I am married to the most beautiful woman in Yorkshire, if not the world.' This comment caused his wife to blush and look down at her plate.

After lunch and extracting a promise from Sara that she would drive safely and be back home by nine p.m., he took Jeremy for a walk in the meadows to the west of the village, where they spent the late afternoon together and identified plants and birds. In the evening Jeremy impressed Somerled Yellich by being able to tell complicated times such as twenty-five minutes to two and seventeen minutes past nine. Jeremy was, according to the school he attended, quite advanced for a twelve-year-old.

Somerled and Sara Yellich had, like all parents of children with learning difficulties, been disappointed to learn of their son's condition, but slowly, over the years, a whole new world had opened up to them. They met and befriended parents of similar children to Jeremy. Somerled and Sara had also learned to revel in the abundance of love and warmth which their son showed, knowing that he would never be a surly and difficult adolescent. With support and care and stimulation Jeremy could, they were told, achieve the functioning level of a ten-year-old by the time he reached adulthood and then be capable of semi-independent living in a hostel where he would have his own room and be able to prepare his own meals if he chose to do so, but where staff would be permanently on hand should difficulties arise.

Somerled Yellich put his son to bed at eight thirty and waited for Sara, who arrived at nine fifteen, panting her apologies. It had, Yellich thought, been a busy week and by then he felt very tired. He retired to bed, leaving Sara, who elected to stay up to watch the late film, and he slept a full and a nourishing sleep.

Thompson Ventnor spent that Saturday afternoon cleaning his house, doing the week's accumulated washing up and shopping for food to sustain him during the coming week. That evening he took a bus to the outskirts of York and alighted at a bus stop at the extreme edge of the city's suburban development. He walked slowly from the bus stop to the gates of a Victorian era mansion and strolled up the drive. At the building itself he opened the front door and was met by a blast of hot air. He signed in the visitor's book and then ascended a wide, carpeted stairway and entered a large room in which elderly people were sitting against the walls and being attended by two women in nurses' uniform. In the far corner of the room one elderly man's face lit up with pleasure as he recognized Ventnor, but by the time Ventnor had crossed the floor to where the elderly man was seated, and said, 'Hello, Dad,' the elderly man was staring vacantly into space and giggling softly to himself.

Ventnor returned to the centre of York and decided to 'kill' the remaining light hours by taking a bus to Harrogate. He spent an hour walking the streets of the spa town until dusk, at which point he returned by bus to York. At York he walked into a pub and had a beer, then another, then another. From the pub he went to Caesar's Nightclub and got into a conversation with a lady who had, he thought, plastered her make-up upon her face in layers. He left the club alone and, finding it a pleasant summer's night, decided to walk home to Dringhouses.

It was Sunday, 02.35 hours.

# FOUR

Monday, 5 June, 10.00 hours – 19.45 hours

*In which Reginald Webster acts upon a whim and by thus doing causes an interesting development, and the courteous reader is privy to another demon in George Hennessey's life, but also to the joy therein.*

'So . . .' George Hennessey leaned forward, placed his elbows on the surface of his desk and clasped his hands together, 'what has happened, somewhat embarrassingly,' he looked down as he spoke, addressing his assembled team of Yellich, Pharoah, Ventnor and Webster, 'is that we pursued a man for the murder of James Wenlock, even unto the point of charging him, and it has subsequently transpired that he is proven innocent of that murder. But by means of compensation, in the process of pursuing him for the murder of Mr Wenlock, we have in fact proved his guilt in respect of another murder – an earlier murder – which we did not know had happened because up until last week Henry Hall was known only to be a missing person. So . . . to use Carmen's phrase we have avoided getting "egg all over our faces", but we are still no nearer to the solution of the mystery of the murder of James Wenlock than we were one week ago tomorrow when Mrs Bartlem presented at our enquiry desk with a collection of postcards.'

'It does mean that we have to give full credibility to the postcards, sir. That's a step forward in itself.' Yellich cradled a mug of tea in his hands. 'The fact that Shane Bond was in custody when James Wenlock was murdered was never made public. It probably, in fact almost certainly, means that the person who wrote, or rather typed, the postcards knew only that Shane Bond was not the person who did murder James Wenlock because that person knows the identity of the actual killer.'

'Yes, good point.' Hennessey looked up and smiled at Yellich. 'Good point indeed, Somerled. So we accept that the sender of the cards knew not only where we could find the corpse of James Wenlock but must know, must also know, the identity of his murderer . . .' Hennessey paused. 'And typewritten postcards . . . any thoughts there, anyone?'

'Typewriters went out with horse-drawn transport,' Pharoah offered, 'the only place you'd likely to be able to buy a typewriter these days is a charity shop or a curio shop . . . or you'd have to take one down from the attic, dust it off and hope to blazes that the ink in the ribbon hasn't evaporated because you can't buy typewriter ribbons any more . . . at least, I assume you can't.'

'Significance?' Hennessey asked, appealing to the group. 'Come on . . . throw anything into the pot, any thoughts at all.'

'The most likely significance of using a typewriter is that the person who typed the postcards wanted to disguise their handwriting,' Pharoah replied thoughtfully, 'which probably suggests that they are close, they are linked in some way, to the perpetrators of the murder. You couldn't use a word processor to disguise your handwriting because there is the danger of the message being retained by the machine's memory . . . too risky. The use of a typewriter has all the advantages of using a word processor without any of the disadvantages,' she continued. 'It suggests we are seeking someone with a clear mind if not a clear conscience.'

'But why postcards?' Ventnor queried as he sucked on a strong mint to smother his stale-beer breath. 'Why not a blank sheet of paper and a brown envelope? Postcards are read by all who handle them. A threat or an offensive statement on a postcard is deemed to be made in public, the statement could be libellous. Postcards are . . . in fact, highly ill-advised as a means of communication for anything but the most inoffensive of greetings . . . unless . . . unless . . . there is some significance to the cards themselves.'

There was then a lull in the conversation. Each member of the team looked down at the floor, or up at the ceiling, or, in the case of George Hennessey, out of his office window at the ancient walls of the city, upon which at that moment walked the very common sight of a group of brightly dressed, sun-hatted tourists. The silence was eventually broken by Webster, who mused, 'The cards were all of Scarborough, specifically of the harbour area . . . probably something is relevant about the harbour? But at any rate, we might wonder if the town of Scarborough has a significance in all this?'

'The last card received told us to look at James Wenlock's client list.' Pharoah partly put up her hand and then lowered it.

'You're not at school now, Carmen,' Hennessey grinned, 'but yes, that is a very good point . . . another good point. So we are, it seems, making somewhat useful progress.'

'It has to be the link,' Yellich offered. 'It has to be the case that one of James Wenlock's clients has a link of some sort to Scarborough, and that link has some significance to the murder of the man.'

'Right, right.' Hennessey tapped his desk top with his finger-tips. 'So it's a return visit to James Wenlock's employers. Who were they again? A London name . . .'

'Russell Square, sir,' Ventnor advised, 'Russell Square, Chartered Accountants of Saint Leonard's Place.'

'Yes, that's it, Russell Square. So you, Thompson . . .' Hennessey pointed at Thompson Ventnor.

'Yes, sir?'

'And you, Reg . . .'

Webster nodded, 'Yes, sir?'

'I think that it is time for you two to team up and start working together.'

'Very good, sir,' Webster replied.

'The last postcard,' Hennessey advised, 'has been sent to the forensic science laboratory at Wetherby – a bit of a futile exercise, I think, but we might obtain a DNA match or a fingerprint which is on our database, although I have to say that I hold out little hope. So if you two, Reg and Thompson, don't return from Russell Square with a lead of some sort then we'll have to seek a Scarborough connection in Mr Wenlock's private life, but I confess I am most loath to call on his family again . . . not without good reason anyway. So we'll eagerly await your return, and while we do, it's administration for the rest of us, recording on other cases to be completed, and statistical returns for May to be collated. Plenty to do,' he smiled, 'plenty to do.'

Situated at approximately fifty-seven degrees, six minutes north and one degree, seven minutes west, the town of Huddersfield sits high in the Pennines and thus tends to have windy and some-what chilly weather conditions, but which the gracious reader might feel is far, far, preferable to the sulphurous miasma which swirls the streets and alleyways of the steel-producing towns further to the south. Huddersfield is situated at the confluence of the River Holme and the River Colne and is home to nearly 150,000 souls. The town is well endowed with buildings of the Victorian era, a very good example of said heritage being that of the railway station, a Grade I listed building, the proud frontage of which is similar to a stately home, and truly established itself during the nineteenth century, when it became a centre for the production of textiles. It is to the town of Huddersfield and to a certain café on the pedestrianized Packhorse Centre to which we now must turn to continue our tale, as within this café a discussion was taking place.

At the back, as far away from the window as possible, and in the corner, the two women sat facing each other; they leaned forward as they spoke in a hushed near whisper. An observer would note a distinct similitude between the two women, although they possessed sufficient difference that they could not be taken for identical twins. Both had thin faces, both were tall, both well dressed, both married, and both adorned with necklaces, jewellery and gold watches. Both wore expen-sive perfumes. If said observer was near enough to the two women and if he had particularly sharp hearing this is what he would have overheard.

> First woman (F.W.) 'It was quite a risk.'
> Second woman (S.W.) 'Oh, yes, very, very risky. It had
>     to be done, though. It just had to be done. There was
>     no road round it.'
> F.W. 'Oh, I agree. I am not upset, I am just commenting

upon the element of risk involved. But, as you say, there was just no road round it. Just no road at all.'

S.W. 'It's a shame the police were not as much on the ball as we had hoped.'

F.W. 'Yes, a pity . . . but it had to be done.'

S.W. 'Yes, because, as we have both agreed, they had to get the right man. No one else would do.'

F.W. 'We'll have to get rid of the typewriter now.'

S.W. 'Oh, yes, it's done its job. No further need for it now.'

F.W. 'None at all.'

Here the conversation between the two women paused as a high-pitched sound from a coffee-making machine filled the café for a few seconds. Then their conversation resumed.

S.W. 'They'll be closing in now. The police will be closing in on him. If they find the typewriter and they are able to match the typeface to the cards we posted . . . well . . . it will be disastrous . . . curtains for little us.'

F.W. 'Where shall we put it? Any ideas?'

S.W. 'The river at the bottom of the hill beyond the university. It's the best place.'

F.W. 'It's a bit shallow, isn't it?'

S.W. 'It's deep enough and the water will wash any fingerprints off the typewriter.'

F.W. 'All right, if you think it's safe to do that. When should we go? Now, do you think?'

S.W. 'In a little while, so not yet, not just yet. The police change their shift at two p.m. There is a little bit of a lull in police activity half an hour either side of then. Few officers are patrolling – the fewer eyes the better, methinks.'

F.W. 'So . . . if we leave about now we'll arrive at the river at the beginning of the lull?'

S.W. 'Yes. But don't get anxious . . . calm down. We'll leave in a few minutes. It's time for another coffee, then we'll go down to the river.'

Upon leaving the café, the two women, as if in a practised manner, fell quickly into step with each other as they walked side by side, commencing up a route which would take them past the library, past the covered market and into Queensgate, where they would follow the curved road as it went down towards the canalized river. They both wore cream-coloured, three-quarter length, lightweight raincoats and carried a shopping bag between them in which, dear reader, was the typewriter. Upon reaching a bridge over the river which was but a few feet beneath them and, after glancing in either direction and without a word being spoken, when there was a convenient gap in the passing traffic, they tipped up the shopping bag so that the type-writer, which was of the small, portable variety, fell into the river, making a small splash and disappearing from sight amid the thick, green weeds.

> F.W. 'Huddersfield is a useful place for us to meet like this, in this manner.'
>
> S.W. 'Very useful So pleased you suggested it.'
>
> F.W. 'We are not known here and it's a pleasant town to visit on top of it all.'
>
> S.W. 'No, no, we are not known at all.'
>
> F.W. 'I am relieved we have got rid of the typewriter. Very relieved indeed. It was weighing on my mind.'
>
> S.W. 'Yes, less of a worry now. No worry at all, in fact.'
>
> F.W. 'Indeed. Well, it's home for me.'
>
> S.W. 'And it's home to hubby for me.'
>
> Without a further word spoken the two women turned and walked away from each other. Neither gave a backwards glance.

'Scarborough?' Clarence Bellingham stroked his chin and seemed to Ventnor and Webster to be pondering an issue. 'Well,' he said at length, 'I think we can let you look at our files, or rather James Wenlock's files. In the circumstances I don't think that we will require a court order compelling us to do so. A murder inquiry, a murder of one of ours, and the fact that any private information about a client's finances will

be at least ten years old . . . no . . . I don't think the partners
will object to me allowing you access.'

'That is very good of you, sir, we appreciate your cooperation.' Ventnor inclined his head. 'We would only be looking
for a connection with the town of Scarborough.'

'Or perhaps even a client of that name,' Webster added, 'if
you know of one?'

'Well, I certainly don't . . .' Again Bellingham stroked his
chin. 'I wonder who might be able to help there?' He paused
and then suggested, 'You know who I think might? A gentleman
by the name of Nicholson. Andrew Nicholson. He's retired
now, but I believe he is still with us and still active and still
with a brain. He'd be the man to talk to.' Bellingham glanced
round his office at the shelves of books, dark furniture, dark,
deep pile carpet and the window overlooking St Leonard's
Place. 'Andrew Nicholson took over James Wenlock's accounts
when James Wenlock vanished, you see. He did so in a care-
taker capacity. He was winding down to retirement when James
Wenlock disappeared and he was asked if he could look after
the accounts in a reactive manner – don't work the cases, just
sit on them and react to anything that happens . . .'

'Yes,' Ventnor replied, 'we understand.'

'So if there was a Scarborough connection, he'll likely know.
Save you picking your way through his files. Andrew Nicholson
will be a sprightly sixty-five now.'

'Sixty-five?' Webster queried. 'I assumed he'd be older. I
mean, if he retired about ten years ago . . .'

'No, you see he went at fifty-five, lucky man that he was,
and still is, so right now he'll be sixty-five or thereabouts.'

'Where can we contact him?' Ventnor asked. 'Do you know?'

Clarence Bellingham reached forward and picked up the
phone on his desk. 'I'll get his home phone number from my
secretary, then I'll phone him and explain the situation. I am
sure he will agree to me allowing you to have his address. He
always was a very accommodating sort of fellow, very accommodating indeed.'

'That would be most appreciated,' Webster smiled. 'Thank
you.'

*     *     *

'Oh, bless my old soul . . . was there ever a Scarborough connection? Well, bless my dear old soul.' Andrew Nicholson revealed himself to Ventnor and Webster as a tall – exceedingly tall – athletically built man in his late middle years. He was, thought the officers, unnecessarily well dressed in a suit and tie despite being at home, relaxing in the middle of the day, as though he had got dressed in his suit and tie when he knew he was going to receive visitors who were calling in an official capacity, and did so as to be in observance of antiquated rules of social conduct. Both officers found his attitude both pleasing and eye-opening, as had been the case in their individual experiences before when calling on people who belonged to an earlier era, and thereby witnessing outdated customs and manners. Webster had once described it to his wife as 'Suddenly finding myself in the midst of a vanished England'. 'I can tell you that there was never a client of that name,' Nicholson continued, sitting in 'his' armchair in the living room of the house whilst his wife was sitting in 'her' chair, 'so were there any connections with the town?' He looked up at the ceiling as he trawled his memory. 'Were there any connections with the town? Delightful place, but then I have only ever visited in the summer. I can imagine the wind off the North Sea makes it quite unpleasant in the winter months. Quite unpleasant indeed, I would imagine.'

'It is.' Ventnor smiled. 'Take it from me, sir, you can do without visiting Scarborough during the winter months.'

'So . . .' Nicholson pondered the ceiling of his living room of his detached house in the village of Barnton, close to Driffield, 'we had one or two foreign clients . . . yes, we did have one or two foreigners.'

'Foreign?' Ventnor queried.

'Yes,' Nicholson replied with a warm smile. 'Foreign as in outside York, as in clients whose homes and/or businesses were located in other towns, and all communication is done by phone or post. There is no reason why one should live in the same town or city as one's accountant. Living in Newcastle and having an accountant in Portsmouth is just as efficient as living next door to your accountant.'

'I see. I dare say it is.' Webster glanced out of the window across the flat rural landscape. It seemed pleasant at the moment but he imagined, like Scarborough, it could become desolate in the winter, as that awful gnawing east wind sliced across the fields.

'So, Scarborough . . . James Wenlock,' Nicholson muttered. 'Was there any account with a connection to Scarborough . . . ?'

'Oh, do hurry up, dear!' Mrs Nicholson was a small woman, quite finely built, thought Ventnor, and neatly dressed, further giving the impression that, as soon as they had permitted Clarence Bellingham to inform the police of their address, they had both hurried upstairs and dressed 'to look their best' prior to receiving their visitors.

'Yes, dear,' Andrew Nicholson turned to his wife, 'yes, I shall hurry, dear. I shall do as you say, as always, dear.'

'Well, please do so, Andrew,' Mrs Nicholson responded shortly. 'These two young men have come a long way and I am certain indeed that they will not be very impressed with your dilly-dallying. Not one little bit, that I can assure you.'

'Oh, really, Mrs Nicholson, it's not that far,' Webster offered, 'it's just half an hour's drive, if that.'

'Yes, no distance at all,' Ventnor added, sitting beside Webster on the settee, which was positioned between Mr and Mrs Nicholson's chairs, 'and quite a pleasant drive, in fact, so we are not at all inconvenienced.'

'I don't know, Andrew, I really don't.' Mrs Nicholson breathed deeply and folded her arms in front of her. 'I confess, I do freely own that I think you are like a huge sloth some-times. I swear if you moved any slower you'd go backwards. You know, Andrew, it might help you to think and remember if you were to make these two young gentlemen a cup of tea each, and some scones, buttered, of course, if you please. And a cup of tea for myself also.'

'Ah, yes, dear. I am so sorry, gentlemen, where indeed are my manners?' Andrew Nicholson lifted his bulk from his chair with a display of minimum effort which impressed both Webster and Ventnor. 'Tea and scones – buttered, of course, coming up.' He turned and left the room, dipping his head below the door frame as he did so.

Claire Nicholson watched him go, then she addressed Webster. 'You know, he is a lovely, lovely man but he can also be so very trying at times, so very trying. He has been trying my patience for the last forty years. And you know he's not even a proper accountant.'

'Certified?' Webster asked.

'Yes. He's only a certified accountant,' Mrs Nicholson confirmed.

'But still impressive.' Webster smiled. 'In this investigation we have got to know the difference between certified and chartered accountants. It's really been quite interesting.'

'Yes,' Ventnor echoed, 'really quite interesting.'

'An education,' Webster offered.

'It is interesting.' Mrs Claire Nicholson unfolded her arms. 'In fact, my father was a chartered accountant and I learned from him that the world of accountancy can be a fascinating one. But Father . . . dear Papa, he was not best pleased when I married Andrew. He was a big, slow, ambling sloth of a man then and he is a big, slow, ambling sloth of a man now. I have found in life that all large men are very self-satisfied.'

'You think so?' Webster was intrigued.

'Oh, yes, I do believe so . . . indeed I do wholly believe so.' Mrs Nicholson sniffed. 'Small men have always seemed to me to be possessed with a desire to succeed; they are much, much more driven, as if to compensate for their lack of stature. I am the daughter of a short man and I steered both my daughters towards small men when I was looking for husbands for them. My husband and I certainly did make a strange pair in the far-off early days, the little and the large, we were, the mountain and the molehill.'

There then occurred a brief period of silence which was sustained until the ambling, lofty Andrew Nicholson returned with a tray of tea and scones. He laid the tray gently upon the pine wood coffee table which stood in the centre of the lounge and then sat in his chair.

'Well, go on, Andrew,' Mrs Nicholson turned to him. 'You be mother. I am sure I cannot reach it from here.'

'Of course, dear.' Andrew Nicholson smiled his reply. 'I am just allowing the tea to infuse.' He then turned to Webster and said, 'I can only think of the Mel-Kart account.' He then looked at Ventnor. 'It's the only account I can think of which has a strong Scarborough connection. In fact, it's the only account with any connection at all with Scarborough.'

'Mel-Kart.' Ventnor took out his notepad and a ballpoint pen.

'Yes, it was an account or part of an account which involved the purchase of a parcel of land on which to build a go-kart racing track aimed at holidaymakers.'

'I see.' Ventnor wrote 'Mel-Kart' on his notepad.

'I understand that it was a bit of a gamble.' Andrew Nicholson leaned forward and stirred the tea, then poured it into four cups. 'As I said, the idea, I believe, was to ride piggyback on the tourist trade. The land was bought and planning permission was sought, which then ran into difficulties. If I remember,' he paused, 'it's all beginning to come back to me now . . . the land occupied an area, a localized area of natural beauty, or it was the only undeveloped land in a residential area and so local opposition was fierce.' Nicholson handed out the cups of tea, first to his wife and then to Webster and Ventnor. 'Yes, that was the issue . . . the land allowed the residential area to "breathe", as it were, a place for children to play and for dog owners to walk their dogs, and to have that taken from the area and for it to be replaced with a go-kart track with karts with those horrible noisy two-stroke engines and floodlit during the evenings on top of that. I can fully understand the local opposition. Milk? Sugar? Do help yourselves, gentlemen.'

'So can I.' Ventnor picked up the milk jug, added a little milk to his tea and then passed the jug to Webster, who did likewise.

'The first application to build the track was narrowly rejected, but the second application was successful, by just two votes. The initial vote saw a rejection by just one vote. So it was a close-run issue.'

'The council was not particularly sympathetic to the residents?' Webster observed.

'No, no they were not. The council seemed to be very interested in the money the go-kart track would bring in. A very high level of rates could be charged for that sort of land use, you see. At the end of the day it was all about money.'

'Do you know who owned the company which bought the land in question?' Webster asked.

'Yes, it was bought by a gentleman by the name of Mellish, one Peregrine Mellish. An easy name to remember.'

'Peregrine Mellish,' Ventnor wrote the name on his notepad, 'an easy name to recall, indeed.'

'Yes . . .' Andrew Nicholson offered the plate of buttered scones to the officers and then to his wife, 'and hence "Mel-Kart" as the business name.'

'Yes.' Ventnor accepted a scone.

'I made that connection,' Nicholson replied. 'I got the strong impression that Mr Mellish was a local Mr ten-per-cent, fingers in many pies sort of chap rather than pursuing one business interest, and I am sure he was also a brown envelope merchant. I recall that I once glanced at his account and noted many tax deductible payments were put down as "expenses". That can cover a multitude of sins.'

'Yes, so we believe.' Ventnor smiled as he ate the scone.

'Did you do anything with the account?' Webster asked.

'No . . . no I didn't. Over and above glancing at it, there was no need to work on it. The tax returns had all been filed before James Wenlock vanished.'

'So if we were to examine the account, or rather if our forensic accountants were to examine it, we might find irregularities?'

'Yes, yes.' Andrew Nicholson nodded his head gently. 'You might. I was familiarizing myself with the account among others, having nothing better to do one dark and rainy winter's afternoon, and I did notice a lot of hard cash withdrawals on the business bank account statements and, as I said, many outgoings labelled "expenses". That will always make an accountant suspicious.'

'Interesting,' Webster said softly as he helped himself to a buttered scone.

'But there were no complaints; there were no allegations, no police interest, nothing like that. All I was asked to do was "sit on" the account until it was reallocated to another accountant at Russell Square, and I confess at that time my mind was focused mainly on the delightful prospect of my early retirement.'

'My father worked until he was sixty-five.' Claire Nicholson sniffed and folded her arms once more. 'And he was chartered.'

'Fair enough,' Webster replied. 'Can I ask if you ever met Mr Mellish personally?'

'No, no I didn't.' Andrew Nicholson sat back in his chair. 'I had no contact with the gentleman at all, no phone, no fax, no email and no eye contact, ever.'


'We called on you at Russell Square,' Webster explained. 'They told us where we'd be likely to find you; we were told you used to socialise with James Wenlock.'

'Well, you've found me.' Noel Varsh completed his meal and placed his knife and fork on the plate. 'A late lunch, as you can see.'

'Yes.' Webster glanced at the table top. 'Do you mind if we join you?'

'I'm not coming apart, but please do if you wish.' Varsh grinned, gently.

Webster and Ventnor sat opposite Noel Varsh. 'Thank you.' Ventnor glanced at the blonde, slender waitress who carried a meal to another customer in the dimly lit pub.

Webster glanced once at the flat-screen television screen to his left, which was showing racing from Newbury, and then he gave his full attention to Noel Varsh. 'We have become interested in a client of James Wenlock, one Mr Mellish, Mr Peregrine Mellish. Does the name mean anything to you? Did James Wenlock ever mention him to you?'

'Like the hawk?' Varsh asked. 'What is it called? The Peregrine Falcon, fastest hawk in the UK – that is to say, the fastest of our native hawks.'

'We presume that that is how he spells his Christian name. We have yet to meet the gentleman,' Webster explained. 'Right now we're just looking for background information, anything anyone can tell us about Peregrine Mellish and the Mel-Kart account.'

'I see.' Varsh delicately wiped his mouth with a paper napkin. 'In fact, that name does ring a bell. Not loudly, but quite distinctly, I confess, quite distinctly.'

'Go on,' Webster prompted.

'Well, this gets a little difficult but since James is no longer with us . . .' Varsh paused. 'I think it was the case that James and Mr Mellish had some form of business arrangement.'

'A business,' Ventnor queried, 'as in business partners?'

'I know no details . . .' Varsh began and then fell silent, as a black-skirted waitress approached the table.

'Was everything all right, sir?' The dark-haired waitress appeared as if from nowhere and picked up Varsh's plate. She spoke with a distinct Scottish accent.

'Yes, excellent, thank you,' Varsh replied warmly. 'Very nice indeed.'

'Would you like anything else, sir?' The waitress hovered.

'No, no thank you,' Varsh replied with conviction, finality and warmth.

'No details at all,' Varsh continued as the waitress retired and was swallowed by the gloom, 'but I believe that there was some arrangement between them which was over and above his professional relationship with Mr Mellish. I recall James telling me something of this – it's the name Peregrine, you will always remember a name like that . . . and James seemed worried about something between him and Mr Mellish. I sensed that the business relationship between him and Peregrine Mellish was a little fraught . . . strained . . . rocky.'

'Interesting,' Webster mused. 'Caused by what? Do you know?'

'Probably because it was not wholly ethical.' Varsh looked uncomfortable. 'I think poor James had got himself into some deep water and that he came to realize that he was swimming with crocodiles and piranhas. Not a clever place to be in.'

'Strange you should say that.' Ventnor's keen eye was caught by another black-skirted, svelte waitress. 'That sounds interesting.'

'Oh?' Varsh asked in a worried tone. 'Why?'

'Because we have also heard that Mr Mellish is not wholly ethical,' Ventnor explained. '"A brown envelope merchant", was a phrase used to describe him and in fact on our way here, driving back from out Driffield way, we radioed in and we asked for a CR check to be done on Mr Peregrine Mellish.'

'CR?' Varsh looked puzzled. 'What does that mean?'

'Criminal Records,' Webster clarified. 'Anyway, it turns out that Mr Mellish has quite a lot of track . . . all white-collar stuff though. Can we ask if you ever met Peregrine Mellish?'

'No, I didn't,' Varsh replied. 'Never met the man. In fact, James only mentioned him when he was a little drunk; the alcohol had loosened his tongue, you see. Initially he was enthusiastic and said that Mellish had helped him solve a little money problem he had.'

'Now that is interesting,' Webster commented. 'But you say that he didn't remain enthusiastic?'

'No, but again he only ever spoke about Peregrine Mellish when the demon drink had got the better of him,' Varsh replied. 'He never gave out any details – he was discreet – but it did seem that things which had started so well between him and Mr Mellish had very soon all gone sour. But I am sure Mr Mellish will be of assistance to you.'

'Or of hindrance,' Webster replied. 'It depends if and what he has got to hide. Right now we just want some background information, as we explained.'

'You'll be reading his file?' Varsh queried.

'Our forensic accountants will. Those sorts of files are all double-dutch to simple folk like us.' Ventnor leaned slowly back in his chair. 'Mr Bellingham indicated that he believed that Russell Square would allow us access to Mr Mellish's file but we'll be getting a court order anyway. We must keep ourselves right from now on and not do anything which might upset the applecart, so we would appreciate a little diplomacy from your good self, Mr Varsh.'

'Diplomacy?' Varsh asked. 'What do you mean?'

Webster put his finger to his lips. 'That sort of diplomacy,' he explained.

'Not a whisper,' Ventnor added, 'not even a dickybird to anyone. And we mean anyone.'

'You have my word,' Varsh replied solemnly. 'I am an accountant after all, well versed and thoroughly drilled in the concept of confidentiality. I will keep my mouth shut, you gentlemen may rest assured on that issue.'

\* \* \*

Reginald Webster entered the drop-in advice centre on a whim. He had been walking in the crowded centre of York and, acting upon a similar whim, turned into a snickelway, being one of the alleys which thread through the centre of the ancient city like a street system within a street system, and which thoroughfare had brought him, quite by chance, to Gilleygate, almost opposite St Chad's Church. He crossed Gilleygate, walked to the drop-in centre and pushed the door open for no good reason that he could think of. So this, he thought, is the place where the lady who started the investigation into the murder of James Wenlock gives her free time to help the lost and lonely, the downtrodden and the needy. He found the drop-in centre warm and welcoming, softly decorated with comfortable chairs, a machine for making tea and/or coffee, posters pinned upon the wall of sun-drenched, far-flung lands with palm trees and ocean views. It was a place, indeed, to drop in for a chat and ask for and hopefully obtain a little useful advice on some personal issue. It had not perhaps the extreme privacy and confidentiality of the Samaritans but was nonetheless an escape, a bolt-hole. Two elderly women sat by the coffee machine but were not talking to each other. A young man with a long, straggly beard and old, unwashed clothes sat alone staring into space and not seeming to register the room or even the world about him, thought Webster. The room itself smelled of furniture polish, and classical music played softly in the background. The volunteer on duty by her name badge was 'Kate', and she was small and cheerful, so Webster found. She had bright, sparkling blue eyes and a ready smile. Webster showed her his ID and Kate's ready smile evaporated. 'I hope there is no trouble,' she said in a pleasant speaking voice.

'None . . . none,' Webster reassured her. 'I just called in on the off chance that Mrs Bartlem might be here.'

'Julia?'

'Yes.' Webster noticed with a professional eye that the production of his ID had caused the straggly bearded youth to turn and eye him with suspicion. 'Yes, Mrs Julia Bartlem.'

'No, I am afraid she is not here.' Kate's smile had returned. Webster thought that she was probably in her mid-forties. 'Can I perhaps be of assistance?'

'Well . . .' Again Webster continued to cast a police officer's eye around the room, 'I just called in on the off chance that she might be here but perhaps you might be able to help. You doubtless will know of the postcards that were delivered to the centre?'

'Yes . . . how interesting . . . and why little us, I wonder? Why were we thought useful in that we'd know what to do with them?' Kate pursed her lips. 'Why not send them direct to the police?'

'Yes,' Webster nodded, 'we also wondered that. Did they arrive separately?'

'Individually?' Kate asked.

'Yes, one at a time?'

'Yes, that's how they arrived, one day at a time,' Kate confirmed. 'They all came in the post. They certainly foxed us; in fact, the first one was nearly chucked out with the waste paper because we couldn't make head nor tail of it . . . lots of numbers like it was a code, but Julia . . . yes, it was Julia, she seemed very anxious to rescue it, she wanted to save it.'

'She did?' Webster asked. 'She was anxious to save it, you say?'

'Oh, yes. She saw something in it that no one else saw, or at least she seemed to.' Kate spoke enthusiastically, 'She seemed to think that someone was telling us something, which I confess I thought was a little out of character for her. She is not an educated woman and always seems to be out for what she can get, which makes it quite strange, I feel, that she should want to give of her free time to help out here. But she carries herself as if she has an education; she has developed the speaking voice of an educated woman though she left school at sixteen with no qualifications and started her working life in the supermarket as a shelf stacker.'

'She married well, in that case,' Webster commented.

'It seems so, it does seem so,' Kate replied, 'though I never met her husband. I knew her from school, you see, the world being a small place, and it seems to be getting smaller as one gets older. I stayed on at school and went to teacher training college. I left teaching to start my family and I did not return.'

'I see.' Webster nodded. 'Well, her husband has proved very

useful – he identified the numbers as being a grid reference on an Ordnance Survey Map.'

'He did!' Kate gasped. 'Well I never . . . knock me down with a feather. Julia told us she was taking the postcards straight to the police, not taking them home to let her husband see them, to see if he could make sense of the numbers. So he's returned, she never told us that – she never mentioned anything about him having returned. She is a dark horse.' Kate glanced at the floor. 'Mind you, she always was very secretive, even in the old days at school; you never really knew what she was thinking.'

'Returned?' Webster asked. 'Where had he been? Were they estranged at some point?'

'No . . . not estranged, not estranged at all, nothing so simple. He went missing. So he has turned up and returned home? This is news,' Kate exhaled and then inhaled deeply.

'Missing?' Webster echoed. 'As in being reported as a missing person?'

'Yes, yes, in that sense. He disappeared . . . oh . . . let me see, it must have been five years ago now.' Kate paused. 'Yes, a long time before she walked in here and offered her services. She said that she had been by herself for four and a half years and wanted something to occupy her free time. She has been here with us for the last six months. I don't know the details about his disappearance but I believe that they went on holiday, to France, I think. She went with him and came back alone. She told the French police and then came home by herself. She said he went for an evening stroll from their campsite or hotel or whatever, never returned and thus she had been alone ever since then. She puts in two afternoons here each week, not much time really for someone who claims that she wants to fill a void, but it seems to suit her. So he has returned . . . well, well, well, strange that she keeps coming in to help us now that he has come home.'

'This is really very interesting,' Webster mused, 'most interesting. Look, Kate, I would be obliged if you wouldn't say anything to Mrs Bartlem about my visit or about what you have told me about her husband.'

'That will be difficult.' Kate sounded worried. 'I have known her since school days. I would feel that I was betraying her. I couldn't do that.'

'If you could try,' Webster urged, 'you probably won't have to keep it a secret for long. It could do great harm to our investigation, which has been triggered by the postcards, if you mention my visit to her or indeed to anyone who works here. Great harm.'

Kate looked to her left, as if in thought. 'I can take a few days off,' she suggested. 'I can do that very easily. It will be the easiest thing to do, I think. If I am not here then I can't let the cat out of the bag. Yes, that's the answer, I'll do that.'

'And that,' Webster smiled, 'would be greatly appreciated by the Vale of York police.'


'Have you . . . or are you detecting a little turbulence?' Hennessey leaned back in his chair and pyramided his fingers. 'Or perhaps it is a little muddying of the waters you have discovered?'

'Either might be the case, sir.' Webster sat in one of the chairs in front of Hennessey's desk. 'Someone who was once nothing more than a public-spirited citizen who did as all citizens are asked and reported something suspicious. Well, she has now accumulated a cloud of suspicion above her head. Mrs Bartlem clearly told us that her husband had told her that the numbers on the back of the postcards were map reference numbers.'

'Which they were.'

'Yes, sir, and they led us straight to the discovery of the body of James Wenlock, but it also transpired that her husband had been reported as a missing person some five years ago, as I have just said. So unless she has remarried, or is in a common-law union then, well, as you say sir, muddy waters . . . something for us to look at.'

'And in France,' Hennessey growled. 'I hate the damn French, wretched people that they are. Do we know anything about Mr Bartlem's disappearance?'

'No, sir, I checked. We don't have a missing persons file on him because his disappearance was apparently reported to the French authorities.'

'I see . . . but his name was Bartlem?' Hennessey asked.

'We can only assume so, sir,' Webster replied. 'Unless, as I said, she has remarried.'

Hennessey reached for the phone book on his desk. 'Thank goodness he wasn't a Smith or a Brown.' He grinned as he opened the telephone directory and turned to the surnames beginning with BAR. 'I count six listings for subscribers with that surname so that is with a possible further six ex-directory.'

'Six, sir?' Webster asked curiously.

'Yes.' Hennessey picked up his telephone. 'I once asked a lady who worked for British Telecom how much larger the telephone directory would be if all numbers were listed and the answer was twice as large, and she said that without having to think about her answer. So for every number listed there is approximately one ex-directory number. Myself being one such.'

'As we are, sir.' Webster smiled.

'I should think so. It does not do for anyone who works with the public to have their telephone number in the direc-tory. That's really asking for trouble.' Hennessey dialled a number. When his call was answered he said, 'Ah, hello, Vale of York police here, nothing to be alarmed about. We are anxiously trying to locate the family of a gentleman of your surname who was reported missing about five years ago when on holiday in France. Ah . . . not your family, madam? Thank you.' He replaced the phone and then picked it up again and dialled another number, and when his call was answered he repeated the question. It was when he had asked the question of the fourth person he called that, upon the answer, he raised his thumb to Reginald Webster. 'Yes,' he said, 'we are inter-ested, very interested. Will you be in for the rest of the day, sir? Good, one of my officers, Detective Constable Webster, will be with you shortly. Thank you.' He replaced the phone gently. He looked at Webster and smiled. 'Fancy a walk, Reg?'

'A walk, sir?' Webster smiled. 'How far? To where?'

'Yes, a walk, just a most gentle stroll. I'd walk if I was to be the one visiting. But I do confess I can think of a few who'd use a car. The address is in East Mount Road.'

'Sorry?' Webster frowned. 'I don't know that road, sir.'

'Out of the main entrance, left on to Blossom Street, third

left, little cul-de-sac of terraced housing,' Hennessey advised him. 'You can probably see the roof from the CID officers' room.'

'No one would drive that distance, sir,' Reginald Webster stated with indignation, 'no one.'

'I know those who would, I assure you,' Hennessey replied in a matter-of-fact voice. 'Not police officers perhaps, but I still know people who'd drive that short distance. You are calling on one Paul Bartlem.'

'Well, I'll walk.'

Webster stood and walked out of Hennessey's office, and then tapped gently but authoritatively on the door of the address in East Mount Road ten minutes after signing out of Micklegate Bar Police Station.

Paul Bartlem revealed himself to be a short, thin man who stood about five feet five inches tall, Webster guessed. His house, as George Hennessey had said, was in a terrace of nineteenth-century back-to-backs so that one stepped from the pavement across his threshold and into his living room, with the small kitchen being at the back of the house, and bedrooms and a bathroom upstairs. Mr Bartlem was dressed casually in an old pair of jeans, sports shoes and a blue T-shirt. 'You're the police?' he asked.

'Yes, sir.' Webster showed Bartlem his ID.

'Please come in.' Paul Bartlem stepped aside and Webster entered the living room. He found it to be neatly kept, smelling of wood polish and air freshener, with 'low brow' books on a shelf in an alcove and a small television set in the opposite corner. Webster sat, upon invitation, in a leather-bound armchair.

'It was a shock. It always has been a great worry but what else can we do but sit and wait?' Bartlem said after the introductions and formalities had been concluded. He had the manner of a man, thought Webster, who was appealing for charity. 'You see, sir, there were four of us, two boys and two girls, and now it's just the three of us. We always meet on our Edward's birthday and we go to a restaurant for a meal and a drink . . . this is at lunchtime, you understand, not in the evening . . . and before we eat we go into a church and light a candle for him. We see each other at various times during the rest of the year, of course, but we always have that special day for Edward. We still hope that he is alive somewhere but it's a thin hope. And as the years go by the hope gets thinner. We know that, but you do read about people who wake up after being in a coma for years or who suddenly remember their name after a decade of amnesia . . . so there's hope.'

'Yes,' Webster nodded, 'it's true that sort of thing does happen. While there's life, there's hope.' He paused. 'We understand that your brother, Edward Bartlem, disappeared whilst on holiday in France?'

'So his wife said.' Paul Bartlem's jaw then suddenly set hard. 'Frankly, we just don't know what happened. He went on holiday with his wife and her sister, just the three of them in a green and white VW camper van, and only the two sisters returned. You can't help but feel a little suspicious. All sorts of possible explanations start running round your mind as if they're playing leapfrog with each other. One bounces over another, but at the end of the day you're still left wondering . . . and waiting.'

'You think that something sinister happened to your brother Edward?' Webster asked. 'That seems to be what you are implying, sir.'

'Yes . . . oh, yes.' Paul Bartlem nodded with undisguised certainty. 'Nothing at all adds up about the whole story. You see we were, and still are, a close family, and our Eddie would have sent us postcards if nothing else. It was planned as a three-week holiday so we could expect three postcards from him, probably more come to think of it, because they were travelling about in their old camper van, but not one postcard arrived, not one. So whatever it was that happened to our Edward happened in the first few days of their holiday.' Bartlem settled back into his armchair and glanced at a particularly large fly which was buzzing noisily against a windowpane. 'My wife . . . both of us, me and my wife, never did take to the family he married into, the Cleg sisters . . .'

'Cleg?'

'Yes,' Bartlem nodded. 'But with only one "g", like the horsefly. I'd rather be stung by a bee or a wasp than be bitten by a cleg; they sink their teeth into you because they're after your blood, and that's with teeth designed to bite into horseflesh.'

'I know,' Webster winced. He had once had that experience. 'Believe me, I know.'

'So a trip to Europe, it was long planned, and then at the last moment she announces that her sister is going to be accompanying them. The day before they were due to depart she, the other Cleg sister, turns up with all her bags packed saying she's having a bad time with her husband and that she desperately needs to get away for a week or two. If you have a bad patch you work it out if you ask me, you don't run away. My wife passed away recently – she was only forty-seven. That's no age at all.'

'I am sorry,' Webster spoke softly, 'that is unfairly young.'

'Yes . . . a heart attack. There is no justice in life, no justice at all. Old men have heart attacks, not women who are halfway through their life expectancy. Can you believe it? She was still south of fifty and she had a coronary?' Bartlem cast another glare towards the fly on the windowpane. 'But at least we did have twenty-seven years of good and happy marriage.'

'That is something,' Webster offered. 'That is some condolence.'

'Yes, and I like to I think of it like that.' Bartlem stared straight ahead. 'Are you married?'

'Yes,' Webster replied, 'yes, I am.'

'Happily?'

'Very happily.' Webster nodded and smiled. 'Yes, we are very content. I look forward to going home at the end of each shift.'

'I thought so.' Bartlem smiled. 'You have that contented look about you. People who are happily married always have such a look about them. I was often told that I had just such a look. That look of deep contentment. But Julia, she was the boss in that marriage and I just could never see what Edward saw in her. Neither did my wife and neither did my sisters . . . none of us could see the attraction he saw. And he never had that contented look about him, never. Not ever.'

'Your brother was a teacher, I believe?' Webster asked.

'Edward, a teacher!' Paul Bartlem scoffed. 'Good Lord, no
. . . no, no, no. Edward, a teacher! Edward, let me tell you,
was a taxi driver.'

'A taxi driver!' Webster gasped.

'Yes . . . well, I dare say that I am doing his good memory
a great injustice there, a huge injustice. He was a taxi operator.
He owned a small fleet of taxis. Five plates. York, the city
fathers of, will allow only so many taxis on its streets.'

'As does any other city or town,' Webster commented. 'They
all cap the numbers of taxi plates issued.'

'Yes, as you say, only a limited number of taxis per city,
so the plates which permit the car to be used as a taxi are
worth quite a bit of money,' Bartlem explained, 'as you can
imagine.'

'So I believe. Five plates,' Webster commented. 'He was
well-set.'

'His was a minnow by comparison,' Bartlem replied. 'Large
companies in big cities . . . well, those big boys can have more
than fifty plates, but they can keep their cars running twenty-
four hours a day, seven days a week with shifts of drivers,
and they also have their own repair service facilities.'

'Again, so I believe,' Webster replied.

'So anyway, Edward and his wife went to France on a
touring holiday and his sister-in-law went with them at the
last minute.' Paul Bartlem clenched his fist. 'Nothing makes
any sense. Eddie didn't like foreigners . . . and he especially
didn't like the French.'

'He would get on well with my boss.' Webster grinned. 'He
is Francophobic as well.'

'Really?' Paul Bartlem chuckled briefly. 'You see, we had
an elderly relative, Great Uncle George. He escaped at Dunkirk,
and he told us that the French artillery shelled the boats taking
the British soldiers to England until they, the French artillery,
that is, were quelled by a Royal Navy cruiser's six-inch guns.
The French were trying to curry favour with the Germans,
you see . . . changing sides in the middle of the battle when
it became clear that the Germans were winning.'

'I never heard that story,' Webster replied.

'Well, it was the case in our family that Great Uncle George's hatred for the French was infectious. He always said to give him a German any day – at least they'll shoot you in the chest . . . but we four grew up hating the French because of Uncle George's hatred for them and our Eddie, he drove cars for a living so all he wanted was a summer holiday living in a hotel where he didn't have to do any driving. So then he goes to France on a driving holiday. It made no sense at all, not at the time and it still doesn't . . . just does not add up and deliver.'

'Yes, I can understand the puzzle,' Webster said.

'Biggest unexplained mystery in our generation of Bartlems,' Paul Bartlem replied. 'We just can't fathom it. Can't fathom it at all.'

'Can you please elaborate on what you meant by your family not seeing what your brother saw in his wife?' Webster asked. 'How did Julia Cleg seem to you as a personality?'

'Well . . . I . . . I always found her to be very pushy – she was always wanting more. Our Eddie, for instance, he would have settled for one plate, just the one plate and a car. Run the single taxi as his source of income then at the end of it all he'd sell the plate for retirement money . . . but she . . . madam the queen, pressured him into expanding. She bullied him into borrowing money, using the plate as collateral in order to buy another plate, then borrow against two plates to be able to buy a third plate. She forced him to incur massive debts . . . even remortgaging their house. Eddie didn't want worries like that, and he didn't want the problems of employing people, but he did that anyway and they moved into a house in Sutton on the Forest.'

'Pleasant village,' Webster commented, 'from what little I have seen of it.'

'Yes,' Bartlem conceded, 'it is a very nice place to live, but look at this house, my little back-to-back in a terrace – this is the sort of house we grew up in, this is the level of society we are . . . not a large house in a posh village . . . But her . . . Mrs pushy, pushy, want, want, she wanted the world, yet she wasn't exactly born with a silver spoon in her mouth either.'

'Oh?' Webster queried.

'Simple folk same as us and she acquired a criminal record,' Paul Bartlem advised Webster, 'under the maiden name of Cleg, though nothing since she married. Not that we knew of anyway, but secrecy is her middle name, so who knows?'

'I'll look her up,' Webster replied. 'It should make interesting reading.' He paused and then asked, 'Can you tell me anything else about your brother's disappearance? Anything that you think we ought to know?'

'Well . . .' Paul Bartlem looked uncomfortable, 'I can only tell you what Mrs pushy, pushy, want, want told us when she returned from France . . . and that wasn't much, it wasn't much at all.' He breathed deeply as if, thought Webster, he was gathering emotional strength. 'She told us that he went for a walk and didn't return, as I said, and she stuck to that story. They waited for twenty-four hours, so she said, and then reported him as a missing person to the French police. They both returned home, back to England. You know it really was so unlike Edward to do that, to go for a walk by himself in a foreign country, and in a country he disliked. Edward never did like being by himself, he was very talkative. Like a lot of taxi drivers he enjoyed putting the world to rights. He never needed to be the centre of attention or anything like that, not our Eddie, but he did like being part of a gang. He was never really happy with his own company, like some people are. So it's all a mystery, the type of holiday, going abroad, and to France of all places, going off by himself when he couldn't speak a word of the lingo . . . it's all not Eddie, not the Edward we knew anyway, and he was our brother, we knew him very well.'

'Did you meet Julia Bartlem's sister?' Webster asked.

'Only at the wedding,' Paul Bartlem replied.

'Did you – do you – have any thoughts about her?' Webster probed.

'A few thoughts and none of them any good. They were twin sisters; the pair of them were both pushy, pushy, want, wants. They looked similar but not the same and they even seemed to think the same. They are not identical twins but I have often thought it was like they had the same personality divided between two bodies.'

'Interesting,' Webster murmured.

'But, like I said,' Bartlem continued, 'that is based on only the one meeting.'

'Fair enough.' Webster paused. 'So what became of your brother's business?'

'She acquired it . . . and their house . . . it's all in her name now. All of it. Our Eddie was declared deceased two years after he was reported missing. He left everything to her in his will. They had no children, which was quite a sadness for our Eddie. All his hard work and sweat and sleepless nights that went into building that wretched taxi business and she owns it all now and is just sunning herself. It's so unfair.'

'Yes, it can seem like that,' Webster nodded, 'it can all seem very unfair.' He paused, then asked, 'Can I ask if you had any contact from the French police at all, that is in respect of your brother?'

'None, we have heard nothing at all. My sister Helen, the youngest, she often says, "Well that's good, isn't it? It means he might still be alive somewhere . . . it's a case of no news is good news".' Bartlem took a deep breath. 'But my older sister, she's a bit more worldly-wise, she says no contact just means that the body has not been found or if it has been found, it hasn't been identified. Sylvia always was a bit more down to earth than Helen. She, Sylvia, just accepted that we will never see Edward again. Me . . . I am torn . . . I hope Helen is correct, but I fear Sylvia is the one who is the correct . . . and his wife . . .'

'Yes,' Webster smiled, 'I was going to ask about Mrs Bartlem's reaction to his disappearance?'

'She didn't seem concerned. She tried to look worried but she's no actress. I fancied I could almost see her grinning from ear to ear inside her head as if she thought everything was going to plan. I am sure she knows exactly what happened over there in France but she insists on playing the grieving widow.' Paul Bartlem spoke in a cold manner. 'At least she tries to play the grieving widow, but, like I said, she's no actress.'

Webster asked if he saw much of Julia Bartlem.

'As little as possible,' was Paul Bartlem's curt reply, 'and that is practically no contact at all, which suits me and my sisters down to the ground.' He shook his head. 'So Edward did things he'd never do, three went to France and just the two sisters returned, and the other sister, Alice, that's the other strange thing, she went straight back to her husband as though there had been no rough patch in the marriage at all. Then, two years elapse and Julia becomes the outright owner of Eddie's business and their home. Iffy, don't you think? Very, very iffy.'

'Perhaps.' Webster gently and slowly patted his notebook with the top of his ballpoint pen. 'I confess I don't like the sound of it at all. Not at all. If I was in your shoes I would be suspicious . . . but at least we are investigating.'

'Yes, and that is appreciated,' Paul Bartlem replied, still in a soft voice. 'I am sorry if I sound ill-tempered, but over the years no one has seemed to care despite the huge cloud of suspicion.'

'So what do you think happened?' Webster asked.

'I suspect . . . I don't know.' Paul Bartlem looked downwards at the carpet.

'Good enough.' Webster smiled. 'So, within these four walls, between you and me and the gatepost, what's your take on the mystery of your brother's disappearance? What is it that you suspect happened?'

'My take?' Paul Bartlem sat forward. 'You ask for my take? My take is that the twins of evil, the evil sisters Cleg, took him to France in order to kill him, so they could get their hands on his money. They intended to hide the body and then report him to the French police as a missing person. They were driving about in a VW camper van so no home for the police to visit, no scene of crime unless it was inside the van, and I doubt they'd be careless enough to spill his blood inside the van.' Paul Bartlem's jaw set firm. 'And you know, the other interesting point is where he was reported missing . . . I mean, the location that he was reputed to have disappeared?'

'Oh?' Webster was intrigued. 'Why should the location be significant?'

'It is very close to the Belgian border,' Bartlem explained.

'Ah.' Webster held eye contact with Paul Bartlem. 'You

know, Mr Bartlem, I think I can see where you are going with this, but do carry on.'

'Well,' Bartlem continued, 'pull up at a roadside stop one evening, not in a crowded campsite, get him to sit down . . . bang him over the head with a stone . . . not to kill him but to disable him just long enough to put a plastic bag over his head. They need not kill him, in fact; just one minute without oxygen will be quite sufficient to bring on his brain death.'

'Yes . . . so I believe,' Webster nodded.

'I watch those crime dramas on TV,' Paul Bartlem explained. 'In fact, to tell you the truth, I have got very interested in them since Eddie vanished.'

'I can understand that,' Webster replied. 'But do go on.'

'So then, and this is just my take, as you asked, they bundle his body back into the camper van and, being careful and only using the back roads, they drive into Belgium. I think that they would have then stripped his body of all clothing and removed all form of identification; then dumped his poor body in a ditch. If they didn't kill him he would have died of thirst within two or three days, but I suspect that they must have made sure he was dead.'

'I suspect so too,' Webster commented. 'But do, please, carry on.'

'Then they return to France and report him as a missing person to the French authorities. You see, if his body was found I understand that it would be reported to the Belgian authorities, who would file a report and check their own missing persons list, but they would not check it with any missing person reported to the French, or any other European country.'

'Yes,' Webster nodded his head, 'that's what would happen – there is no Pan European missing person database. Was your brother a tall man? Would he have been able to fight off two female attackers?'

'No . . . no, he was small like me . . . and a taxi driver so he wasn't muscular at all. If they attacked him when he was asleep, or attacked him from behind when he was sitting down, he would have had no chance to defend himself . . . I fear that my sister Sylvia is right. I fear that his body is likely to have been discovered, given a name and buried in a Belgian cemetery with a simple graveside service. Yes, my sister Sylvia is right; my sister Helen is wrong. My brother Eddie is dead.'

Webster stood. 'Thank you, Mr Bartlem. I'll go and talk to my boss . . . then we'll contact the Belgian authorities. Where exactly was your brother reported missing?'

'A small town called Mohon in the Ardennes, to the north of Rheims. I looked it up and I promise you, you just couldn't get closer to Belgium. But thank you, thank you so very much. I am so relieved, so grateful that the police are taking an interest at long last.'

'It seems to link with another inquiry.' Webster wrote 'Mohon' on his notepad. 'It is often the way of it. But rest assured, we will now be looking closely at Mr Bartlem's disappearance.'

'So, do they link, Reg?' Hennessey clasped his hands behind his head, grinned and raised his eyebrows. 'What do you think?'

'The twin sisters?' Webster shrugged. 'It's much too early to say yet, sir.'

'And do they link somehow in some way to the murder of James Wenlock?' Hennessey leaned forward and once again cast his eye over Julia Cleg's criminal record. It was all 'low-end stuff' as Webster had told him, shoplifting mainly and also one conviction for 'disorderly conduct' – hardly a blip on the radar, he thought, and noted that there was nothing at all added to the file since she left her teenage years behind her and she became Mrs Julia Bartlem. 'Or are we looking at another red herring?'

'We can't say that yet either, sir,' Webster replied calmly. 'But we mustn't lose sight of the fact that the last red herring led us to a conviction for a murder which we didn't know had taken place, so that diversion was not such a red herring after all.'

'Point taken . . . but we must also not lose sight of the fact that we have to investigate the murder of James Wenlock and not get involved with any investigation the French police might be undertaking in respect of the disappearance of Edward

Bartlem . . . That holiday in France does indeed sound so very, very suspicious. Everything Edward Bartlem did on that holiday was allegedly so wildly out of character, and why on earth should Mrs Bartlem tell us that her husband is a living and healthy geography teacher when in fact he is missing, and almost certainly a deceased, taxi driver?'

'Only she can tell us, sir,' Webster replied. 'Shall we bring her in for a quiz session?'

'No, not yet,' Hennessey stroked his chin, 'I think we should be a little more circumspect. She seemed most anxious that we find the body of James Wenlock. So why would she want us to do that, I wonder? But . . . we'll be cautious, we will be very cautious here. She is not going anywhere. Can you contact the French police at . . . where was it?' Hennessey appealed. 'These obscure French names.'

'Mohon, sir.' Webster grinned.

'Sounds like a French verb,' Hennessey growled. 'Anyway, tell the blessed frogs we are developing an interest in Mr Edward Bartlem's disappearance, just a courtesy notification at this time, I think, and if you would, prepare a media release for the French/Belgian press.'

'Very good, sir,' Webster stood. 'I'll get on that straight away.'

'Thank you, Reg. Tomorrow I think we turn to the connection between Mr Wenlock and Mr Mellish,' Hennessey glanced out of his office window, 'and that will most definitely have to be a two-hander.'

George Hennessey sedately drove home and, as he did so, just as he left the suburbs and had joined the open country, a motorcyclist came up behind him at speed and roared past him, thus awakening his other demon, and once woken it rose and occupied the forefront of his mind for the remainder of his journey. It would probably have tortured him late into the evening had it not been for the fact that, on that day, joy awaited him.

After the motorcyclist had overtaken him his mind turned to his boyhood in Greenwich, helping his beloved older brother polish his equally beloved Triumph motorcycle each Sunday morning, and how he would be rewarded for his assistance by a trip as a pillion passenger up to town, round the sites and back, south of the river, over Westminster Bridge and round Blackheath Park. He recalled there was the day that Graham caused worry and grief to their parents by announcing that he was giving up his safe job at the bank in order to train to become a photographer, but Graham's mind was made up and he would not be dissuaded from his new-found ambition. Then, there fell that fateful night, when George Hennessey lay abed listening to his brother kick life into his machine, rev the engine and ride away, changing up the gears as he drove along Trafalgar Road towards the Maritime Museum and the Cutty Sark. Once the sound of his brother's bike had faded it was replaced by other sounds: ships on the river, an Irishman tramping slowly up Colomb Street chanting his Hail Mary's in a drunken, slurred voice as he passed beneath George Hennessey's window. Later . . . later that night came the dread knock, the distinct police officers' knock . . . tap, tap . . . tap . . . a knock he was to come to use, then the hushed but urgent conversations . . . his mother's shriek followed by her prolonged uncontrollable wailing, his father coming to his room, fighting back his own tears as he told the young George Hennessey that Graham had 'ridden his bike to heaven . . . to save a place for us'. It had, it transpired, been the case that Graham lost control of his bike as it ran over a patch of oil in the road.

The gap in George Hennessey's life where an older brother should have been was a permanent void and he could only wonder what sort of man Graham would have become – certainly a good father to some lucky children and a good uncle to Charles. He would also, George Hennessey believed, have been a damn good photographer, a crusading photojournalist capable of changing world opinion with just one photograph; not for Graham Hennessey would be the sleazy world of glamour photography or the privacy-invading, life-ruining world of the paparazzi, but noble photography which people remember. Upon his brother's death he had then met for the first time the incongruity of a summer funeral, how wrong it all seemed for his brother's coffin to be slowly lowered into the ground amid bloom and green and fluttering butterflies and with the sound of 'Greensleeves' being heard coming from a distant and unseen ice-cream van. It was the same incongruity he was to meet again, twenty years later as he scattered his wife's ashes in an abundant summer garden. All that could have been were it not for a small patch of oil or if Graham's line of travel had been one inch to the left, or one inch to the right.

As George Hennessey approached his house he saw a silver BMW parked half on and half off the kerb outside his house. His heart leapt at the sight and his face cracked into a broad grin. Half an hour later, after a barking, tail-wagging Oscar had been greeted, Charles and George Hennessey were sat on the patio at the back of Hennessey's house, looking out over the garden whilst each sipped a mug of tea.

'Where are you this week?' George Hennessey broke a short moment of silence which had developed.

'Leeds,' Charles Hennessey replied. 'My man is going NG to a serious assault upon his lady wife. He seems to think that said lady wife will withdraw her complaint as she has apparently done on many previous occasions.'

'Enough is enough, she is saying, I assume?' George Hennessey's eye was caught by a swirling, darting house martin clearly pursuing a flying insect.

'Yes, that's what she is saying, but he is still refusing to go "G" and so get an automatic one third off his sentence upon conviction. There are many witnesses, you see. He was, I also learned, in the habit of using his wife as a punch bag in the street, in full view of many sympathetic neighbours. Anyway, he refused to take my advice and his solicitors' advice . . . and we have to take his instruction . . . so, hell mend him, really.' Charles Hennessey stretched his arms and yawned.

'As you say. How are the children?' George Hennessey looked towards the ground at Oscar criss-crossing the lawn, having evidently picked up an interesting scent.

'They are very anxious to see Granddad Hennessey again; they want to know when you'll be taking them out for the day once more.' Charles Hennessey smiled. 'You spoil them rotten.'

'I know. I love doing it.' George Hennessey laughed softly.

'So you'll be sending us more work.' Charles Hennessey yawned a second time. 'More felons for us to defend?'

'Hope so.' George Hennessey also yawned. 'We are working on a ten-year-old murder at the moment and in the process discovered a murder which we didn't know had been committed. One felon is in the pipeline, who will need a very good defence counsel unless he does the sensible thing and pleads guilty, as he seems intent to do. Another is out there, awaiting arrest.'

'So, your friend,' Charles Hennessey queried. 'When do we meet her?'

'Soon,' George Hennessey replied, 'soon. She is anxious to meet you also . . . but all in good time.'

It was Monday, 19.45 hours.

# FIVE

*In which more is discovered about the Cleg sisters and a dying man gives information.*

George Hennessey sat at his desk and kept his eyes downcast. 'To recap for the benefit of all, it now seems to be a wheels-within-wheels situation. We have two sisters, two twin sisters, though only one of whom we have thus far met. The husband of one is missing somewhere in France but suspiciously near the Belgian border. The same sister tells us her husband is a geography teacher so that we will know the significance of the numbers on a postcard which was posted to the drop-in centre where she works. We would rapidly have realized what the numbers meant but she was clearly very anxious that we find out sooner rather than later. It transpires that her husband is not an alive and well geographer at all but a taxi driver missing, presumed deceased.'

'In France,' Webster added, 'which is difficult for us.'

'Yes,' Hennessey nodded, 'he is a self-employed taxi driver or taxi-fleet owner to give him his proper due, and went missing on a holiday he took with the twin sisters. Three left the UK, two returned.' Hennessey glanced at his team: Yellich, Webster, Ventnor, Pharoah. All were attentive, waiting for him to continue speaking. 'Did we contact the French police, Reg?'

'Yes, sir,' Webster replied, 'via Interpol, as you requested. No reply yet.'

'All right.'

'Their response will be interesting,' Carmen Pharoah offered. 'I mean, there is no proof that he was reported missing at all, just Mrs Bartlem's word, and her word is becoming suspect.'

'Good point, Carmen.' Hennessey smiled at Carmen Pharoah. 'In fact, you have just talked yourself into a job

– can you please chase up the French contact, confirm that Mr Edward Bartlem was reported missing, where he was reported missing and enquire as to what information the French authorities were provided with?'

'Yes, sir,' Pharoah replied briskly, efficiently.

'He will have been reported,' Hennessey continued. 'They will definitely have done that. It would be far, far too suspicious if they have not reported him, but check anyway – we must cross all the t's and dot all the i's.'

'Very good, sir.' Again Carmen Pharoah's response was instant.

'You know,' Hennessey continued, 'I am taken by the notion of Paul Bartlem's that his brother Edward, or rather the body of Edward Bartlem, was left in Belgium and his disappearance reported in France. So, can you contact the Belgian authorities as well as the French, please, Carmen? Again, just being thorough.'

'Yes, sir.'

'Provide details of Mr Edward Bartlem's description and ask if it matches the description of any deceased males who might have been found in the border area with France at about or shortly after the time of Edward Bartlem's disappearance.' Hennessey paused and glanced out of his office window. 'I am nearing my retirement but in my time as a police officer I have known many instances of corpses being found in various states of decomposition; they could not be linked to any locally reported missing person and so they were given a name and buried. But ponder, if you will, how easy it would be to lure somebody to England from Ireland or from the Continent and despatch them somewhere in Britain and allow the corpse to be discovered and start only a local murder investigation?' He paused again and turned to his team. 'If you ask me, police forces are just too inward looking, and I ask you, has that benefited the criminal or has that benefited the criminal?' He drummed his fingers on his desk top. 'So why was Mrs Bartlem suddenly so anxious for us to find Mr Wenlock's body ten years after his murder? Who posted the cards and who uses a typewriter these days?'

The officers sitting in front of Hennessey's desk shrugged

their shoulders and gently shook their heads. Eventually Yellich replied for the entire team by saying, 'Well, that's the question to be answered, sir. Answer the first question and we'll most very probably find the answer to the second.'

'All right,' Hennessey leaned back in his chair, 'time for action. Carmen, once you have sent the messages to the French and Belgian police, I'd like you to team up with Somerled.'

'Yes, sir.' Carmen Pharoah glanced approvingly at Somerled Yellich, who nodded at her.

'I'd like you two to visit Mrs Bartlem,' Hennessey continued.

'Yes, sir,' Yellich replied.

'See what you see, find what you find. We'd like to hear her version of her husband's disappearance. Ask her why she told us her husband was a geographer and try to find a connection between her and James Wenlock.'

'Understood, sir.' Yellich replied again for both himself and Carmen Pharoah.

'Reginald and Thompson . . .' Hennessey turned to Webster and Ventnor.

'Sir?' Ventnor answered.

'I'd like you two to go and take the measure of Mr Mellish and, if you can, find the link between him and Mr Wenlock, but do be tactful . . . do be circumspect. In fact, all four of you be circumspect – please remember that we are still only making inquiries. We have no suspect or suspects at this time and we don't want to send anyone running for the hills by making accusations or arrests which are too early in the piece. Remember . . . softly, softly, catchee monkey.'

'Understood, sir,' Yellich replied as all four officers stood.

Mrs Julia Bartlem welcomed Somerled Yellich and Carmen Pharoah and invited them into her home in a warm, calm and self-assured manner. The Bartlem house was a detached, nineteenth-century house. It was clearly very well kept and seemed to sit very confidently in about half an acre of land.

'Just a few questions, if you don't mind, Mrs Bartlem,' Yellich began as he and Carmen Pharoah accepted Mrs Bartlem's invitation to take a seat and then sank into deep armchairs, whilst she, the lady of the house, chose to sit on the settee, elegantly so and upright, hands folded on her lap, legs together and angled to one side. She wore a figure-hugging three-quarter-length purple dress, and shiny black shoes with a modest heel. 'It is just the case of dotting a few i's and crossing a few t's – nothing for you to worry about.'

'I see,' Julia Bartlem smiled as she replied. She seemed calm but Carmen Pharoah, as one woman observing another, detected a wariness bordering on fear behind the smile and the dilated pupils.

'There are,' Yellich continued, 'just a few things which to the police just don't seem to add up.' He took his notepad from his jacket pocket.

'Oh?' Mrs Bartlem inclined her head. She did indeed, Pharoah observed, seem very middle class. She had all the correct mannerisms and had clearly risen up from the council schoolgirl and the late teenager with convictions for shoplifting and breaching the Queen's peace.

'Well, yes.' Yellich sat back in the armchair. 'For example, can you please explain to us why you saw fit to tell us that your husband was a geography teacher, when he is in fact missing and presumed deceased, and when with us was a self-employed taxi driver? In fact, he owned a small fleet of taxis; he was much more than a humble driver of a taxi. He was rather a successful businessman.'

'Ah,' Mrs Bartlem bowed her head, 'I can really see your suspicion, I really can, but I was just being public spirited; it was nothing for the police to find suspicious . . . I wished only to help you out, you see.'

'So why mislead us?' Yellich held eye contact with her.

'Oh, I wasn't misleading you, I can assure you,' Mrs Bartlem sounded shocked. 'Oh no, I wasn't doing that, it is . . . it was . . . simply the case that I knew the numbers to be map references but I thought that if I told you that my husband was a geography teacher and recognized them as such it would give some credibility to the claim, get you there quicker, all the more speedily.'

'Get us where?' Yellich snapped.

'To the identification of the numbers as being map references,' Mrs Bartlem replied defensively.

'You think we wouldn't have seen them for what they were?' Yellich's voice was heavy with anger. 'We are not brain-dead numpties, Mrs Bartlem. We have police officers who are graduates, even postgraduates.'

'Yes, even postgraduates,' Carmen Pharoah echoed. She glanced round the room. It was well appointed; she noted expensive furniture and carpets, a flat-screen television and hard-backed books on shelves.

'I just said that to help you along,' Mrs Bartlem repeated. 'I was being public spirited.'

'It did that but we would have got there quickly enough ourselves, as I said,' Yellich replied coldly. 'The map reference led us to the grave of an accountant who had vanished some years ago, a gentleman by the name of Wenlock, James Wenlock. Did you know him, by any chance?'

'Wenlock?' Mrs Bartlem shook her head slowly. 'That name means nothing to me. Wenlock, you say? No . . . the name rings no bells, no bells at all.'

'All right, but it seems to be the case that you wanted Mr Wenlock's body to be found.' Yellich pressed forward.

'I didn't want it to be found. How could I? I didn't know it was there. It just seemed to me that the cards looked somewhat suspicious,' Mrs Bartlem protested. 'In fact, some of the staff at the drop-in centre wanted to tear them up but I thought they were dubious and so brought them to the police station. It seems it was a good job that I did, I'd say,' Mrs Bartlem added indignantly. 'The body would still be undiscovered if I had not done what I did. Has that occurred to you, I wonder?'

'Yes . . . that is a fair point,' Yellich agreed, 'but we are police officers, so when folk lie to us we tend to become very suspicious, even if they lied to help us. Can I ask if you are employed, Mrs Bartlem?'

'I own my late husband's taxi firm,' Mrs Bartlem replied, somewhat smugly in Carmen Pharoah's view. 'I employ someone to manage it for me, so I have much free time, hence doing charity work at the drop-in centre.' Julia Bartlem smiled gently. 'I really do enjoy the work I do there. I enjoy helping people . . . giving advice . . . it's very deeply rewarding.'

'I see.' Yellich paused. 'Can I ask – do you own a typewriter?'

'Not any more,' Julia Bartlem answered quickly.

'You had one?' Yellich asked.

'Once. Over the years we had a succession of the things. What businessman did not own a typewriter?'

'What did you do with them?'

'Threw them out years ago,' Mrs Bartlem explained. 'When the word processors came in, the typewriters went out.'

'Very well.' Yellich tapped his ballpoint pen on his notepad. 'So, your husband, can we ask you about him?'

'Yes . . . Edward . . . it is so distressing not knowing what happened. It was awful.'

'You don't know what happened?' Carmen Pharoah asked.

'No.' Mrs Bartlem shook her head vigorously. 'No, I don't. As I have just said, I don't know what became of him.'

'He disappeared . . . we believe.' Yellich raised an eyebrow.

'Yes, we were holidaying in France about ten years ago.' Mrs Bartlem gave a quick nod of her head. 'We had a camper van. He went for a walk one evening and he simply never returned.'

'Was it normal for him to go away by himself?'

'Oh . . . not generally . . . he was not a man who liked solitary pursuits but it became quite normal during that particular holiday. He just needed time to himself each evening,' Mrs Bartlem explained. 'I think he was tired of the company of myself and my sister . . . we argued a lot during the holiday, you see, me and my sister, I mean, and Edward got fed up with it all. He'd walk away after supper for an hour or so . . . but never went far and he always came back; then one evening he didn't return.'

'I see.' Yellich once again tapped his ballpoint pen on his notepad. 'That was near the Belgian border, we believe?'

'It was . . . yes.' Mrs Bartlem's voice faltered. 'You have been doing your homework.'

'We chatted to your brother-in-law, Paul Bartlem,' Yellich explained.

'Paul?' Mrs Bartlem glanced up at the ceiling. 'I bet he had little good to say about me.'

'He was . . . shall we say, helpful . . . he was very helpful.'

Yellich avoided eye contact. 'You reported your husband as missing to the French authorities?'

'Yes, yes,' Julia Bartlem replied, 'of course we did.'

'But not to the Belgian authorities?'

'No, there was no reason to do that because he went missing in France,' Julia Bartlem replied, once again defensively. 'We didn't think to report him as a missing person in Belgium.'

'Despite the area where he went missing to be right on the Belgian border? He could easily have wandered into Belgium.'

'No,' she shook her head, 'despite that. It never occurred to us. In fact, Belgium was beyond walking distance for Edward. He could manage about two or three miles, that's all. We were at least ten miles from the border when we stopped for supper that evening.'

'It's all right,' Yellich smiled, 'we have been in contact with the Belgian authorities anyway.'

Julia Bartlem paled in an instant.

'Just before we came out here, in fact,' Carmen Pharoah added, noting with interest as she did so how Mrs Bartlem's complexion lost all its colour.

'If it should transpire that a missing person was reported to the Belgian police at the time of your husband's disappearance, and that person proves to be your husband by description and DNA matching,' Yellich continued, 'and if his corpse shows signs of violence . . . then . . . well, then that will be murder inquiry for the Belgian authorities, and if that does prove to be the case then I am sure they'll want to interview you. You have no plans to go anywhere, I hope?'

'No . . . no plans,' Julia Bartlem replied with a shaking voice. She cleared her throat. 'No plans at all, not of that sort, anyway.'

'Good.' Yellich stood, as did Pharoah. 'We'll see ourselves out. Thank you for your time and your cooperation.'

The house, observed Webster, was of a solid, self-assured appearance, timber framed with plaster infill which was painted a pale yellow, with the timber being picked out in black gloss. The house was set back from the main road at the edge of the village of West Lutton, approximately ten miles to the east of York. It had, he estimated, a full acre of neatly cared-for garden. Webster parked the car at the verge of the road and he and Ventnor walked side by side up the paved driveway to the front door of the house. They were not, much to their surprise, greeted by freely roaming guard dogs. At the front door which had, they saw, been treated with a liberal coating of varnish, they halted and Webster rapped on it using the large metal knocker. The sound of the knocker was heard to echo loudly in the house, but other than that the only sound the officers heard was that of songbirds and the occasional car passing along the road behind them. Eventually the door was opened casually by a woman who instantly gave Webster the impression that he had seen her before.

'Police.' Ventnor showed her his ID and Webster did likewise.

'Yes?' The woman smiled; she stood confidently on the threshold of her house, remaining calm and casual in her manner. 'How may I help you, gentlemen?'

'Well, we are actually looking for a Mr Mellish,' Ventnor explained. 'Is this the correct address?'

'It is . . . I am Mrs Mellish. My husband is at work at the moment.'

'I see.' Webster replaced his ID card in his jacket pocket. 'When is Mr Mellish due to return, please?'

'Whenever he feels like it is the answer to that question, I'm afraid.' Mrs Mellish looked beyond the officers for a brief moment and then returned her attention to them. 'He is self-employed, you see, and so he does not keep to a routine. He is starting up a new venture at the moment and seems to be working exceedingly long hours.'

'Can I ask the nature of the business?' Webster asked as he tried to place the woman. She seemed to him to be so familiar somehow.

'Frankly,' Mrs Mellish replied, 'he hasn't got one. Unlike someone who has a particular skill, my husband's business is everything and anything. If it makes money he will work it and take the necessary risks, but he is very good at assessing the risks involved and wins much more than he loses.'

'Yes,' Ventnor cast an eye over the house, 'he certainly seems to be successful.'

'He frequently buys struggling businesses, turns them round, makes them a going concern and then sells them for a handsome profit. He is good at that but he has other irons in the fire. As I said, he does anything and everything.' Mrs Mellish gave a slight shrug of her shoulders. 'He definitely has the Midas touch.' She wore a lightweight summer dress, of pale yellow, which blended well, Webster thought, with her house. 'With a little bit of seed money he can build up a very nice business,' Mrs Mellish added. 'He has earned the nickname "Mr Mustard", of which he is quite proud.'

'Mr Mustard?' Webster queried.

'Yes . . . as in a large tree growing from a small seed.' Again Mrs Mellish looked beyond the officers for a second as if, Ventnor thought, searching for someone, then once more she returned her attention to Webster and Ventnor.

'Well, again,' Ventnor remarked, 'he seems to have earned that nickname.'

'Yes. I am very lucky to have a house like this to manage,' Mrs Mellish replied. 'It's bought and paid for, no nonsense about a mortgage. This and our house in Norway.'

'Norway?' Webster could not contain his surprise. 'That's a little out of the ordinary.'

'Yes,' Mrs Mellish smiled warmly. 'Unusual, don't you think? Most people have villas in Spain or somewhere, but we have a small house in Norway and we holiday there each year, if my husband can afford to take the time off. That's the constraint – not the cost involved, but whether he can afford the time. It's in a little town called Voss, by a lake, halfway between Bergen and Oslo. Do you know it?'

'Can't say I do,' Webster replied.

'Me neither,' Ventnor added.

'Oh . . . I tell you . . . it's delightful . . . the midnight sun effect, the endless pine woods – it is all so mystical. If you go into the woods when the sun is casting long shadows you can see why the Scandinavian folklore is always full of trolls and goblins . . . you see such strange shadows in the half-light. My husband also owns a few houses in York which he lets to university students. He sees those properties as a sort of safety net. If all else fails, then we still have the rental

properties to provide an income for us. We could retire now
on what rents they generate.'

'I see.' Ventnor nodded. 'What is the nature of his present
venture?'

'It is a "park and ride" idea,' Mrs Mellish explained. 'It is not
an original idea by any means. Many local authorities run such
schemes but this will be a wholly private venture and that, I
confess, is all I know. It is, in fact, all I am permitted to know.
My husband . . . well, he does not and never has included me
in his business life. I am to take care of the house and not to
ask questions – not too many, anyway. I am a rich man's wife
and I am expected to look the part. I must also manage his house
and help to entertain his guests. I just don't get to be part of the
wheeling and dealing of my husband's business world, nor in
fact do I particularly want to be part of it. Running this house
is a full-time job as it is.'

Still Webster could not place the woman, and was beginning
to feel irritated that he could not.

'Can you tell us,' Ventnor asked, 'if your husband ever
mentioned a man called Wenlock, James Wenlock?'

A look of alarm flickered in her eyes. Both officers noticed
it. Her head jolted slightly but Mrs Mellish replied, 'No.'
Though the name clearly meant something to her, she nonetheless replied, 'No, I think I would have remembered that
name, Wenlock . . . Wenlock . . . It isn't the name of a relative
or of a family friend and, as I said, I am not privy to his business dealings and contacts.'

'Are you sure?' Webster pressed.

'Yes,' she persisted, 'very, very sure.' But a distinct edge
of nervousness had crept into her voice.

'Mrs Mellish,' Webster continued, 'if you are hiding something
then I must warn you . . .'

'I am hiding nothing,' she replied indignantly, 'nothing, I tell
you . . . nothing. I know nothing of my husband's business
affairs, nothing but the bare outlines and no one called Wenlock.'

'This would have been about ten years ago,' Ventnor added.

'You're both like a dog with a bone!' Mrs Mellish hissed.
'I don't remember what I did yesterday, never mind ten years
ago.'

'He . . . that is, Mr Wenlock, was an accountant with Russell Square,' Ventnor continued. 'It was Russell Square who provided us with your address. Mr Mellish, your husband, was one of Mr Wenlock's clients . . . if that might jog your memory.'

'Well, it doesn't, will you please listen to me? I tell you, there really is no memory to jog. I can't make it any plainer than that.' Mrs Mellish was adamant. 'And as I said, if my husband, Mr Mellish, had dealings with an accountant then I would definitely be the last one to know. I just would not have been involved. I am the little woman at home, remember? His to come home to . . . slippers by the fire and supper on the table and I am kept well in my place. It's just my lot in life, but I do not complain because my husband has provided us with a very high standard of living. I am content with that.'

'All right,' Webster smiled, 'just so long as we are clear about that. Can we ask where your husband's business premises are?'

'In York.' Mrs Mellish seemed to relax, rapidly so. 'I don't know the address but it's in the *Yellow Pages*. Mellish Finance is the business name. I will have to phone him and let him know you have called here and that you will be calling on him. He will expect me to do that.'

'And we would also fully expect you to do that,' Ventnor replied, 'but thank you for your time.'

Walking away from the house, Ventnor said, 'The name Wenlock meant something to her.'

'I know,' Webster replied, 'I also saw that look flash across her eyes. As you say, the name holds significance for her.' He fell silent as he and Ventnor continued to walk back to the road and their car. Then he added, 'But as well as that, as well as the fact that she was hiding something, I am convinced that I have seen her somewhere before. I can't place her . . .'

'It'll likely come to you,' Ventnor offered encouragingly.

It likely came to Webster as Ventnor, who drove the car on the return journey, slowed to a halt at the set of traffic lights. He buried his head in his hands and then turned to Ventnor and said, 'I know who it is . . . her . . . back there. I know I haven't seen her before, I've seen her sister. That is Mrs

Bartlem's twin sister, I know it is. Mrs Mellish and Mrs Bartlem
are . . . or they were, the Cleg sisters. They were the Cleg
twins. The evil Cleg twins. It was her, Mrs Mellish, who was
on holiday with Mr and Mrs Bartlem when Edward Bartlem
allegedly went for a stroll from which he never returned.'

'Allegedly,' Ventnor repeated softly, 'allegedly . . . but if
you are right, and she is the second Cleg sister . . . then she
certainly becomes a person of interest.'

Alice Mellish closed the door on Ventnor and Webster and
walked calmly to the lounge of her house, curled on to the
settee and sat in a feminine posture with her legs folded under
her. She examined her left-hand fingernails as she calmly
reached for her mobile phone with her right hand. She keyed
in a number, pressed 'call' and when her call was answered
she didn't introduce herself, said only, 'They've visited. Just
left a minute ago.'

'Suspicious?' asked the other person.

'Yes,' Mrs Mellish smiled, 'deliciously so. It was like
watching a fish swallow a hook or rather like watching two
fishes swallowing a hook each.'

'You didn't overact, I hope?' asked the voice on the phone.

'No . . . no . . . I was very careful. They mentioned James
Wenlock's name, as we expected, and when they did so I
allowed the slightest hint of recognition of the name to cross
my eyes. I definitely know they saw it because they then
warned me about withholding information.'

'Good, so the net is closing.'

'Slowly and steadily,' Alice Mellish replied, still examining
the nails of her left hand, 'slowly and steadily, as we planned.'

'Is the file still where you put it?'

'I will of course go and check,' Alice Mellish replied calmly,
'but really you know there's no reason why it shouldn't be
there . . . no reason at all.'

'It's essential that you do confirm it's there before I send
the final card,' Julia Bartlem advised. 'We'll look like very
silly sisters if it has been removed by someone at some point.
Ten years is a long time for anything to happen.'

'Will do. I'll have to phone him at work, tell him the boys

in blue are on their way – it'll too look suspicious if I don't. Then I'll make sure where the file is and phone you back.'

'Very well, you've waited a long time for this, so don't mess it all up now. Keep calm. Don't do anything inappropriate.'

Peregrine Mellish showed himself to be a powerfully built man. He was, thought both Webster and Ventnor, well over six feet tall. Both officers had the unusual and the unnerving experience of having to look up at him. He was square-jawed with piercing brown eyes, broad-chested, and he betrayed no sense of humour or warmth. He was in fact cold, angry and determined, so found the officers. He was, they thought, the sort of ruthless individual who makes fortunes at the expense of the ruination of other people's lives. Peregrine Mellish dwarfed his small office in a new-built development at Stonebow in the centre of York. His surroundings were spartan: there were no comforting or softening photographs or prints of paintings, and there were no photographs of loved ones proudly displayed. It was, Ventnor and Webster both felt, as if Mellish was a robotic moneymaking machine and his office was one of the components. 'My wife phoned me a few moments ago.' Mellish had a cold, hard voice with a slight trace of a local regional accent. 'She told me that you'd be calling.'

'Yes, she said that she would notify you,' Webster replied. 'We are making enquiries about a man called Wenlock, James Wenlock.'

'I don't know anyone of that name,' Mellish snarled.

'Really?' Webster smiled. 'That's a strange thing for you to say to us because he was once your accountant when he was employed by Russell Square.'

'I still don't know anyone of that name,' Mellish repeated the snarl. 'Note the present tense, if you will. Yes, I did once know a man of that name and yes, he looked after my finances . . . but I don't know of him now. He vanished, I believe? Disappeared, as some people do.'

'All right, fair point,' Webster nodded briefly, 'but at least we are talking about the same man.'

'Yes, and I thought you might be calling about him at some point, trying to unravel his life, calling on his family and his colleagues and his business contacts. I've seen the TV news and read the newspapers; his body has been found and my wife said that you mentioned his name when you called on her just now.'

'What do you know about his murder?' Ventnor asked quietly.

'Nothing at all.' Mellish snarled again as he spoke and his eyes pierced Ventnor's eyes. 'I know nothing at all about it.'

'We understand that you had a business interest in Scarborough?' Webster probed, not liking Ventnor's more direct, aggressive approach. 'Is that true?'

'Yes. That is not a past tense issue,' Mellish replied. 'I still have a business in Scarborough, a go-kart track. It makes very good money, especially in the holiday season, but it's an all-year-round business really. Bad weather shuts it down but we can keep going most of the time. Coastal weather, you see. It rains, it's very windy . . . that east wind, I tell you that can bite through anything, but it rarely snows and it's snow and ice that stops the track from operating, not wind or rain.'

'So you have a number of business interests?' Ventnor queried.

'Yes . . . yes I have.' Mellish paused. 'But . . . also in a sense I have none; in a sense I am penniless.'

'In what sense?'

'Well, I am trying to put together a park and ride scheme . . . park your car outside the city in a large car park and get bussed in and bussed back out again.'

'Your wife mentioned that to us,' Ventnor replied.

'I am just getting it off the ground but it's been a bit expensive purchasing the land outside York, concreting it over to make it a year-round car park,' Mellish explained, still speaking in a cold, hard voice. 'Purchasing the buses . . . they're not cheap. Four of them Volvos I had liveried, bright red with "Park 'n Ride" in yellow. I borrowed all the money. OPM – it's the business golden rule in business.'

'OPM?' Webster queried.

'Other people's money.' Mellish smiled an unpleasant smile. 'If it takes off then I can pay off the debt; if it folds, well, they lose their money and I escape, because all my money and property, all my business interests are in my wife's name. The creditors can't touch it; they can't get their paws on it. Standard business practice, like OPM.'

'You must trust your wife?' Webster observed.

'Oh, I do, you know, we have a marriage made in heaven. We have done this numerous times before. She has always re-signed them back over to me.' Mellish began to sound smug. 'She's a good woman. She does her duty.'

'I see . . . that's quite interesting,' Webster spoke softly. 'So you have no idea of anyone who would want to murder James Wenlock?'

'No, no one. James, I remember him – he was a quiet, home-loving family man. He had no enemies. Not that I knew of,' Mellish replied confidently. 'He was a nice bloke. Can't imagine anyone wanting to hurt James, let alone murder him. I can't imagine that at all.'

'Well, he was murdered, that's a fact, as you have read in the papers, and he was buried in a deep sort of shallow grave, as shallow graves go,' Ventnor replied icily. 'So someone didn't like him and that someone didn't want his body to be found. Not ever. Interesting, don't you think?'

'If that sort of thing tickles your fancy then it could be interesting . . . but me . . . the only thing that is tickling my fancy right now is getting my park and ride scheme up and running. So, gentlemen,' Mellish gave another icy smile, 'if you have no more questions, I have work to do.'

'No more questions,' Ventnor replied equally icily. 'For now.'

'For now!' Mellish snapped angrily. 'What's that supposed to mean?'

'It means we have no more questions . . . for now,' Webster replied.

'Am I under suspicion?' Mellish sounded alarmed.

'Yes,' Ventnor replied, 'you are. But only because everybody who knew Mr Wenlock in any capacity whatsoever is under suspicion.'

'Inquiries are continuing,' Webster replied calmly. 'Let's just leave it like that. For now.'

George Hennessey thought that the man had a hard face, with a thin-lipped, spiteful, cruel-looking mouth and cold, cold eyes. The room in which the man was slumped in a wheelchair beside a single, unmade bed had an odour about it, which seemed to Hennessey to come from the man and which Hennessey could only describe as a stench.

'I only see the top man,' the man wheezed. 'Only ever see the top man. Only the top man for me because I am the top man.' The man caught his breath and winced with pain. Outside the building another man, in short sleeves and a wide-brimmed straw hat, was cutting a privet hedge with a large pair of shears. Clip, clip clip. The man spoke with difficulty. 'Hear that?' he demanded aggressively.

'Yes,' Hennessey replied, 'I hear it.'

'That sound I recall from my boyhood, my father cutting the privet in our back garden. That sound hasn't changed in nearly a century. No reason why it should. Same plant, same sort of tool.'

'No reason at all,' Hennessey replied. He had received the phone call in the middle of the afternoon when he was alone in the CID room at Micklegate Bar Police Station, all the other members of the team having been committed to investigative visits. He had let the phone ring thrice before picking it up, leisurely so. The switchboard operator had then advised Hennessey that he had a call from the matron of a hospice in Malton who was most anxious to speak to the officer in charge of the James Wenlock murder inquiry. 'I reckon that must be me,' Hennessey replied warmly. 'Please put her through.'

'It's one of our patients,' the matron had explained, having introduced herself as Matron Temple. 'He is a difficult patient, with the name Grypewell, spelled with a "y", but pronounced "Gripewell", and I tell you, sir, he does nothing but gripe. Ever since he has been here he does nothing but complain . . . griping about this, griping about that.'

Hennessey had then 'allowed' his smile to be heard down the phone.

'Oh, I kid you not; you could not find a more appropriately named man, especially given his Christian name of Earnest.'

Hennessey laughed, 'Really?' Earnest Grypewell the complainer . . . ?

'Really . . . griping in earnest from morn till night, and if he's awake, from dusk till dawn. And it's not a sudden change of personality; he's been like this all his life, so we believe. No one ever visits him, though we know he has blood relatives. He has apparently succeeded in driving everybody away from him during his life with his terrible and insufferable personality.'

'I know the type,' Hennessey replied. 'Then they wonder why they are alone.'

'Oh . . . exactly,' Matron Temple replied. 'Exactly.' She paused. 'Now, the reason I am calling is that, despite his awkward personality, he is fully compos mentis. His body is ravaged but his mind is still as sharp as a tack. He keeps abreast of current affairs by watching his little black and white portable television and he has requested – nay, insisted – that I contact the senior police officer in charge of the James Wenlock murder.'

'I see.' Hennessey reached for his ballpoint pen and his notepad. 'He has information, do you believe?'

'It would seem so, but he will only talk to the most senior officer involved in the case or the "top man", as he says. So even if you are not the senior man you'd better tell him you are or he'll take his information to the grave . . . and frankly that could be any time now. So if you believe he has credibility, then time is of the essence.'

'Is he serious, do you think? Is he genuine?' Hennessey leaned forward, becoming very interested in what he was being told. 'What do you think about the issue of his credibility, Matron Temple?'

'Yes . . . you see, as he complains about the slightest pain it is significant, perhaps, that he has refused morphine. He wants to remain conscious to make his statement.'

'Oh . . .' Hennessey leaned forward. 'That does give him quite some credibility. Well, pleasing for him, I am the "top man". I'll leave immediately and be with you shortly.'

'Thank you. It's Saint Simon's Hospice, 12 Crossley Close, Malton, new building, single storey, flat roof, large sign at the entrance. You can't miss it.'

'Can you give him a little morphine,' Hennessey asked, 'to take the edge off the pain but keep him conscious?'

'Yes, yes I'll do that – he won't gripe about that.' Matron Temple also allowed her smile to be heard down the phone.

'Thank you,' Hennessey replied. 'I'll be there within the hour.'

Alice Mellish walked to the bottom of her garden, stood by the side of an old potting shed and then slipped on a pair of washing-up gloves. She knelt by the shed, probed underneath it and, locating an object within a plastic bag, she then withdrew her hand and, smiling gently to herself, stood by the shed. Surrounded by rich foliage and birdsong under a blue sky she took her mobile phone and keyed a pre-dialled number. When her call was answered she said, 'Yes, it's all right. It's still here.'

When George Hennessey arrived at the address he found it to be exactly as Matron Temple described it to be: new built, bricks gleaming in the sun, single storey, flat roof, and set in large grounds to afford peace and privacy to those in their final days, hours, minutes. He walked up to the front door and at the reception desk swept off his panama, identified himself to the receptionist and asked for Matron Temple. Matron Temple, when she arrived hurriedly in the reception area, revealed herself to be a small, somewhat overweight lady with a brisk manner yet a warm and deeply caring attitude. She shook hands with Hennessey and escorted him to Earnest Grypewell's room, where Hennessey sat in the bedside chair and matron stood beside him with her hands held together in front of her.

'I only ever seen the top man,' Grypewell hissed, giving the clear impression that he was fighting great pain.

'I am he,' Hennessey replied softly. 'I am the top man in the Wenlock murder investigation.'

'That's good because I am the top man and I only speak to other top men,' Grypewell gasped.

'Fair enough.' Hennessey held eye contact with Grypewell's icy stare. 'I am told you wanted to talk to me, Mr Grypewell. Do you have information for us?'

'Yes . . .' He pointed to the portable TV set which stood on a chest of drawers beside his bed. 'The news about James Wenlock,' Grypewell wheezed. 'I know what happened. I know all about what happened.'

'Yes, sir?' Hennessey prompted gently.

'I was on Scarborough Council, years ago. I was the only councillor who was worth anything . . . none of the others were up to the job. Only me.'

There was a short pause.

'Mellish put in his application to build a go-kart track . . . little cars racing each other. He got a lot of opposition because he wanted to build it in an area of natural beauty, important for wildlife . . . small wildlife . . . newts and butterflies, things like that.' Earnest Grypewell winced with pain and took a shallow breath before continuing. 'But there was a lot of approval as well. In the end it was a hung jury . . . one vote either way . . . and Mellish made it worth my while. Who'd want to end up like me? I mean, look at me . . . I struggle all my days, never do anyone any harm and this is what I get. I never had any justice, never no fairness . . . never.'

'Are you saying you took a bribe, sir?' Hennessey asked.

Grypewell nodded. 'Yes, I am saying that. A hefty sum but all it did was pay off my debts so I never benefited. I never saw any of it.'

'I see . . . please carry on,' Hennessey replied softly.

'Well, Mellish, the idiot, left a paper trail to my door. His accountant found out . . .' Grypewell caught his breath.

'Blackmail?' Hennessey sat forward. 'Is that what you are saying, sir?'

Grypewell gritted his teeth and nodded. 'It would have totally ruined me as a politician. Me! A man of my calibre . . . me!'

'Yes,' Hennessey sat back in his chair, 'it would have done that all right, and no mistake.'

'Mellish paid him off. He had to pay him off because I couldn't. I never had any money. Not a penny all my days.

But that lazy accountant was greedy. He wanted more . . . He contacted me again . . .' Grypewell caught his breath again. 'Anyway, a few days later Mellish told me that the accountant had been "taken care of".'

'"Taken care of?"' Hennessey repeated. 'What did Peregrine Mellish mean by that?'

'I assumed . . .' Grypewell again winced with pain. 'I assumed it meant he'd paid off Wenlock and that Wenlock was satisfied because we never heard from him and we were all happy. Mellish had his go-kart track, I had enough to pay off the moneylenders and prevent my legs being broken and Wenlock got his six-figure wedge.'

'Six figures!' Hennessey whistled. 'That's big money.'

'It was high six figures,' Grypewell repeated. 'If I had that sort of money when I was twenty-six then that wretched girl would have married me. Instead she went off with a lawyer with a big, black car and I was a bachelor all my days . . . I never did have no luck.' He gasped for breath. 'Never no luck with nothing. Then I lost my seat on the council soon after. Now, I watched my little TV and saw that Wenlock's body had been found.' Again he pointed to his small television set. 'Then I knew what Peregrine Mellish had done and I didn't want to pass over keeping that information from the police.'

'Good man. If I write out a quick statement, will you sign it?'

'Yes,' Grypewell wheezed. 'But make it quick . . . I think you had better make it quick.'

Hennessey glanced up at Matron Temple who said, 'There's paper in the office,' and she walked quickly from the room.

Five minutes later Earnest Grypewell signed the statement which Hennessey had written and read out to him in the sombre presence of Matron Temple. It was to be the last act of Earnest Grypewell before he slid from this world to the next. Where, dear reader, we hope that he found the peace and contentment which so clearly eluded him in this life.

It was Tuesday, 16.40 hours.

# SIX

Thursday, 8 June, 10.35 a.m. – Christmas Day, 01.35 hours

*In which a confession is obtained, the tender and the too genial reader is privy to George Hennessey's other great joy and in northern France a young man walks under a starry sky, and our tale concludes.*

Paul Bartlem remained silent for a few moments and then he slowly, very slowly, stood and walked to the window of his living room and stared vacantly out into the narrow street and to the black houses at the other side. Eventually he turned to Webster, who had remained seated, and said quietly, 'It is a relief. I am relieved . . . and at least we can now have closure. My sister Helen will have to come to terms with it but eventually she will accept it and she, too, will have closure.'

Webster remained silent.

'But in a ditch . . . in a ditch . . . and naked . . . how ignominious is that? And he was found just ten days after they had reported him to the French authorities as a missing person?'

'Yes,' Webster replied. 'I am very sorry.'

'So where is Nouzonville?' Paul Bartlem glanced to his left as a car drove slowly down East Mount Road.

'It's about five miles . . . or eight kilometres north of the French border, sufficiently within Belgium for the Belgians to have treated it as one of theirs and not to have contacted the French police. A couple of hundred yards from the border and then they might have asked the French to check their missing person reports but five miles . . .' Webster replied apologetically.

'And no identification,' Bartlem appealed, 'nothing at all?'

'Nothing.' Webster felt awkward, helpless. 'The height and the age at death are so far the only indication that he is Mr Edward Bartlem, that and the location, being about fifteen miles from where he was reported missing.'

'Yes,' Paul Bartlem allowed anger to creep into his voice, 'but with a very useful international boundary between his body and where he was last seen and where the missing person report was made.' He fell silent again and then asked, 'What happened to him? I mean, what happened to his body?'

'He was given a name and he was buried, just a simple graveside service . . . the undertaker, a police officer and a priest,' Webster explained. 'We would do the same.'

'Not cremated?' Bartlem queried.

'No, sir, in such circumstances an unidentified deceased person is always buried – again, we would do the same,' Webster continued. 'It is the policy to do that in case a relative should come forward at some time in the future. The relative can then request the body be cremated but of course the reverse can't happen.'

'Fair enough. That's fair enough, I suppose.' Bartlem folded his arms in front of him. 'So, tell me what happened to him.'

'I can't, I'm afraid,' Webster replied. 'We don't know. All that the Belgian police have reported is that his body bore no signs of violence . . . no injuries at all. It is only the absence of anything that might identify him which is strongly indicative of foul play . . . that I grant you . . . but it isn't evidence . . . so we probably will never know what did happen to your brother. I am very sorry.'

'Again, that is fair enough, I suppose.' Bartlem looked down at the carpet at his feet. 'I can't say I like it but it's fair enough. But are you definitely sure it's him? Are you sure it's Edward?'

'No,' Webster replied and thus caused Bartlem to glance at him questioningly, 'it's not certain until we have a familial DNA match,' Webster explained. 'We'll need a few of your scalp hairs or a buccal swab of your saliva to match DNA taken from the body. If they match then, and only then, will we know whether the body found in the ditch in Belgium is that of your brother, Mr Edward Bartlem.'

'Do you want to take the samples now?' Paul Bartlem asked eagerly. 'I am of course very willing . . .'

Webster held up his hand. 'Not just now, sir, thank you. One of our forensic chemists will be calling on you in a day or two to take a sample of your DNA. We'll send it to Belgium and they will notify us of the results. As soon as we hear from the Belgian police we'll notify you.'

'Thank you.' Paul Bartlem nodded slowly. 'But I know that it will be our Edward's body. You know, I've never been to Belgium. I have a reason to go now . . . we have a grave to visit, me and my sisters.'

Antoine Chadid reached for a pair of scissors and cut out the short news article appealing for witnesses, then went up to his bedroom and rummaged through a collection of old photographs and, finding the particular photographs and the negatives, he placed both in an envelope to await his brother's return from overseas. He and Jules had always done everything together, and they would, he believed, continue to do so.

The red recording light glowed softly. The twin cassettes spun slowly. Hennessey sat beside Yellich. Opposite them Peregrine Mellish sat beside his lawyer who had introduced himself, for the benefit of the tape, as 'Percival St John of Ellis, Burden, Woodland and Lake, Solicitors and Notaries Public of Saint Leonard's Place, York.'

Hennessey noted that Peregrine Mellish looked nervous and withdrawn and sat with his arms folded, his eyes downcast. The four men sat in silence. It was broken eventually by Hennessey, who said, 'It doesn't look good, Mr Mellish. For you, that is, it doesn't look good at all, especially now that we have acquired the possible murder weapon.'

'Possible,' St John repeated. 'You say possible . . . can you explain that, please?'

'Yes, as we have said quite simply, I mean that forensic tests have still to be completed, but if the blood on the file is that of Mr Wenlock, if the file fits the damage to Mr Wenlock's ribs . . . you see, the distinctive V shape is the key. The Home Office Pathologist, Doctor D'Acre is testing that now, and if your fingerprints are on the handle . . . then it's the murder weapon.'

'Can you lift fingerprints after ten years?' St John asked. He was a portly man in his early middle years, wearing bifocal lenses, an expensive-looking suit, a gold watch, and reeking of aftershave.

'It is possible,' Hennessey replied. 'It's certainly possible. The file was found tightly wrapped in a plastic bag and sealed, so yes, it is possible.' Hennessey paused, and then he turned to Peregrine Mellish. 'And the murder weapon, if it is the murder weapon, was found on your property, Mr Mellish, and you had a powerful motive: he was blackmailing you. That plus the deathbed statement of Mr Earnest Grypewell, given, freely so, at his request and signed in front of an independent witness in the form of a nursing home matron of good character.'

'The Crown Prosecution Service has run with less and still got a result,' Somerled Yellich added. 'Much less. Much, much less.'

Mellish glanced sideways at Percival St John, who shrugged his shoulders in a manner which clearly said, 'I can't help you, not unless you are willing to plead guilty, then we can argue for a reduction in sentence, a reduction in the minimum time to be served'.

'You need to do some hard thinking,' Hennessey said. 'You need to start working for yourself instead of against yourself.' He paused. 'We'll give you a little time to talk to Mr St John here. This interview is terminated at . . .' he glanced at his watch, '. . . eleven thirty-four hours in the forenoon this day as has been previously indicated.'

The recording light glowed softly; the twin cassettes spun slowly. Hennessey and Yellich sat opposite Julia Bartlem, who smiled confidently. She sat alone, having politely declined the offer of legal representation.

'This is being recorded?' she asked.

'Yes,' Hennessey growled. 'It keeps us both right.'

'Even the silences?' Julia Bartlem smiled. 'I confess I quite like the silences.'

'Yes,' Hennessey replied, 'even the silences. Silences are useful; the longer the silence usually means the interviewee is withholding something.'

'Or has nothing to tell you.' Julia Bartlem continued to smile. 'Do I get a copy of the tape?'

'Yes,' Hennessey hissed, 'that's why there are two cassettes – one for you and your legal team if you should engage one and one for us and the Crown Prosecution Service.'

There followed another long period of silence, then Hennessey leaned forward and said, 'Shall I tell you what I think, Mrs Bartlem? Shall I tell you what I think happened?'

'Oh, please do.' Julia Bartlem also sat forward. 'I think I'd like to hear what you think, Mr Hennessey.'

'I think you and your sister helped each other to get rid of your husbands,' Hennessey spoke coldly. 'I think you cooked the whole thing up between you and I think that it was years in the planning. You both did that to acquire their wealth.'

'Ah . . . the evil Cleg sisters . . . sometimes also called the evil sisters Cleg.' Mrs Bartlem inclined her head to one side. 'Do you know what a cleg is, Mr Hennessey?'

'A horsefly,' Hennessey growled.

'Yes, found in northern England and Scotland,' Julia Bartlem replied. 'It bites you for your blood. If ever you've been bitten by a cleg you'll know it, that I can promise you.'

'So I believe,' Hennessey snarled. 'I have never had that experience. But I will take your word for it, Mrs Bartlem.'

'Me and my twin sister got taunted at school because of our surname. You know what children can be like to each other, how cruel they can be . . .' Julia Cleg spoke as though she was beginning to tell a story and so Hennessey didn't reply. He wanted her to talk; he wanted her to implicate herself in something, somehow. His experience and intuition told him to remain silent. She continued. 'The chief tormentor was a girl called Sarah Gosling but nobody could torment her and call her "duck" or anything because she was a big girl – I mean, very big. She took after her father who was a farm labourer. One boy once made fun of her name and she broke his nose with just one punch. She was that sort of a girl; she could do it to others but no one could do it to her.'

'I have met the type,' Hennessey commented.

'So she lived in a tied cottage, remote,' Julia Bartlem continued. 'It was, probably still is, and when the weather was bad she used to go home using a shortcut through a small wood. So one day, when it had been raining hard for two days and with no let-up in sight, she went missing and they found her in a ditch with her head all bashed in . . . they said that she was a real mess, blood and bone everywhere.'

'That's interesting,' Hennessey commented.

'There was chaos and confusion, all sorts of police running round asking questions, but they never arrested anyone and no one ever suspected us, the two little innocent Cleg sisters, but things changed for us after that . . . no one called us the "horsefly twins" again.'

'You murdered her!' Hennessey raised his voice. 'Is that what you are admitting to?'

'I'm not admitting to anything, Mr Hennessey. Besides which, she was bigger, like I said, than us, a real farm labourer's daughter.'

'She wouldn't have been bigger than both of you,' Hennessey growled, 'and if you got the first blow in and put her down . . . and the rocks to bash her skull in with were all most conveniently to hand.'

'Dare say the rain helped,' Yellich added. 'It would have muddied the scene quite nicely. Any footprints would be washed away. Can you remember how long was it before her body was found?'

'I think nearly two days because her father had forbidden her to walk through the woods and so they spent a lot of time looking in the wrong place.' Julia Bartlem smiled. 'But I dare say that you'll have a record of it all. An unsolved child murder . . . you can give it to your cold case team.'

'You know, we might just do that.' Hennessey clenched his fist. 'We might just do that, Mrs Bartlem.'

'We'll be most cooperative.' Julia Bartlem smiled at Hennessey and then at Yellich. 'Most cooperative.'

'I am sure you will be,' Hennessey growled his reply.

'But you were going to tell me what you think, Mr Hennessey.' Julia Bartlem continued to smile. 'I don't know how we got on to the story of poor Sarah Gosling.'

Hennessey paused and collected himself. 'What I think is that you bullied your husband to take you on a touring holiday in France in your camper van and your sister Alice came along, apparently at the last minute, but that was well planned.

When in France you murdered your husband Edward Bartlem, probably by pulling a plastic bag over his head when he was sleeping so as not to cause injuries . . .'

Julia Bartlem continued to smile as she listened intently.

'Then you drove along back roads until you were safely in Belgium and, having removed anything that could identify his corpse, you rolled his body into a ditch. You probably brought his clothes back to England and donated them to a charity shop.'

'My, Inspector Hennessey,' again Mrs Bartlem smiled, 'what a wicked imagination you have. Really most wicked.'

'After Mr Bartlem had been presumed deceased you then acquired ownership of the house and his business. And you now have someone managing the business for you.'

'You have that bit right.' Julia Bartlem raised a finger. 'That's correct.'

'What is correct?' Hennessey replied quickly. 'The murder?'

'No, no . . . the fact that I now have a man to manage the fleet of taxis for me. That is quite correct.'

Hennessey sighed deeply and then continued. 'In your sister's case, Mrs Bartlem, she had on previous occasions cooperated with her husband by allowing him to sign his assets over to her whenever he was starting a new business venture, and when it was safe to do so she would re-sign all the assets back to him, thus giving her credibility as a faithful and a trustworthy wife. Then Mr Mellish murdered James Wenlock because Wenlock was blackmailing him . . .'

'And you can prove that?' Julia Bartlem asked.

'Yes, we will prove it.' Hennessey nodded and smiled. 'Well, that is to say we won't have to prove it because Peregrine Mellish will confess to the murder. He is talking to his solicitor as we speak and I fully expect him to confess because it's the best thing that he can do. By confessing he will get a lesser sentence and an earlier parole hearing. I have been doing this job for a very long time and believe you me, I know when someone is going to come clean. Peregrine Mellish is about to come clean and start working for himself.'

'Well, we will just have to wait and see, won't we?' Julia Bartlem held her smile. 'We'll see, but do carry on.'

Her smile, thought Hennessey, was infuriatingly and unshakeably confident. He realized that Peregrine Mellish was close to making a full confession. Julia Bartlem and probably her sister, Alice Mellish, certainly were both very far from confessing.

'Then,' Hennessey continued, 'your sister, probably having played some part, some greater or lesser part in the murder of James Wenlock, obtained the murder weapon with her husband's fingerprints and James Wenlock's blood upon it and secreted it in a safe place, tightly wrapped in plastic so as to preserve the evidence implicating Peregrine Mellish in the murder of James Wenlock. Over the years Peregrine Mellish's fingerprints would most probably have decayed but James Wenlock's blood would not. That is enough to convict with the fact that it was found under Peregrine Mellish's potting shed in his garden; that, together with Earnest Grypewell's confession, is a certain conviction.' Hennessey paused before he continued. 'She waited . . . then she and you waited . . . until once again Peregrine Mellish signed all his assets over to his wife, your sister, when he was starting another new business venture, and then, once it was all in her name, it was then that you and she started to send anonymous postcards to the drop-in centre, where you insisted on handing them to the police, knowing they would lead to Mr Mellish's conviction. Mr Mellish will be sent to prison for a long time, leaving your sister in possession of his fortune, just as you acquired your late husband's wealth once he had been presumed deceased. That, Mrs Bartlem, is what I think.'

Julia Bartlem looked to her left and then to her right and then at George Hennessey. 'That,' she said calmly, 'is a most fanciful tale, it is quite the most fanciful tale I have heard for many a long year. All you have to do now is to prove it.'

The red recording light glowed softly, the twin cassettes spun slowly and silently. Hennessey and Yellich sat together facing Alice Mellish across the surface of the highly polished table in interview room three. Mrs Mellish sat alone, similarly having declined the offer of legal representation and after listening to Detective Chief Inspector Hennessey she looked to her left and then to her right and said, smiling, 'That is a most fanciful tale, it is quite the most fanciful tale I have heard for many a long year. All you have to do now is to prove it.'

The red recording light glowed softly, the twin cassettes spun slowly and silently.

'My client wishes to make a full confession,' Percival St John stated.

'Good man.' Hennessey smiled, he leaned forward and clasped his hands together and beamed at Peregrine Mellish. 'It's always the best course of action in the light of so much evidence.'

'This will help me?' Mellish appealed. 'I know it's murder but I still want to do as little jail time as possible. I don't see myself as a criminal. I know that I've done some dodgy things but I don't mix with criminals.'

'We will note your confession,' Hennessey assured him, 'and the judge will take it into consideration. You can also argue duress caused by Wenlock's blackmailing of you. Cooperation from you when in prison, a genuine show of remorse and you could win an early parole. You will receive a nominal life sentence,' Hennessey explained, 'but you could be out within ten years.'

'Ten years,' Mellish echoed. 'Ten years.'

'Make full use of the facilities,' St John advised. 'Register for an Open University degree . . . that always impresses parole boards and the anticipated sentence was not ten years . . . it was within ten years.'

'It does?' Mellish glanced at his solicitor. 'I mean the OU degree course?'

'Yes, yes it does,' St John replied. 'You're bettering yourself, aren't you? Moving away from crime.'

'I see.' Mellish had a vacant look about him. 'Yes . . . yes, I'll do that . . . I'll do that. I've always been interested in history . . . time to study . . . it has an attraction. I can use prison time to my advantage.'

'All right,' Hennessey refocused the conversation. 'What happened?'

'But I have given it all to her,' Mellish complained. 'I'll come out to nothing.'

Hennessey remained silent.

'Nothing . . . I am penniless and without a property. I bet it was her who betrayed me. Was it? Was it her?'

'I can't tell you,' Hennessey replied. 'Not at this stage, anyway. It might come out in the trial.'

'The newspapers said postcards had been sent to the police?' Mellish asked.

'Again, we can't comment,' Hennessey replied. 'Just tell us what happened.'

'I bet it was her,' Mellish appealed to Hennessey, 'her and her sister. You know, sometimes they talk like they're one person, like one personality in two different bodies stringing whole sentences together without any form of rehearsing.'

'So we have heard.'

'It was them,' Mellish continued. 'I know it was those two, they gift wrapped me and handed me to you on a silver platter.' Mellish buried his head in his hands. 'She waited until . . . oh . . .' he glanced up at Hennessey, 'her brother-in-law . . . her sister's husband. She suddenly announced that she'd been invited to go on holiday with them and off she went . . . only the two sisters returned.'

'So no marital discord between you and your wife at the time?'

'None,' Mellish shook his head, 'none at all. Oh, my . . . you should . . .'

'We are.' Hennessey smiled, anticipating him. 'The disappearance of Edward Bartlem is being investigated. We have been in touch with our Continental European counterparts, we have appealed for witnesses in the French and Belgian media . . . that is in hand.'

'Why did I marry her?' Mellish appealed to Hennessey. 'Why did I marry into that family? Those two are not human. What did I marry . . . ?'

'Let's just hear your story, please,' Hennessey pressed.

'Yes, I'm sorry . . .' Mellish paused. 'Well, Wenlock had the bite on me, you know, blackmail. He came round to my house. I invited him to come round so we could talk about it, never expecting him to agree but what did he do?'

'He agreed,' Hennessey replied.

'Straight into the lion's den. I banged him over the head. I don't think I did any damage but he went down . . . we . . .'

'We?'

'Me and Alice,' Mellish explained.

'I see . . . all right.' Hennessey smiled. 'Just clarifying things.'

'Yes, so we turned him over and I pushed the file into his chest . . . he gave a shudder and that was it. I had killed a man . . . there was hardly any blood.'

'There wouldn't have been,' Hennessy explained. 'The point of the file went straight into his heart.'

'Julia told me it would; she told me where to put the pointed tip of the file.'

'That is interesting – as though she had done it before?' Hennessey asked.

'Yes.' Mellish nodded. 'Just like that . . . as though she had done it before . . . like she knew what she was doing.'

'All right, carry on, please,' Hennessey encouraged Mellish. 'You are doing well. Very well.'

'So after we had killed him we waited until evening and bundled him into our car – he wasn't a big man – and drove out to the country . . . Dug a hole . . . it took me all night but I have . . . I had the strength and the stamina for it and in he went and we covered him up.'

'We?' Hennessey clarified. 'You and your wife?'

'Yes, we bought two spades. I did all the digging but Alice helped with the filling in, in fact she did most of the filling in because by then I was totally exhausted.'

'I can imagine.'

'We then planted some oak saplings we had taken with us to try and explain the disturbed soil. It seemed to work because no one questioned the soil being disturbed. He'd still be down there if I hadn't signed everything over to Alice . . . such a dear, sweet woman is she.'

'And the file?' Hennessey asked. 'What did you do with that?'

'Alice assured me that she had thrown it into the river as I had asked her to do.'

'In fact,' Hennessey leaned back in his chair, 'she had wrapped it up in a plastic bag and pushed it under the potting shed in your garden, and then waited.'

'Yes . . . and waited.' Mellish also leaned back in his chair. 'And in the interim, while she was waiting, Alice helped her sister get rid of her husband.'

'Probably . . . probably,' Hennessey replied, 'but that still has to be proved. All right, let's get this down in the form of a written statement.'


Christmas Eve – 22.00 hours

The man and the woman sat in silence in the softly illuminated room, sipping mulled wine. They had enjoyed the ghost story broadcast on Radio Four and had then switched the wireless off. The previous day the man had given evidence in the trial of Shane Bond, who had unexpectedly insisted on pleading not guilty to the murder of Henry Hall, and who had subsequently been found guilty and sentenced to life with a minimum tariff of fifteen years, after a trial lasting three days. Peregrine Mellish's trial, by contrast, was over in less than a minute. He stood as the charge was read, said, 'Guilty,' the judge said, 'Life,' and he was led down to the cells.

'So,' the woman said softly, 'all over before Christmas. Just.'

The man glanced round the room; the log in the grate gave a pleasant warmth, while a respectable number of cards bedecked the mantelpiece and other surfaces. In the hall a recently felled pine tree sapling stood by the door, beneath which were parcels to be opened the following morning. 'I wish I could feel the same but it is . . . once again . . . we have glimpsed what happened but have been able to prove but ten per cent of it. We know now what probably happened to the bullying Sarah Gosling. Julia Bartlem's "admission" is on record, but that case still remains open. The Bartlem family reburied Edward in a grave of his own in Belgium rather than bring his body home, letting him lie where he fell, like a battlefield casualty . . . at least they now have closure. But the

Cleg twins, they murdered Sarah Gosling and Edward Bartlem. One of them, at least one, conspired in the murder of James Wenlock and the disposal of his remains. Alice Mellish might not have pushed the file into James Wenlock's chest but she still would have collected life for her part in his murder. Of course, she's not admitting it. She's not admitting anything and we can't prove anything.' He sipped his drink. 'Though by means of compensation, we did solve the murder of Henry Hall, who up until then had been only a missing person . . . so he got some justice, God rest him.'

'So what happened to the Cleg sisters?' the woman asked, as the sound of children's feet running along the upstairs landing was followed by the closing of doors and silence.

'They were liquidizing everything the last we heard of them, totally selling up . . . their husbands' business interests, their homes . . . everything. They are probably moving to the beautiful south. Probably they'll buy a house together and with any luck they'll trip themselves up somehow and we could possibly nail them for something even if it's for only one of the murders – even that would be something, but at the moment there is the annoying sense that they have used the law and the police to become two wealthy women. All we can hope is for a witness to come forward or a new piece of evidence; as it is they seem to have got away with it. But they'll never sleep easily; they will live in fear of the seven a.m. knock on their door.'

'H.D.O.W.A.O.,' the woman offered.

'Sorry?' the man queried.

'Husbands, disposal of, wealth acquisition of,' Louise D'Acre explained. 'Well, it's gone quiet up there. Shall we go up?'

George Hennessey drained his glass. 'Yes,' he said, 'let's go up.'

## Christmas Day – 01.35 hours

Antoine Chadid walked slowly home through the small village close to the Belgian border in which he had lived all his life. The sky was cloudless and myriad stars seemed to him to be pinpricking the blackness. The midnight mass had, he felt, uplifted his soul and he enjoyed a profound sense of peace and contentment. As he walked he glanced to the north and he identified the Plough and using the pointers he found the Pole Star. Antoine Chadid's thoughts then turned to Jules, his beloved older brother who was a geologist and who, at that moment, was combining the laying of foundations of his career with a young man's lust for adventure, being at that moment in the great dead heart of Australia where he was working for a company who were drilling for oil. All received geological wisdom, all fossil evidence, Jules had once told him 'indicates that Australia must be sitting on a vast ocean of oil, and a fortune awaits the company which finds it'. His brother's contract of employment was due to expire in the coming April, whereupon he intended to spend the money he had earned on an extended holiday in Australia and New Zealand and he planned to return home to France when his money was spent, probably, he anticipated, the following October.

It was upon Jules's return that Antoine Chadid would show him the newspaper cutting and the photographs that they had taken the day when, hidden from view, they had been bird watching some three hundred meters from the incident, but had changed the wide-angle lens to the telephoto lens and had captured the image of two women lifting the body of a male into a green and white camper van, and had then also photographed the van as it had driven away, obtaining a clear image of the United Kingdom number plate. When no report of a crime had been published the two brothers had assumed that the man had consumed too much red wine and had been carried by his two female companions into the back of the camper van so that he might sleep, and so they mentioned it to no one and thought no more about it. They were then twelve and thirteen years old.

Antoine Chadid stepped off the road and walked up the pathway to his house as an owl hooted, and another owl answered. Yes, he could do that, there was no need to hurry, there was no urgency. He would allow his brother to rest for a few days upon his return, and then at some quiet moment he would show his brother the news item he had cut out of the newspaper earlier that year, in the midst of the summer, about a man whose body had been found ten years earlier in a ditch in Belgium and who had only just been identified. The British police had appealed for witnesses and had added that the man had been reported as missing to the French police by two women who were believed to be driving a green and white camper van at the time.

Antoine Chadid silently unlocked the door of his small house, so as not to wake up his wife and their infant son. Yes, he thought, yes, he would wait, because he and Jules always did everything together and he knew Jules would want to be part of reporting what they had seen. And after a delay of ten years, what did a further ten months matter?

It would be no time at all.